The Dragon's Name, Reign of Shadow Book One

Printed in the United States of America

ISBN-13: 978-0-9967959-5-1

Visit raynalstiner.com to learn more about the
author and her other works.

Join the conversation on facebook.com/raynalstiner
or Instagram @rlstiner.

This is a work of fiction. Names, characters,
places, and incidents are the products of the
author's imagination or are used fictitiously. Any
resemblance to actual events, locales, or persons,
living or dead, is entirely coincidental.

THE DRAGON'S NAME

REIGN OF SHADOW, BOOK ONE
BY RAYNA L. STINER

TAGORBI PUBLISHING, LLC

ACKNOWLEDGMENTS

As always, to my alpha reader, partner, mate, best friend and cheerleader, James. Your dedication to supporting me in being an author over the years is saint-like. You've been by my side during early morning writing stints, and cooked dinner for late-night editing sessions. You're my sounding board for plot and character development, and a compassionate ear through frustrations and self-doubt. There's no better man in the world and I am lucky enough to have you in my life.

Thank you, current beta readers Jessica and Randy, and past beta readers Dan and Fran, and Danny and Anthony. I'm humbled to have your thoughts, expertise and detailed feedback that pushes me to excel.

Special thanks to friends and family who read past versions of this story, encouraged me to revisit Riana and the world of Tyrinth, even after I trunked the novel.

Another acknowledgment goes once again to Jessica, for sincere faith, constant encouragement, regular accountability check-ins, and believing in me when I did not believe in myself. A friend as true as you is a rare and special gift. I'm humbled to call you friend.

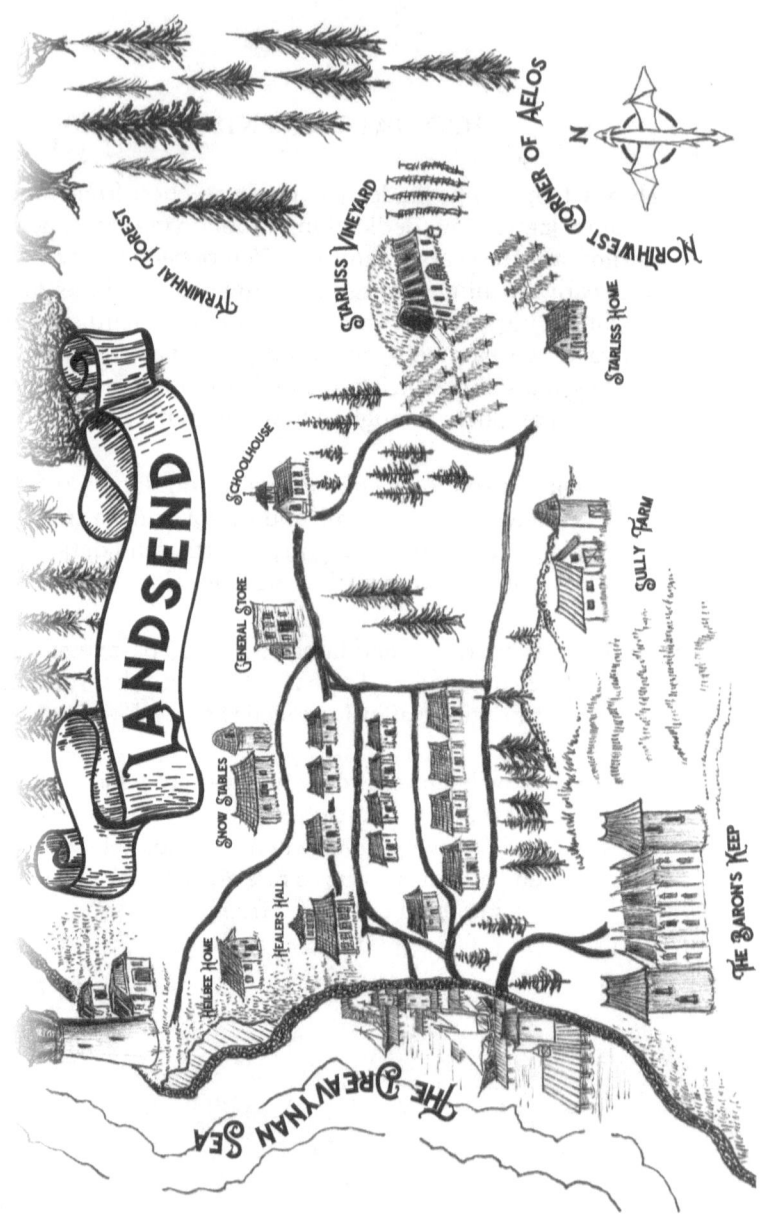

CHAPTER ONE

Riana fought to stand firmly in the crowd while bodies jostled her. The cacophony of screams rose. She moved to escape the thick of it but was shoved forward by Landsend's townspeople behind her. Elynda's green gaze appeared through a gap in swaying bodies.

"Riana, here!" Elynda said, her eyes wide in her porcelain face under a dark clutch of curly hair. She reached for Riana.

Riana took her best friend's hand, gritted her teeth, and squeezed her way through the throng. When she emerged from the crush of people, she cried out, wanting to escape back into the masses. Here, at the foot of the stage, she had more of a view than she'd bargained for.

"Why are we here, Elynda?" Riana asked, desperation in her voice.

"We can get past them better this way." Elynda pointed in front of the crowd, into a small empty space between the stage and the roped-off area where Landsend's townspeople gathered.

Riana nodded, tears slipping down her face. She lurched after Elynda, still holding her hand tightly. A voice rang out, a shout above the screams of the crowd.

"Where do you think you're going?"

Elynda stopped so abruptly Riana ran into her with an oomph.

"Uh..." Elynda started.

"Stay right where you are. You've the best view. The folks in the back'll be jealous."

Riana peeked around her friend's shoulder, breathing raggedly. The woman was dressed in the black and gold colors of the High King. She was stern and beautiful, with a wicked scar marring her tan face.

Pinned to the double-breasted coat she wore was a sigil Riana had only ever heard of: a circle divided into four quarters with gems signifying the four elements. This was a Tyrmini guard, a wielder of elemental power sanctioned by the High King of Aelos to enforce the law on magic. The law that stated that if you came of age at sixteen summers and discovered you wielded elemental magic, you turned yourself in to the High King. You would be run through a series of tests where the High King would decide if you could control the elemental power or if the elemental power controlled you. If it was the latter, or you failed to report yourself, you were executed.

Elynda backed up as she spoke. "Yes, jealous." She spat the words out at the Tyrmini guard, but the woman had shifted her attention to the stage.

The crowd cried out in exultation as a young man was marched onto the raised platform for the town to see. Escorting him was another Tyrmini guard, this one a large man with sandy hair and blue eyes. He too carried scars; these along his neck, as if something very big had swiped at his throat. The guard held a bird cage, but inside were no birds.

Riana yelped and put a hand over her mouth. She recognized the creatures flitting behind the bars. She couldn't help the tears rolling down her face. She hoped the people on the stage took it for fear instead of sympathy and compassion.

She knew elemental creatures could be dangerous. They could wield elements, and humans who were not Tyrmini could not. Because Tyrmini could protect themselves from elemental attack, throughout history the association had been made that Tyrmini often adopted elementals as familiars, or at the very least lived peacefully beside them. Anyone caught in the presence of an elemental-wielding creature could be accused of being Tyrmini.

Riana's gaze went from the fire nymphs to the young man bound in manacles on both his wrists and ankles. More tears fled her eyes. She knew him.

"Elynda, that's Tomas Perry," Riana said.

"Yes," Elynda said, looking up at Tomas, her own tears streaking down her face. "Mother told me she'd heard it was him the guards found."

"I stand before you today," started the Tyrmini guard on the stage, "to call to justice a rogue Tyrmini who abstained from reporting his condition to the High King when he came into his power at sixteen."

The crowd went wild. Vegetables, rotten fruit, stones, and worse were hurled at Tomas.

"No!" Riana shouted, but no one heard her, except for Elynda.

Tomas turned his head to one side but did nothing else to guard himself from the onslaught. Soon, his face dripped with vegetable juices and one eye was red where it had been struck. He doubled over when a stone hit him squarely in the stomach. His knees buckled when another struck him in the leg.

"And now we have found this Tyrmini with elementals on his property, clearly marking him as one who possesses outlawed magic. What do we say to those who are Tyrmini and put their fellow community members at risk by not reporting themselves?"

The crowd jeered.

"We say burn him!"

"Hang the demon!"

"Slit his throat!"

"Keep us safe!"

"Yes," the man said, walking to and fro on the stage, the cage of fire nymphs rattling against his leg. He waited for the crowd to quiet. He went on. "Tyrmini must be taught to use their oddities to serve the High King, to serve you!" He jabbed a finger into the crowd.

"We must be tested, we must be trained, we must be tamed, or else we pose a risk to all humanity, as once we suffered under the hands of the Tyrmini before the Great High King stamped out the rebels and murderers wielding elemental magic.

"Do you recall, here in this very town of Landsend, the great battle between the High King and the water-air Tyrmini Serena?"

The crowd shouted.

Riana cast about her, the faces of the people she lived and worked with turned wild and red with rage.

"Five hundred years ago, Tyrmini were born, Serena among them, living here in the northwest region of Aelos. She could not control her magic. And you know what happened. She drowned the town in a deluge, a monstrous storm of her own making! Nearly the entire town died that day. Only a few remained.

"Your Baron's ancestor, Aiden Tarbyrwyn, and our High King's ancestor, Achyla the First, joined forces to take the Tyrmini down. Along with her elemental familiars: creatures like the haleosphere, a blood-sucking monster that conceals itself in storm clouds; and the water elemental amatsu that moves massive amounts of water, causing tsunamis; and the berubula that eats humans whole if you step into its boggy home.

"And these," he lifted the cage into the air and shook the fire nymphs. "Fire nymphs who seek the refuge in the aura of a Tyrmini. A Tyrmini who nearly killed his entire family with their flames!"

"That's not true!" Tomas shouted. "I would never hurt my family."

Riana looked away from Tomas, searching until she found the face of his mother and father in the crowd. The two pulled their youngest daughter into a shared embrace. The mother, a brown-haired and slender woman in a plain dress and stained apron, bent her cheek to her daughter's head and sobbed. The father looked at his son with a stern mask of anger.

"You shoulda told us, Tom. You shoulda said somethin. We woulda taken ya to the High King. He coulda helped you control this. Instead, you turned your back on your family and nearly burnt down our entire season's crops. I'm ashamed you're my son."

Riana gasped. How could he say such a thing to his child?

"No," Tomas whispered, the crowd suddenly silent as they listened to the dialogue between father and son. "Dad, I never meant for that to happen. The nymphs just found me in the field. I tried to get them to leave, but they wouldn't. I'm not powerful. I bake bread. I stoke the fire and make sweets and confections. I can pick the best grain and I know exactly when the fruit is perfectly ripe for the most delicious pies. How is that even dangerous?"

"You. Nearly. Burned. Down. All. Of. Our. Fields!" his father shouted.

The Tyrmini guard stood by, a smirk on his face.

"What's the next accident, son? Our house? With us in it? With your mother and your sister? You're dangerous. You put your family at risk with your secret." His father shook his head, his arm wrapped firmly around his wife and daughter. "Shame on you," he said.

"And this is the danger, friends. Tyrmini gone rogue have no control of their power, much less their elemental familiars. The elementals and the Tyrmini thrive in the presence of each other. These creatures and Tyrmini are the same. They cannot be trusted with that raw power, unchecked.

"His disobedience to the Throne is treason!"

The crowd screamed for justice. Tomas's father among them.

Riana sobbed.

Elynda clutched onto Riana's arm and shoved her. "We have to go. They'll carry out the sentence in moments."

Riana swiped at her tear-stained face but moved. Tomas caught her gaze. His eyes were soft brown. He was a sturdy young man, gentle and quiet. He'd been one of the few people at school who'd been genuinely kind to Riana. A year ahead of her and Elynda, he'd graduated and took up work at his family's bakery in the spring the year before.

Tomas gave Riana a soulful gaze, and then he said to her in a voice low enough for no one else to hear, "I'd never hurt anyone. You know that."

Riana nodded. "I do!"

5

"I'm glad I'll die knowing someone understood that. Without doubt." Tomas bowed his head, breaking his gaze with Riana.

Riana's legs turned to jelly as she cried out with hurt and anger. They couldn't do this. It was murder.

"Traitor, traitor, traitor, traitor..." the crowd cried out, some pumping fists in the air to the rhythm of the chant.

"What do traitors get?" asked the guard, raising his arms out to the crowd, ready to receive their answer.

"Justice!"

"Death!"

"The grave!"

Elynda pushed Riana hard. "We don't want to see this, Riana. Move!"

Riana peered over her shoulder at her friend, and then finding a sliver of strength, she pushed her wobbling legs forward, swiping savagely at her tears to clear her vision. She took hold of her friend's hand and pulled her through the angry mob. A mob comprised of people she knew. She ducked her head and shoved her way through the horde.

Riana looked back to the stage once more as the guard set down the bird cage and pulled a sword from the scabbard at his hip. She cringed and turned away, pulling Elynda after her, back through the mass of people.

The crowd reached an exultant crescendo of cheers.

It was done.

Tomas was dead.

Screeching filled the air. To Riana's horror, the Tyrmini guard had begun the execution of the fire nymphs. It was hideous. The crowd continued to cheer while Riana and Elynda escaped.

CHAPTER TWO

Riana stood in the barren strip of land between two worlds. On her right, even rows of vines were lined with neat precision. On her left, the TyrMinHai forest loomed. She stared into the ancient forest. A flicker of light caught her attention. It sparked away as quickly as it had appeared. Riana searched through the trunks and limbs for another glimpse. A glimmer of light illuminated the shade. She crouched, instinctively reaching into her skirt pocket for her notepad, and crept toward the trees.

At the end of the row of vines, she pushed herself into the vegetation and curled up, notebook and pencil ready. She waited for the light.

"Riana!" an old but powerful voice boomed out over the expanse of vines.

Riana cringed, mentally shushing the voice that would disturb her secret art session. The voice belonged to her adopted grandmother. Riana was an orphan twice over. Orphaned at birth and orphaned again by her adopted mother, Loralee Fraely, daughter of Sela Starliss. Sela had taken Riana in at the age of eight, after Loralee passed away. Her adopted father had never liked Riana. In fact, Roy Fraely had abused her soundly, most especially when her adopted mother had turned ill.

Riana looked through the twiggy fruit vines and thought maybe she'd be concealed enough to claim she'd been too far away to hear her grandmother's call.

"Riana Rose Starliss, you bring your skinny behind up here this instant! If you're out in the forest again, I swear you'll get a tanning—I don't care if you are fifteen summers!"

Riana exhaled and hung her head.

"I can see your hair!" her grandmother added.

Riana growled and pushed herself to standing. Her hair, which was silvery white, always got her in trouble. It was one more attribute that made her different than others in Landsend. Between being an orphan of unknown parentage and her silver hair and eyes that shifted colors, people had a hard time accepting her as one of their own. She was teased for looking like an old lady, like her grandmother, that her hair was colorless while her eyes had too many colors. She was called a freak simply for the fact that nothing about her matched anything about the other people in Landsend.

"Coming, Grandmother!"

"Riana!" her grandmother shouted again.

"Yes, Grandmother, I know you can see me. I'm coming," she said impatiently. She didn't hurry, but stalked toward her grandmother, disappointed she'd missed spotting the owner of the flicker of light.

Riana rounded a corner and stepped into another row of vines. Her grandmother, Sela Starliss, owner of Starliss Vineyard and Winery, stood at its end.

"Wait! Stop!" Grandmother Sela said, her voice suddenly shrill.

Riana obeyed. "What is it, Grandmother?" she whispered.

Grandmother Sela stared above Riana's head, her sea-blue eyes wide, mouth slack in surprise. Slowly, she raised a hand to point.

Riana's scalp tingled, setting off a cascade of shivers down her spine. She slowly raised her head. A small creature with skin of royal blue hovered on fast-beating wings above her head. The creature had captured a strand of Riana's hair and rubbed the silver lock over her face, seeming to thoroughly enjoy the feel of it.

Riana could barely breathe. She'd never seen a fire nymph so close. The last time she'd seen them they'd been caged and then slaughtered. She was still haunted by their screams even months after the last Tyrmini execution. Her gut churned.

Finally, she inhaled. The nymph darted away, only releasing Riana's hair at the last moment so that it yanked at Riana's head.

"Ow," Riana said.

The fire nymph burst into flames and circled over the vegetation.

"Not here!" Sela shouted.

Flames dripped off the nymph and fell onto the vines.

The vegetation immediately crackled in fire.

Riana inhaled in shock. "No!" she said.

The little nymph zoomed away, back into the forest, leaving a trail of golden light streaming across the evening sky. Riana yanked off her cloak and smothered the fire. Her grandmother rushed toward her, joining Riana as she stamped at the escaping flames. Smoke rose away from the blackened vines as the viticulturist rounded the vine row.

Sela turned toward Riana. "Let me handle this. Do not say anything," she told her, meanwhile reaching into one of her many pockets.

"Not the Rumalska! There are so few!" the viticulturist said. He rushed toward Riana and Sela, barely noticing his boss, and gingerly touched the smoking vine. He knelt down, looking at the trunk, poking at the slightly charred bark.

"I'm so clumsy," Sela said. She opened her hand to show him a cigar and a box of matches—a somewhat new invention Riana was still enthralled with. "I dropped my match when I was trying to light my cigar. But, no worry. Riana jumped straight to action and put the flames out." Sela turned toward Riana. "Well done, dear."

Mr. Freeman looked up at his boss, then Riana. "You had something to do with this," he accused.

Riana opened her mouth, but a stern look from Sela made her snap it closed.

"Did you not hear me, Mr. Freeman? I am the one who did this. Not Riana. Riana moved quickly to put *out* the flame."

"I don't believe it. She's always causing trouble," he said.

Riana snorted and rolled her eyes. It was so easy to blame a kid who couldn't defend herself. Although she had to admit guilt to at least some of his accusation. Riana seemed to stumble into trouble, mostly by stumbling into elementals. And she couldn't blame the elementals. Otherwise, she'd end up in the very same place as her schoolmate Tomas and his companion fire nymphs. Riana swallowed a lump in her throat, worried about yet another appearance of elementals near her.

"Mr. Freeman," Sela Starliss said, the sharp note to her voice making the viticulturist whip his gaze from Riana to his boss. "I know how well you tend our fruit. I understand you are protective. But that is no reason to go around blaming my granddaughter for something that is not her fault."

Mr. Freeman tilted his head up, grinding his jaw to one side, then the other.

"I was lucky enough that Riana was quick to smother the fire—and at the ruin of her apparel, I'd add."

Mr. Freeman cast a dark glance in Riana's direction. "Lucky," he muttered. He turned back to the plant, gently touching the smoking vines, and frowned.

"Come, Riana, let's go find you a new cloak," Sela said. She stuffed the cigar and matches into her dress pocket, firmly grasped Riana's shoulders, spun her around, and steered her out of the vineyard row.

Riana was struck by several things at once. Her grandmother was hiding the existence of the fire nymphs and their interaction with Riana. Also, her grandmother smoked cigars. She was shocked.

When they were out of earshot, Sela stopped, halting Riana and turning her back around to face her. Riana felt a little annoyed at this gesture. It had been ages since her grandmother had handled her like this. She wasn't five summers anymore.

"You do know you must never speak of this, don't you?"

"Yes, Grandmother," Riana groaned, folding her arms and leaning heavily on one leg.

"Good. Because the last person who had elementals around them was put to death by the Tyrmini guards."

"Grandmother," Riana said, frustrated, "I know. I was there, remember? Remember how it's mandatory for everyone to attend? I remember it all very clearly. Tomas was a classmate, Grandmother." Riana hung her head. She would forever hear Tomas's voice begging her to remember he'd never hurt anyone. She wrapped her arms around her middle. Tears slipped from her eyes.

"Oh," Grandmother said. "Oh, dear. I'm sorry. It's even more difficult when you've known the person."

Riana nodded.

"I just don't want that to be you up there, Riana," Sela said.

"I know, Grandmother," she said. She worried that fate would catch up with her and she'd find herself atop the stage instead of at the foot of it.

CHAPTER THREE

Riana approached the schoolhouse under cover of mist. The fog was so thick and wet that the particles of moisture floating through the air caught on every surface; hair, cloak, dress, book bag. Riana was sopping by the time she climbed the three short steps to the porch and front door.

Her best friend, Elynda, met her with her mother, Mrs. Heilbee. Ribbit, her other best friend, was nearby with his father. Donny Derringer approached, flipping his head to one side to move his overly long hair that obstructed his view.

"Riana," he hailed loudly so that the rest of the classmates would turn to look in his direction. He made sure he had their attention before tossing his hair out of the way again. "No one here to announce your apprenticeship? Probably because you don't have one."

His friend, Finnigan, lurked behind him and chuckled at Donny's joke. "No one wants a freak for an apprentice," added Finnigan.

Riana hadn't even put her books away and they were already starting in. She shrugged past Donny.

Donny followed.

"Go find an egg and suck it, Donny," Elynda said and pushed past the hulking boy who was becoming a man.

"What she said," Ribbit said and followed Elynda.

Riana hung her bag and cloak in one of the white cubbies lining the back wall, ignoring Donny and his crony. Donny was a hulking kid who had haunted Riana's every step since she was old enough to go to school. Before her adopted mother had died, Riana would go from home where her adopted father had berated, yelled, and hit her, to school where Donny pinched, punched, tripped, and scoffed at her. Then her mother had died, Grandmother had taken Riana in, the abuse at home had stopped, and Elynda and Ribbit had rallied to Riana's side. Things had gotten better. But Donny was forever trying to get under her skin.

She turned to her friends. They each looked at her, nerves clearly written on their faces.

"Well?" Ribbit asked.

"Oh," she said. "You're worried too? Grandmother will be here in a little bit. She had to run wine to the Baron's Keep this morning."

They both sighed in relief, hugged her in turn, and then went to their desks to wait for the class's announcement of apprenticeships. Over the years, they'd watched all the classes who had come before them. Year after year, the eldest of the class chose, applied, and were awarded apprenticeships. Most went into their family's business. Some didn't have that option or hated their family's trade.

Riana made her way to her desk and slid in, pulling her dress out of the aisle. She'd learned if it stayed there, Donny would step on it.

Mrs. Tomly, their fierce and lovable red-haired teacher rang the bell to announce the commencement of class.

"Good morning, class," she said. Her cheeks and the tip of her nose were rosy. Her pleasingly plump frame was donned in a floral ivory dress with lace at the neck and sleeves. "This morning marks the first of our new year. And as you know, that means announcements of apprenticeships." She clapped with excitement. "First up is Elynda Heilbee. Elynda, will you and your guest please make your way to the front of the class?"

Riana wiggled in her chair, excited for her best friend. Elynda walked to the front of the classroom with her mother ushering her along. The children, all different ages, sat astute, hands folded neatly on their desks. Mrs. Tomly sat down at her desk at the front of the classroom.

The door to the schoolhouse opened and Riana's grandmother joined the group of adults at the back of the building near the hulking woodstove.

Riana's heart jangled in her chest. Only Elynda and Ribbit knew about her apprenticeship. And of course, Riana knew about Elynda's and Ribbit's.

Elynda stood in front of the class, fingers gripped together in front of her dusty blue dress. Her mother wore a similar style of cotton dress, jade and burgundy plaid with white ruffles at the end of the sleeves. Mrs. Heilbee and Elynda were mirror images of each other. Both had raven dark hair with thick curls. Both had long, dark eyelashes over stunning almond-shaped eyes. One of their few differences, aside from the obvious age, was that while Elynda had green eyes, Mrs. Heilbee had one blue and one green.

Mrs. Heilbee was holding something between her hands. "Good morning, class," she said.

They greeted her in unison.

"After a lot of thought and preparation, Elynda has chosen her apprenticeship, which we at Healer's Hall accept wholeheartedly." Mrs. Heilbee unfolded the thing she'd been holding. She stepped behind Elynda and draped the healer's apron over her head. After tying it at the back, she stood next to Elynda, turned toward her, and said, "Welcome to the healing team, my dear. Your father and I are so proud of you!"

Elynda smoothed the white apron down the front of her dress, her eyes glittering with overwhelming pride and achievement. There was an assortment of pockets on the front of the apron for the various tools, medicines, and tinctures she would supply to her patients. She turned to her mother and wrapped her arms around her to the applause of the class.

"Congratulations, Elynda!" Ribbit shouted above the clapping. He was next in line for his announcement. There was never any question to Riana what he'd end up doing. As Elynda and Mrs. Heilbee made their way back from the front of the classroom, Ribbit and his father, Mr.

Snow, walked toward the front of the room. Well...Mr. Snow walked; Ribbit trotted behind him, two steps for every one of his father's. Mr. Snow stood head and shoulders above his son, despite his son being sixteen summers and nearly fully grown.

Ribbit and Mr. Snow were as opposite as Elynda and Mrs. Heilbee were alike. Mr. Snow had graying dark hair; Ribbit had blonde hair. Mr. Snow was a looming six feet and several inches; Ribbit was smaller than Riana. Mr. Snow was dressed in a handsome but humble jacket and pristinely clean shirt and cap; Ribbit's overalls hid none of the wrinkled shirt and weathered pants. Mr. Snow was respectable and solemn; Ribbit waved at the class like a celebrity. Once they stood at the front of the class, Mr. Snow withdrew a horse whip from his belt loop.

Ribbit flinched away. "Whoa, dad. Not in front of my classmates."

Mr. Snow rolled his eyes and shook his head. "And if this kid slows down to take anything seriously, I'll let him apprentice to be the Master of Snow Stables." Mr. Snow held out the whip, which Ribbit took ceremoniously, much to the surprise of the class and Mr. Snow. The room erupted in applause. Ribbit bowed, cheeks burning.

Next up was Donny Derringer. Donny's family were pig farmers, but his eldest brother had gone into the Baron's Guard. Riana knew pig farming was not in Donny's future and sure enough he was not accompanied by a parent but by the Captain of the Baron's Guard, Steph Weylin. She wondered if Donny's parents were nervous about the future of their business.

Captain Weylin of the Baron's Guard escorted Donny to the front of the class. "Before we begin," he said, "I'd like to make a quick announcement." The class straightened, a soft murmur whispering through the room, even to the group of adults in the back.

Riana looked over her shoulder at her grandmother, wondering if she knew what this was about. Her grandmother didn't seem surprised at this sudden opportunity to make an announcement. In fact, she seemed annoyed, but begrudgingly offered quiet acceptance of whatever the Captain had to say.

"We've had a lot of elemental sightings lately," Steph said.

Some of Riana's classmates' eyes popped wide. A little shrill of fear went tracing up Riana's spine as well, but not for the same reason as the rest of the people in the room. Donny Derringer shuffled from one foot to the other before swiping at his nose with a knuckled fist. He shook his head to whip his hair out of his eyes before peering over at the Captain.

"I'm sorry to announce we've recently had a death to one of our guard and member of our community." Captain Steph clapped a hand on Donny Derringer's meaty shoulder. Donny stuck out his chin, as if he dared anyone to feel sorry for him. "Jack Derringer, older brother to Donny, was attacked and killed by an elemental the countryside hasn't seen in over a hundred years. A shadow wolf."

Donny was her personal bully, but Riana's heart pinched in empathy for Donny's loss. What an awful thing to lose your brother. She imagined losing Elynda, the closest thing she had to a sister, and blinked at the sting of tears.

"Donny," Mrs. Tomly said, her voice showing the shock. "I'm so sorry for your loss. I had no idea." She clapped her hands to her chest, a handkerchief miraculously appearing to dab at her tear-soaked eyes.

"Yes," Captain Steph said, "the wolf is still at large. Luckily, Donny has decided to take his brother's place on the guard to help us hunt down the beast and rid the community of these dangerous creatures and search out any rebel Tyrmini."

The class erupted in applause. Riana looked around and put her hands together, but more for the show of it. She could understand Donny wanting to avenge his brother, but she wasn't sure the creature was to blame. It was a creature with an appetite. Certainly, one had to be careful, but to exterminate it? Riana wanted to side with the creature, which felt like a betrayal to her fellow community members.

Donny made his way down the aisle. Riana caught his eye. "I'm sorry for your loss," she told him.

"Worry about yourself," he spat. "I don't need sympathy from a freak who can't even get an apprenticeship."

Riana sat stunned, unable to form a response. After all the teasing and tormenting, Riana was willing to extend Donny a smidgeon of common decency, and he couldn't bring himself to reciprocate. Why did she even bother? The blooming hurt withered and was replaced by a simmering anger. Riana clenched her hands into fists until her nails pierced her skin. She was mad at herself for not being able to conjure a response. Then again, an immediate response really wasn't necessary.

Donny returned to his seat and Steph took up a space at the back of the class with the other adults. Riana was shaking with anger and hurt. She pushed herself out of her desk and made her way to the front of the classroom. Sela joined her. The class fell silent. When Riana arrived to the raised platform at the front of the room, she turned and looked at her classmates. Their faces displayed a range of emotions from shock to surprise. Except for Elynda and Ribbit, who smiled broadly at Riana.

Sela stood next to her adopted granddaughter and placed a warm, maternal hand on her shoulder. "Riana has grown up at the vineyard and winery. She is familiar with its inner workings from an intimate perspective. That is why I have asked Riana to be my apprentice, learn how to assist me, and ultimately take over ownership of Starliss Vineyard and Winery."

Riana fought a smug smile as Donny stared slack-jawed at Sela.

Riana stood at the entrance to the winery and let the sun warm her face. Afternoon had chased away the morning's ocean mist and dried the day out. Riana looked out at the fields of vines, the coastline, and the looming TyrMinHai forest standing like a guarding army of trees, which were all contained on her grandmother's property. A wild need to be out in nature called to her.

"Come on, Riana," her grandmother said. "Wineries don't run themselves."

Riana straightened, training her eyes to the inside of the winery instead of the vast fields, forests, and streams behind it. A bolt of nerves shot through her middle for what lay ahead after today.

"Yes, ma'am," she said and followed her grandmother. The winery was built into a hillside, using the Tyrinth's soil like a protective layer to keep the fermenting wine at just the right temperature. The winery's soil ceiling sprouted with wild grasses and flowers. Riana stepped over the threshold, turned, and shoved the big, oaken door back into place. The song of the sea ceased, replaced by an echoing silence.

Under the brick ceiling stood a tall crushing vat to Riana's right. The empty wooden pool was stained from ages of grapes. It would remain empty until this summer's harvest.

Humongous barrels lined the wall near the crushing vat where the grapes and their juices rested and fermented. Papers were posted on the barrels with scrawled notes about the dates and flavor. On Riana's left, wine presses stood waiting to be used. Now was the growing season. And it was always aging season, with vintages stored in the bowels of the winery older than her grandmother.

Today they were picking the wine supplied to the Baron for his big Spring Ball at which the major landowners and merchants would announce any new apprenticeships—including Riana's. Pride welled within her. Riana was an outsider and an orphan, and she would be apprentice to the owner of Starliss Vineyard and Winery. One day, she would fully operate the place she'd grown up in while her grandmother enjoyed a well-deserved retirement.

Maybe then people would treat her differently.

Grandmother Sela Starliss was a fashionable woman and a force to be reckoned with. Her silver hair was swept into a twist and bun. Her dress was a sturdy color of green with an overlay plaid of blues and rusts. Her hat was pinned to one side. Sela moved with purpose through the open expanse of the crushing room, Riana on her heels.

The office was at the back of the main winery room, near the entrance to the cellars. The vintner, viticulturist, and cellar manager stood inside the office, talking among themselves.

"Good morning, everyone," Sela said as she slid through the door of the office.

"Good m-morning, Ms. Starlis," the vintner, Mr. Tellnar, said through his usual stutter.

"Mornin'," Ms. Highhouse, the cellar manager, said without smiling.

Mr. Freeman, the viticulturist, simply nodded his capped head in Grandmother's direction. He didn't look at Riana. He leaned against one of the two oak desks occupying the office. Grandmother rescued a small green ceramic pot in which thrived a miniature evergreen from the leaning Mr. Freeman. The tiny evergreen had been an occupant of the office for as long as Riana could recall. Sela looked sternly at the viticulturist as she moved the plant to the second desk. Mr. Freeman took no notice.

Riana darted glances all around the room, not wanting to look any of the managers in the eye. She could only imagine how they were going to react, especially Mr. Freeman, after yesterday's incident.

Grandmother motioned Riana over to her.

Riana obeyed and found the toes of her boots most fascinating.

"I have something to tell you all," she said and placed a hand on Riana's shoulder.

Ms. Highhouse gave a wide-eyed dancing glance first to Mrs. Starlis and then to Riana and back again.

Here it comes, Riana thought.

"I've chosen Riana to apprentice me," Sela said. She wrapped an arm around Riana's shoulders and squeezed.

Riana wasn't sure if she was doing this out of affection or protection.

Highhouse crossed her arms over her middle and set her gaze to flat disappointment. Mr. Tellnar's eyes went wide while his mouth opened. His head and neck shimmied on the edge of shaking a silent no.

A hacking noise unhinged itself from Mr. Freeman's throat. He pushed himself off the desk and leaned toward his boss. "You can't seriously apprentice her?" he asked.

There it is, Riana thought. Her guts squirmed. She couldn't help but feel like an imposter being given a huge gift and responsibility, and not even being blood-tied to the woman who gave it.

"Mr. Freeman, why ever not?" Sela asked.

"She is trouble," Ms. Highhouse said, her voice was deep for a woman.

"Y-yes," Mr. Tellnar said.

"What are you talking about?" Sela asked, incredulous.

"Have you already forgotten yesterday's...shenanigans?" Mr. Freeman bellowed.

Riana shrank back.

"The Rumalska is completely ruined for the year," Mr. Freeman said.

"Mr. Freeman, I assure you—as I already mentioned yesterday—the Rumalska was this clumsy, old woman's fault."

He snorted.

"Need I remind you of the incident in the cellars with the five-year red we were just about to bottle?" Ms. Highouse cut in.

Oh, she was still sore about that. Riana cringed. When Riana was eight and new to her adopted grandmother's winery, she'd wandered down the cellar halls until she'd stumbled onto one of many elemental discoveries. The creature had been coiled atop the stack of barrels. Riana had climbed onto the barrels for a closer look, even then carrying a small notebook and scratching out sketches of her discoveries.

The creature had woken. They'd stared into each other's eyes for a breath before the elemental screeched, spread its wings, and evaporated in a puff of fire, a blast of air, and plume of black smoke.

Riana had been blasted by the elemental's use of air and fire and slipped, setting off a cascade of loosed barrels, many of which cracked and spilled their contents onto the dirt floors. She'd received a sound scolding for climbing the barrels, which she'd endured all the while itching to sketch out her new elemental discovery. She'd learned by then not to speak of elementals and stowed her secret love for dangerous things. Looking back, she felt lucky the elemental had not blown up the barrels—or Riana.

"Sh-she spoiled last year's sweet white. A whole vintage ruined because of her," Mr. Tellnar accused.

"I didn't do that!" Riana said, thankful for something she could deny.

"I saw you touching them barrels. The very next day I did a tasting. Ruined."

She'd been touching them because they'd smelled funny. They smelled funny because they'd been left on the first floor in the heat for too long. Riana opened her mouth to tell him he should have been tending the temperature of the wine more closely when her grandmother jumped into the conversation.

"I think you go a little far," Sela said to Mr. Tellnar.

"She's b-b-bad llllluck," he replied, his voice almost whining.

"Every time she shows up here, she is followed by Catastrophe." Mr. Freeman personified catastrophe, as if it were an invoked elemental. "How on Tyrinth do you expect her to be able to run Starliss Vineyard?" He cast an encompassing arm toward the whole of the vineyard.

Her grandmother went silent, her even breath whistled into the pause of flinging accusations.

Riana knew they were right though. It did seem like more times than not she caused heartache for the workers at her grandmother's vineyard. But, if they knew it really wasn't her at all, they'd like her even less. She simply took the blame.

Grandmother let the silence stretch while her gaze grew cooler. Riana always thought her grandmother's eyes were like reflections of the Dreavynan sea. When she was angry, the sea was dangerous. The energy of her sturdy anger filled the room until the three vineyard and winery workers seemed to choke on it. Only after the workers shifted from foot-to-foot, rolled shoulders or crossed arms, did she speak.

"I hear your voices," she began, "and would remind you whose name hangs on the sign over the entrance to this establishment. And who pays you handsomely to produce the region's most exceptional wine."

"She'll ruin you. She'll ruin your legacy. She'll ruin every life that depends on you for their livelihood. Please, ma'am. I implore you to reconsider," Mr. Freeman said.

Riana rubbed her nose and fought back the eye roll building in her head. Mr. Freeman was being dramatic. The Rumalska would be just fine. Grandmother had said so.

"Riana is my apprentice. She may cause you a particular amount of grief because she is young, but that will not always be the case." Grandmother paused. "One day, she will own this vineyard and winery and you will report to her. It would be wise of you to mend your attitude and your relationship with her."

If they were committed to following their employer's words, it didn't show. Each of them fixed Riana with a stare ranging from anger to disgust.

Riana stared back, daring them to argue with Sela Starliss.

"You may go now," Grandmother said to them. They filed out of the room, their anger following them.

"That went well," Riana muttered.

"They'll get over it," Sela said, waving a hand in front of her face as if to clear her nose of a foul odor. "Now, then, let us get to business, my Apprentice." She fixed Riana with a joyful gaze so infectious Riana could do nothing but grin.

"The Baron has approved your apprenticeship. Not that he gets a choice in the manner. Soon you'll learn, Riana, power does not come only by way of title."

"Yes, ma'am," Riana said.

"Your school announcement is done with now." Grandmother Sela seemed to be more pleased at this than Riana. "And next is the Baron's Ball," she intoned. She giggled and gripped Riana with strong, if slightly trembling, hands.

Riana gulped back nervousness that crawled up her throat. She may have always looked forward to the ball, but it was for the public announcement of her acceptance in the community, not to attend a people-filled event. She would be stuffed into the finest dress Landsend could procure or create and paraded around to each and every person her grandmother could think to introduce her to. Including the Baron.

"This Ball affords us the opportunity to introduce you to all of Landsend's traders and merchants. Cementing these relationships determines the success of the vineyard. You can make excellent wine, but if you give them sour grapes, you'll fail a dozen times over."

Riana suppressed another eye roll at the cheesy statement. "Hopefully, they'll hate me less than your own staff."

"Don't worry about them, Riana. Just focus on doing the work; it will speak for itself. And as far as building relationships, I will teach you everything I know. And then, of course, you'll win them all over." Grandmother fixed her with a sly smile.

"You'll share all your secrets?" Riana asked.

"All of them," Sela said, rolling her head around to encompass the vastness of her secret knowledge, her sea blue eyes wide and sparkling.

"Okay, okay, then I guess I'll go," she teased, knowing there was really no choice in the matter. "But, do I really have to wear a dress?" she asked.

Her grandmother pinched the brow of her nose and shook her head. "Oh, dear. I've fought so hard to build an appreciation for fashion in you."

"I'll be more pleasant in a pair of leathers and a tunic, Grandmother. Surely, that helps with negotiating."

"Pleasant never served me. A woman leader in a dress puts a man merchant, sailor, or royalty at ease. When they are at ease, they are easier to ply."

"Well," Riana started. "What if I just give them wine first and then start negotiations?"

"Oh, I do that as well, my dear."

"So, is it the dress or the alcohol that plies them?"

"Riana! Never make a woman question her charms!" She put her hands on her hips and set her gaze to steely.

"Apologies, Grandmother," she said, but grinned while she said it. "I am your student. Mold me."

CHAPTER FOUR

Riana straightened in her chair, tilting her head back then left and right to relieve the pressure in her neck from bending over the paperwork.

"How goes it?" her grandmother asked.

Riana looked down at the inventory logs she'd been scouring for hours. "Well, if I'm calculating correctly, it seems our cellars are only at about forty-seven percent capacity. Is that about right, from your estimation?"

Her grandmother gripped her chin, casting a gaze into the ceilings and her memory banks. "Yes, that seems about right from eyeballing it."

Riana smiled, excited her counts had been accurate.

"Now that that's done, let's take a look at the report from Mr. Freeman on his estimations of fruit production for the year."

Riana looked through the papers on the desk, looking for the report.

A knock scraped at the office door, interrupting Riana's shuffle of papers. Grandmother pushed herself up from the desk and paced toward the door. As she reached to open it, it swung in. She backed up.

From the second desk where Riana was tallying the records of wine bottles, she could see only the door and her grandmother. Sela Starliss frowned at the concealed visitor. Riana leaned back, hoping to get a glimpse.

"You're very early," Sela said. "By several days. It's not ready yet." Her words came out chopped and anxious yet irritated. She cast a quick glance at Riana and returned her focus to the person on the other side of the door.

"His majesty is quite thirsty." The voice of the person on the other side of the door was male and low and familiar. Riana recognized it as belonging to the Captain Steph Weylin of the Baron's Guard, the man who had announced Donny's internship and given the warning about extra elemental activity in the area.

"What happened to the reserve I left last month?" Sela's eyes grew wide, her head and neck trembled.

"All gone," Captain Steph said.

Grandmother Starliss cast a quick glance at Riana, then back to Steph. "Please give me a moment, Steph, and then we shall speak in private."

The door wiggled and then Steph's head appeared around the blocking door. "Oh, hello, Riana."

Steph was a tall, muscular man with thick, auburn hair that Riana had come to think of as luxurious. His mustache was well-trimmed. The lines on his face gave away his age, but the kindness in his hazel eyes belied his station as one who fought against disorder.

Riana nodded in the Captain's direction.

"My apologies for the intrusion, Sela. I'll wait out here until you're ready."

The door closed. Sela turned to face her granddaughter. "You've done a lot of work today. Why don't you take a stroll on the grounds while I conduct this business with the Baron's Guard."

"Shouldn't I stay to learn?"

Grandmother waved away Riana's question, shaking her head along with her hand. "No, no, no, my dear. There are some things I wish not to hand off to you. This business will end with my retirement."

Puzzled, Riana placed the dip pen in its dry holder and replaced the inkwell lid. She slid from her seat and went to the door. She pulled her cloak from the coat rack and then turned to her grandmother, who waited patiently for her to leave. "Grandmother, is everything alright?"

Grandmother smiled, but Riana could sense weariness under the gesture. "Oh, yes, my dear. Everything is just fine. Don't you worry. I've been dealing with the Baron of Landsend since I was a child."

"Very well," Riana said, and pulled the door open.

Captain Steph of the Baron's Guard turned from his surveillance of the empty winery and faced Riana. His Baron's Guard uniform was deep navy blue with shining brass buttons down the center of his chest and stomach. The coat flared out around his legs, almost forming a skirt. His emblem of office was a golden cord, looped twice with tassels hanging off his left shoulder.

"Riana," he said, "good to see you. How are your studies?" He clasped his gloved hands in front of him and rocked from toes to heels.

Riana cast a gaze over her shoulder, looking to her grandmother for support on whether she should mention her apprenticeship.

Grandmother Starliss inched her way forward and squeezed next to Riana just over the threshold to her office. Wrapping an arm around Riana's shoulders, she made the announcement for Riana. "Her studies have become more focused. Riana is my apprentice to one day take ownership of Starliss Vineyard. And give this poor, old woman a rest."

Riana was looking into her grandmother's face. When she turned to the Captain, it was to see him ashen-faced and gaping. Riana's throat swelled. No one would accept her, it seemed.

"Well?" Sela said to Steph.

"Oh," Captain Steph said. "Um—congratulations, Riana. Sela, does the Baron know?"

Grandmother's arm fell away from Riana's shoulders. "What do you take me for? You think I'm new to handling the local royalty?"

"Forgive me, Ms. Starliss. I am surprised the Baron—"

"Careful, Captain," Grandmother growled.

"Well, what I mean is, I am surprised the Baron would venture to argue with your judgment."

Ms. Hightower walked past the group, toward the entrance to her domain in the cellars.

Grandmother eyed her as she spoke, raising her voice to carry. "He doesn't. And if the Baron doesn't argue with my choice of apprentice, neither should you—or anyone else."

Ms. Hightower cast a quick glance in Grandmother's direction, caught her intense blue gaze, then ducked her head and scurried down the ramp.

"A valid perspective," Steph said. "Let us then to our business, so I can let you return to the task of training." Steph stood aside and Riana walked past him.

Grandmother pushed open the door to the office, entered, and held the door open for Steph. Once Steph was inside and out of Riana's eyesight, Grandmother turned to her. "Take your time, Riana. You deserve a nice leg-stretch."

Riana nodded and watched the door inch closed. She looked around. The winery was empty. The door to the office was marginally cracked open, golden light spilling out onto the stone floor. Riana's heart jangled inside her chest as she considered eavesdropping. She tiptoed forward, careful her boots didn't scrape on the stones.

The door swung open again and her grandmother stood framed in the lantern light. "Go on, then. Be outside, Riana."

Riana jumped, guilt washing over her as she turned and fled from her grandmother.

The day outside was cool. Riana pulled her cloak tight and buttoned it against the chill. The vineyard stretched away in front of her in rolling hills, vines bare and tweedy. The grass was still dead and the fruit trees slept too. Everything was quiet and colorless.

Everything except the TyrMinHai forest, which backed the furthest stretches of the vineyard land. In fact, Starliss Vineyard property went far into the forest. No one much cared how much of it her grandmother owned because no one set foot into the forest without a very good reason.

Riana marched straight for it.

The trees seemed to speak to her, calling her name, as they always had. Everyone in Landsend was afraid of the forest, but Riana never felt more at home. She wouldn't say it to another living soul, but the magic in the forest didn't scare her; it thrilled her.

She'd caught glimpses of elementals in the trees when she was young, and it'd been her dream to study them closer. She hunted the elementals but not because she wanted to kill them. She wasn't like the rest of the people in Landsend. And it wasn't just her strange hair and eyes. Often, she saw and understood deeper things others seemed to miss. While others could poke and prod at what made her different because it was apparent and overt, they never wanted their own differences and weaknesses exposed.

She'd never understood that.

Thinking and walking, Riana cut through the maldaine grape vines. She surveyed the skeletal vines twisting around posts, where once they'd made their ambitious way to the lattices that crossed over her head. The dead vines lay over the supporting structure, their winter sleep undisturbed by the girl passing beneath them who would soon be their Master.

Riana touched a vine and shivered. Maybe it was just her imagination, but she could almost sense their sleepy contentment. She passed through the long tunnel of grape vines, mist accompanying her steps.

At the end of the row, Riana stepped into the barren strip of land between the vineyard and the forest. She stood in the borderland and soaked in the eerie emptiness, the embodiment of nonpartisanship. Her boots swished through the short, winter grass, her skirt hem dragging through the stalks. Sunlight shone weakly through a thin cover of cottony gray clouds. Once she was standing among the first outstanding trees that marked the entrance to the forest, she breathed a deep sigh of relief.

It was as if she were coming home. Her steps lightened as she navigated over roots bulging from the Tyrinth. She reached out and touched the giant sentinel of an evergreen, almost hearing the rush of energy along the network of waterways and fibers within it. The release of joy within her was so overwhelming, she threw her arms around the trunk of the tree and held it in a grateful embrace, sighing in relief.

A sound somewhere deeper in the trees plucked at Riana's attention. She pushed herself away from the tree, patting it gently, then moved into the forest. The foggy afternoon light fell away as the evergreens grew closer. After she had made it deeply into the forest, the familiar terrain wrapping around her, she picked up the noise she'd heard earlier and headed east. She moved with ease over the leaf litter and through bramble, dampening her footsteps by placing her feet with care.

The sound she followed whooshed and stopped, coming and going, but getting louder. Riana's senses buzzed as she stalked her prey. A fiery golden streak whizzed in front of her. Riana tiptoed to a nearby fallen tree and crouched behind its massive girth. From her perch behind the moss-laden log, she watched them.

Quietly, she reached into her skirt pocket, fussing with the folds, and pulled out her paper pad and pencil. She thumbed through the images of elementals captured by her drawing. If she were caught, it would most likely mean her death.

Despite the inherent danger—or maybe because of it—she found herself drawn to these creatures. They were lovely and evocative. They stood apart from humans because humans had made them their enemy. Riana could relate to standing apart. Had people not said it a hundred times over? Calling her a freak for her odd eyes and old-woman hair. Bringing up her orphan status. She was a human, she knew that. But in the midst of elementals, her differences were not so strange, not so unique, and certainly not hated.

At least, she always hoped her differences that set her apart from the elementals would not incite their hatred.

Riana pushed herself up enough to peer over the log. She'd seen the random lone fire creature resting on tree limbs, their fire doused and their normally blue skin taking on the cracked and hardened texture of evergreen bark. The only thing giving them away was their shape and luminescent wings.

She'd never seen what she was seeing now. She calmed her breath and let the pencil capture the scene before her.

The giant evergreens formed a warm and welcoming circle. Amidst their branches and trunks, burnt-out pockets formed homes for the fire nymphs. A nymph of golden flame flew over her head, the sound a whoosh of crackling fire. Riana bit down on her tongue to keep from yelping. She gripped her pencil and waited for her hands to stop shaking.

The creature barreled toward a tree on the far side of the circle, extinguishing its flame as its feet touched down on the threshold of a nymph home. Its blue skin glittered. Its wings twitched as it pulled aside a large swag of evergreen sprigs that served as a door. Riana's hands flew over the sketchpad as her eyes stayed glued to the glimpse inside the nymph home. Another nymph, more feminine in nature, reached out to the entering nymph. Riana couldn't see fast enough. She caught a glimpse of a hammock and the reflection of a pool of liquid to one side. The nymph entering the enclosure unwrapped a pouch from its crude belt and pulled from it a shining bulb of fruit.

The fruit had to be some sort of grape, but she'd never seen a grape glow with such golden light before. Abandoning her drawing, she placed a hand onto the bark, pulling herself closer to the nymph home, curiosity gnawing at her. Before she could identify the fruit, the evergreen swag was replaced and the shining, golden fruit was gone.

She dropped down to her perch, pencil flying over the paper. The drawings seemed to come to life at her insistence, the fruit bulging off the paper, and even though it was only in the gray tones of pencil, Riana could see its shining golden color as she intended to see it.

So obsessed with her work, when Riana felt a sudden warmth she waved it away. When the warmth returned, she only half looked in its direction. The glance fully wakened her from the spell of her drawing.

Riana yelped and scrambled away. The fire nymph that had been inches from her face, hanging over her shoulder and watching her draw with rapt attention, flew backward, head over heels, its silver hair gracefully following its movements to lay perfectly between the joints of its wings. The wings stuttered, the nymph dropped a foot, then the wings buzzed back to their incomprehensible speed and the nymph rose again.

Riana faced the fire nymph and the nymph faced Riana. She recognized the creature from the day before. She didn't breathe for fear the creature would dart away. The curiosity she felt seemed to be mirrored by the fire nymph, her wide, violently black eyes piercing her with a questioning gaze. Her lithe form was encompassed in shifting flames. The fire twisted and swayed, first orange, then red, then blue and yellow. The nymph's facial features were softened in the glow of its robing fire.

The fire nymph opened her mouth and a clear note rang out, vibrating through the air. Riana closed her eyes and let the sound wash over her. The notes created a rhythmic pattern, picking out a melody. When the song ended, Riana felt a question hanging in the air.

"Friend," she answered. "I only want to draw you. Nothing more."

The nymph sang again, notes lifting and falling, their meaning washing over Riana.

Riana answered by lifting the pad and showing it to the fire nymph. The nymph flew closer, blinking its ebony eyes as it regarded the scene Riana had sketched on the paper.

The nymph sang three notes. Riana felt around for the possible meaning but was distracted by a new noise. A loud, wet inhale of breath broke the conversation. Riana's scalp prickled in fear. The nymph froze in place, the buzz of its wings grew louder with what Riana translated as anxiety.

Riana shoved her notepad and pencil safely into the inner pocket on her skirt, buttoning it up to keep her secret sketches safe. Whatever was making the noise sounded large and dangerous.

The nymph scanned the forest, searching for the source of the noise, then turned and let out three long notes as she flew toward the community hidden in the trees. Riana's heart hammered into overdrive as the notes registered in an instinctual interpretation: danger.

Immediately, dozens of fire nymphs emerged from their homes in the branches above. They gathered in the center of the trees. The nymphs flew in a circle until they formed a tornado-shaped funnel.

The strange snuffling resounded through the trees. Riana looked around to spot what was making the noise. Perhaps a boar? She willed the nymphs to hurry. The nymph with whom she'd conversed was on the outside of the group, looking here and there, as if to make sure everyone had made it into the group. Riana saw her leadership and responsibility to the community and decided the nymph must be something like a monarch to the nymphs.

A tiny blue nymph bumbled out from behind a tree. It cried out, anxiety lacing its voice. It was just a baby and could barely fly. Another nymph with orange wings flew from the other side of the tree circle, singing out to the baby nymph. The queen nymph exited the cyclone, darting to the baby nymph, then flying toward its mother with the orange wings.

As she crossed the clearing to deliver the baby, a nymph on the outer ring of the twisting congregation bumped into the queen. She skittered away, still gripping the baby in strong arms, but her flight faltered. Her wing was damaged. The blur of the fire-cloaked nymph cyclone blinded Riana. The leader's flight toward the baby's mother stuttered, falling closer to the ground. The mother flew toward the leader. The baby cried. The cyclone gathered an alarming speed and brightness. Behind Riana, the animalistic grunting noises of an unknown creature grew louder.

"Hurry," she told the nymphs. The leader looked at the cyclone, which was now behind her. The grimace on her face gave away her pain. With a movement Riana could barely track, the leader nymph darted to the mother, placed the baby in her arms, and shoved them both into the cyclone. A moment later, a resounding crack and puff of smoke burst in the center of the trees and the nymphs were gone, nothing but a stirring of air to show they were ever there.

All but one. All but the queen.

She fell to the ground, quickly pulling herself into a sitting position and gripping the broken, translucent wing. Her fire extinguished and her blue skin grew dusky and pale.

The nymph-stalking creature howled, triumphant. Riana whipped around, eyes locking onto the source of the noise. Her breath quickened as she took in the massive beast approaching the clearing.

It was nearly as tall as a horse, with long, white hair hanging from its body. Its legs were dog-like yet overly long. Its feet were overly large, as were its wide pink nose and collection of curved and wicked teeth jutting up from an underbite.

The creature sniffed loudly, its head lowering as it located the nymph by smell. It leaned forward, soil and leaf litter crawling up its legs. The air rushed in toward it. It picked up a foot, extended its leg, and then, before the foot could touch the ground, the creature disappeared.

Riana cast around, searching for where it had gone. With a crack, it reappeared many feet closer. Riana squealed in terror. It was an elemental, one who used Tyrinth and Air to teleport itself, that was obvious to Riana, but she had no name for this creature she was both meeting and running from at the same time.

Riana's gaze yanked back to the little nymph. The queen struggled to rise. Launching herself into the air, she batted her wings, jerked in a semicircle, and then crashed to the ground again.

Riana glanced once more over her shoulder, a molten resolve dropping into her stomach. She scrambled clumsily over the log, leapt to the middle of the tree circle, and scooped the nymph into her hand.

The nymph looked up at her, sadness painted over her face. Riana tucked the creature into the inner pocket of her cloak.

And then, she ran.

Trees whipped by, dark and giant shadows against the fading afternoon sky. Riana was naturally a good runner. She could still outrun the boys who'd finally outstripped her in height and muscle mass. Even with her innate ability, her lungs burned and her heart hammered, and the white elemental galloped behind her. Leaf litter crunched under Riana's boots and her skirts tangled around her knees.

A root snagged her foot. She yelped as she stumbled, arms wind-milling to keep her balance. After several lurching steps, she righted herself. She whipped around, searching for her pursuer. The white creature stood amid the towering trees several yards away. Riana's fear squeezed her throat. The beast loped forward once, air swirled around it, raising its long hair from its body. A pop resounded and the creature disappeared.

Riana scanned the forest frantically. Another pop sounded. The creature appeared in a swirl of air, ruffling the pine needles of the nearby trees.

Riana screamed. The answering bellow of the creature behind her jolted through her. She turned toward the vineyard and ran, closer to the edge of the forest, closer to her grandmother, and closer to safety. She instinctually reached a hand to the small inner pocket of her cloak, felt the warmth there, and allowed herself a small sense of relief.

Riana's silver braid fell victim to the torrents of wind stirring the night. Lye soap mixed with lavender, sap of evergreen, and the mulch of the forest floor met her nose. She could see the edge of the forest. She could make out the hulking winery in the distance.

The snuffling of the creature echoed behind her. An errant puff and snap resounded and then it was there, looming ahead of her. Riana's already hammering heart picked an impossible staccato tempo against her ribs. The nymph held securely in her pocket wriggled.

Riana looked around, searching for a way out. The creature in front of her stood on gangly legs. Riana backed away, watching it warily. This was so much closer than she'd ever been. She held one elemental to her chest while another hunted it. Riana was no longer the silent observer of new creatures spawning in the TyrMinHai. She was intervening between them.

Enough of the setting sun shone through the canopy to see the creature's white, shaggy fur hanging over invisible eyes. She wanted to see its eyes, touch its fur, watch its movement to understand its magic.

The elemental took several loping steps forward. Riana backed up. She knew it wanted the fire nymph, but she wouldn't let it eat the queen. She took another step backward and bumped into the solid mass of a giant evergreen.

"Listen," she said to the creature, still looking around for her best exit. She was trapped. Any direction she could go would be cut short by the elemental who could teleport itself. It lifted its huge, pink nose into the air and sucked in a long, wet whiff. Its fur seemed to lift lightly from its body, then the now-familiar whoosh and pop, and the animal stood feet in front of her.

Riana had to put a hand over her mouth to keep from screaming. She put a shaking hand over the pocket with the fire nymph. Tears squeezed out of her eyes as the creature closed the space between them.

It snuffed the air around Riana with enough force to stir her hair and tickle her skin. Riana's pocket shivered. The creature sniffed at Riana's pocket and a snappish anger shot through her.

"No," she told the creature, pulling the pocket-bearing shoulder away. The creature paused. Riana waited for it to eat her, her breath wheezing, heartbeat tripled with fear.

The beast growled low and then whined high, which sounded to Riana like a noise of irritated dissatisfaction. It plopped on its rear, and to Riana's astonishment, it seemed to sulk. Riana found it hard to believe how quickly the creature went from terrifying monster to the almost lovable creature pouting before her now. It certainly didn't evoke the image of being a man-murdering monster, as all elementals were depicted.

She was aware of the curved and needle-like teeth lining its lower jaw, jutting up and over part of the creature's humongous nose. Riana gauged the teeth to be as long as her forearm. Teeth that would have torn through its prey if Riana had not stood in the way.

The animal leaned its head down and forward, hair sweeping closer to her. It was the length of a woman's hair. Riana wondered if it were submitting to her. She started to reach out to the creature, pulled her fingers away, and then plunged her hand forward. She swept the hair aside. Her breath caught in surprise. The creature had no eyes.

Above its dog-like snout with overly large nose was short fur on an empty face. The creature's hair shimmered, silken strands a similar color to Riana's own. The creature huffed and leaned into Riana's touch.

Stunned, Riana stroked the silver strands, still cupping a protective hand over the injured fire nymph in her pocket.

"We're alike, you and me," she said, absently. She opened her hand, palm brushing the silken tendrils.

A shout echoed from the other side of the tree line.

The creature jolted, half-turned, and growled a deep and vibrating hum. Riana marveled at how the Tyrinth trembled beneath her at the creature's vocalizations. When it turned back to Riana, she could almost sense the regret. It took two steps back. Tyrinth melted up from its giant feet, wind exploded, and then it was gone.

Riana's hand jerked back to her chest. She opened her cloak and peered into the inner pocket. The little blue nymph peered back at her with incredulous black eyes.

"He's gone," she said. "I didn't let him get you."

The fire nymph sang three short notes, then nuzzled deeper into Riana's pocket.

"Riana!"

Frantic shouting scratched at the serenity of the sleepy vineyard, tearing away the final shreds of thrilled discovery.

Riana closed her cloak, rose from her forest seat, and ran to her grandmother.

CHAPTER FIVE

"You're lucky you're not antoli fodder," Sela said.

Finally safely in her room, Riana opened her cloak and peered in on the fire nymph. The creature stood, extending her tiny hands toward Riana. Riana scooped the nymph out of her pocket, placing her gently onto the top of her dresser.

"Antoli," Riana said carefully. "That's what that was?"

"Yes," Sela said, "and that it didn't eat you while you had a fire nymph on your person is a mystery." Sela pulled her cloak from her shoulders while she stared intently at her granddaughter. "Stay here. I'll be right back."

Riana held the name of the creature in her mind, turning over the images of it until she could safely sketch it. She thought about the interaction. The antoli had been set on its target until Riana had spoken to it, and then it had seemed to listen to her. Much the way the queen fire nymph seemed to understand her. Riana moved around her room, thinking about elementals and how they acted around her versus other people, looking for something she could use as a bed for the fire nymph.

Riana's room was a vibrant array of colors. As she'd gotten older, she'd replaced the toys with books and pictures. Where once her desk had been littered with doll clothes, sketches, paper, and pencils had taken over. The bay window once overflowed with stuffed animals but now held stray clothes, her school bag, and cloak. Her modest bed was covered in a blanket stitched in a starburst of oranges, yellows, and reds. The bed was made, but not pristinely.

Atop her chest of drawers, the little nymph tiptoed across the thin layer of dust to Riana's jewelry box. She lifted the lid with effort and peered into its shadowed depths. Plucking out a ring—something plain and silver that Riana's grandmother had given her when she was twelve—she stood in front of the mirror and observed her reflection.

The little nymph was lithe, with blue skin a dusty shade so extremely opposite from when she was on fire. Her silver hair fluffed up on top of her head and flowed down her back between her wing joints. She stood in a wide stance, tilted back her chin, and lifted the little ring up, placing it resolutely on her head. The metal winked against the flame of a nearby oil lamp. She seemed pleased with the fit and look of not just her new crown, but her overall appearance.

Riana stifled a giggle and went about her own business, gathering handkerchiefs and searching for something which might serve as a makeshift bed for the creature. Riana hoped the queen fire nymph would sleep tonight. She looked around the room and finally decided on a nice box that had been filled with decorative and sweet-smelling soaps. She lifted it to her nose and sniffed. It even still smelled pretty.

Riana pulled stuffing from one of her old plush toys and pushed it inside the box, covering it with a handkerchief. She fished a doll blanket from the top of her closet and carried the new nymph bed over to the dresser.

"Here you go, Queen," Riana said.

The nymph yawned and stretched, wincing as the injured wing rose a little too high. She took the ring off her head and replaced it in the jewelry box. She made new tracks through the dust and climbed into the bed, immediately blinking heavily once the blankets were pulled to her chin.

Grandmother Sela came into the room, paused, eyes popping out as she looked the room over, shook her head, and then went over to the dresser without a word. In her hands, she held a shining bottle shaped like a teardrop and containing a shimmering golden liquid.

"What is that?" Riana asked. The liquid was thick, not clear like white wine. It seemed to swirl and sway, even though her grandmother didn't jostle or turn the bottle. The color was so vibrantly golden it seemed to carry light. It reminded her of the fruit she'd seen the fire nymphs bringing back to their home today.

Grandmother Sela sighed. "I had hoped to keep you out of this," she said.

"Out of what?" Riana asked.

"This is a special elixir, Riana. And it heals like no other medicine can. We can only make a very, very small amount. Partly due to your friends, the nymphs."

Riana recalled what she'd seen today and dawning sparked. She pulled the notepad out of her dress pocket and flipped to today's drawing. "It's made from these, isn't it?"

Grandmother Sela pulled glasses from her apron and looked at the drawing. "Yes," she confirmed. "That is Kaely's fruit." She put her glasses back into her pocket and from another pocket pulled a dropper and port glass and handed them to Riana.

Riana held the instruments while her grandmother pulled the cork from the small wine bottle. She then took the dropper from Riana and squeezed liquid into the glass tube. While Riana held the port glass, her grandmother squeezed the dropper of contents in.

The queen sat up, eyes glittering, and reached for the glass. The nymph was no bigger than Riana's hand, but she still managed the port glass, tipping it up and drinking deeply until the liquid was gone. Grandmother took the empty glass. The nymph hiccupped, burped, and slumped back in her bed with a smile spread over her tiny face. Her eyes drooped, then fell shut and she slept soundly.

"Well," Grandmother said, "that was quick." She looked at the bottle of elixir, one white eyebrow raised. Sighing, she held the dropper, port glass and wine bottle in her hands. "Sometimes I think a swig could do this old lady some good."

"Why don't you drink some then?" Riana asked.

Grandmother regarded her. "If I drink the wine, I risk becoming addicted, as the Baron has become. Furthermore, to drink this wine is to take away the amount available to the fire nymphs. I just can't do that."

"Why? You don't believe the elementals are dangerous like everyone else?" Riana asked.

"Oh, elementals can be dangerous, yes. I have my own reasons for feeling protective of them, which I won't go into tonight. It's imperative, Riana, that you tell not a soul about this elixir."

Riana halted her thoughts already heading a course to revelation to her best friend, Elynda, the one to whom she told everything. "Why?"

"Because, my dear, if anyone else were to discover the elixir, then they'd want it for themselves and would not allow our friends the nymphs to survive."

"Well, obviously, I wouldn't tell anyone dangerous. But, what about Elynda?"

"Keep it quiet, Riana. Do not test me on this." The ice in her voice stole through the air and cut Riana's argument short.

Elynda was trustworthy. She wouldn't say anything to anyone. Riana nodded her consent, but in her heart, she meant to tell Elynda anyway.

"This is for your own safety, the safety of the vineyard, all of its workers, and the safety of the elementals hidden in the forest. If they find the elixir, they'll find the fruit. If they find the fruit, they'll find the elementals. If they find the elementals, we're all in trouble, Riana. Knowing about elementals and not reporting them is punishable by death."

Riana knew this. "I won't get caught," she said, tired of the lecture.

"I'm serious, Riana," Grandmother said.

"Don't worry so much, Grandmother," Riana said.

"I do worry, Riana. You know the consequences and yet you still take hefty risks."

"Have I been caught yet? No. I'm careful. I'll be careful with this too."

Sela Starliss crossed her arms and regarded her adopted grandchild with a mixture of heartache and judgment.

Riana was sure her grandmother didn't believe her to be capable. "Grandmother, I promise. Okay? I won't tell anyone, and I'll be careful."

Grandmother held her gaze a moment longer, then finally nodded. "Very well. Now, get some sleep."

"Yes, ma'am."

Grandmother exited her room, closing the door, and at last Riana was able to breathe more easily. Riana slipped into her night clothes and turned down the oil lamp at her bedside. As she crawled in bed and lay under the starburst cover, she watched the fire nymph, glowing in the dark in dusky shades of blue. Something deep inside her recoiled from the state of things. Tomas's last words begging her to know he could never hurt anyone. The screams of the fire nymphs killed by the Tyrmini guard. Guards who possessed the magic the High King outlawed. It was only okay if he said it was okay. Riana wrestled with the hypocrisy of it.

And yet, what could she do about it?

Nothing, a voice told her. You're only a teen girl. Only an apprentice.

Everything, another voice said. You're the only one who can make the change.

Yeah, right, she countered to the second voice, and then slipped into a dark and disturbed slumber.

In her dreams, she flew. She was made of feathers and scales and they shone like another moon under the lunar light. She was free. She cast about the sky, looking left and right so that her one eye could take in all that the missing eye didn't see. Even maimed, she was filled with joy.

The exhilaration of the flight swelled within her chest, twisted in her belly.

Centuries. Centuries had passed. But now she could fly again. Fly... and something else. A new, engulfing emotion took place of the joy of flying. Stomach boiling with anger, heart aflame with indignation, she swung her massive body up into the sky, the moon full in her face for mere moments before she dove again. The castle grew larger in her vision. There on the parapets was her target. She flexed her talons, fixed her eye upon him, screeched into the night, and attacked.

CHAPTER SIX

"Grandmother," Riana hollered from her doorway.

"What is it, child?" her grandmother asked, coming out of her own room. She was already dressed, her bodice tight and skirts wide enough they brushed the door frame when she exited the room. The dress was sage green and dusty purple with lace trims and sleeves. She flipped open her fan and waved it at her cheeks.

"I can't find the blue dress," Riana said.

"You've outgrown the blue dress. I got rid of it. Now hurry up. We're late for the seamstress."

Riana moaned under her breath and went back into her room. She hated dresses. She wished she could wear pants like men.

A movement out of the corner of her eye caught her attention. She turned to see the fire nymph aflame, dancing and flying above the surface of the dresser and watching her reflection.

"Please don't catch my room on fire," Riana said. "Grandmother is already cross with me."

The nymph continued to dance.

Riana searched through the dresses hanging in the closet. Pink. Purple. Green. She yanked the next one back. It pulled free of the hanger and hung in her hand. Grey. The hanger swung wildly on the rod while Riana yanked the dress over her underdress. Thank the Maker she didn't have to wear those stupid hoop skirts. She was banking on them going out of style before she was considered woman enough to wear them. The corset was bad enough, and she often skipped putting one on and suffered her grandmother's chastisement.

The gray silk was less stiff than the other dresses, and the subtle stitching of the flowers was not so overtly girly, so Riana didn't mind it so much. It would be her most comfortable option for getting fitted for yet another dress. She rolled her eyes. She really despised the seamstress shop.

After she'd pulled every article of clothing into place and cinched up her bootstrings, she faced the twirling, fiery nymph.

The sound of Sela's bootheels echoed down the hall before she was framed in Riana's bedroom door. Riana looked from her to the dancing nymph.

"What are we going to do about the nymph?" Riana asked.

"There isn't time to take her back to the forest now. We're already late. Leave her here and we'll take her to the forest when we return from the seamstress," Grandmother said. "But make sure she's locked in your room."

Riana nodded, watching the little nymph arch high before circling clockwise. The streaming flame made a beautiful ring in the air.

Riana closed her door and followed her grandmother down the hall and out into the main living area. Grandmother cast her a harried look.

"What?" Riana asked.

"Your cloak, dear," Grandmother said.

"Oh." Riana dashed back down the hallway and into her room. She snatched her cloak from the coat rack and quickly ran out again.

The seamstress shop was perched on the cobbled streets, squished between the baker and the cobbler. Riana sighed and removed herself from the carriage. Grandmother tied the horses and met Riana on the sidewalk.

The carved, wooden sign hung proudly over the rounded wooden door: "Sew and Sew."

In the shop window, wicker skeletons of women's figures boasted the latest fashions. Riana looked at the dresses and frowned. The latest fashion obviously did not hold into account such activities as chasing after elementals in the forest or hiking up Lighthouse Hill. The closer to womanhood Riana got, the more constricting the clothing became.

"My, aren't those lovely?" Grandmother said. "What a delicate pattern on that green dress! And look at the quality of the petticoats. Those are simply divine!"

Riana rolled her eyes.

When Grandmother snapped out of her reverie, she regarded Riana. "You would look lovely in that green dress, Riana. Shall we try it on?"

Riana stifled her distaste. "Grandmother, if you feel the dress is appropriate as your apprentice, I would be happy to try it on." Even as she said it, she could feel the squeeze of the corset and the bite of the metal cage she would have to wear to poof the dress out as far as the mannequin.

"Sometimes, we have to endure a certain measure of discomfort to fulfil our duties, Riana. And dressing the part to deal with potential buyers is critical. The client judges the wine first on their judgment of you and me."

Riana grimaced as she stepped over a puddle. She thought about her grandmother's wines. This climate was supposed to be horrible for growing grapes. It was too wet and mild. The fog was said to produce weaker fruit, fruit too mild in flavor to produce proper wine. But the grapes, to the complete astonishment of wine experts across Aelos, thrived. They had a distinct flavor, to be sure, but they were bold, warm, and subtle with notes of sweetness. Grandmother's wines were mysteriously good. Unique to all wines in different regions.

"Grandmother, I think you underestimate the power of your wines' reputation. You're famous. And your wine is bold and different. Magical, in a way," she said, not thinking the words through before she spoke them.

Grandmother halted on the sidewalk, turning on her heel to face Riana. "Hold your tongue, Riana Rose."

Riana lowered her head, chastised.

Grandmother stepped toward her. She rubbed her arm and leaned in. "Be careful of using those sorts of words in public," she whispered hoarsely, looking around the cobbled streets.

Riana did the same. Luckily, no one was near. It was careless to say 'magic' in such a public area.

Grandmother looped her arm through Riana's and pulled her through the shop's door. Riana allowed herself to be pulled along. A cheerful chime and the golden glow from a collection of oil lamps scattered throughout the shop greeted them.

Along the walls were hung already-made clothes. Most of them occupied wooden hangers but others clothed more headless manikins.

Grandmother removed her wide-brimmed purple hat with a green sash and stowed it on the coat hanger near the door. After removing her gloves and tucking them into a hidden pocket in the folds of her skirt, she trilled warmly, "Celeste! Are you here, my friend? Riana and I are here to try on dresses for the Baron's Ball."

Grandmother turned around the room to take in the dresses that had appeared since they were in a few weeks ago. She stopped her rotation when Treyor appeared instead of Celeste.

"Oh," she said, her smile faltered then slid from her face. "Hello, Treyor. Where is your aunt?"

Treyor shuffled forward. He was red-haired and lithe with green eyes, a pointy nose, and red lips. When he smiled, there was a wicked set to his pointed eyebrows.

"Terrible thing about Aunt Celeste, ma'am," the young man began. "She has gotten awful sick-like. She wheezes and has turned a real pale shade of green. She sweats like the devil but says she's cold."

Riana regarded him, her skin crawling. He didn't even seem upset about his poor Aunt.

"That's a very unfortunate thing. I would like to see her myself. Young man, please take me back to her quarters and then you will tend to Riana." Grandmother headed for the counter. Treyor opened the waist-high door to let Sela through. They exited through a dark door.

Their fading footsteps turning to measured creaks as they ascended the stairs to the living quarters on the second floor.

As her grandmother disappeared, a cold stone of fear dropped into her belly and splashed up her throat with anxiety. Treyor—a boy her age—fitting her? She didn't want him to get anywhere near her, much less let him pin her for fitting.

Riana removed her cloak and hung it on the coat rack.

The shop was as quiet as dust floating on the afternoon sunlight. She sniffed and hummed nervously, just to make some noise and dispel the silence. She turned again to peer out the window and saw that among the crowds of people passing by, many women regarded the dresses in varying degrees of desire, from simple admiration to downright covetousness.

Riana shook her head at the frills and furbelows and turned away, then ran right into the red-haired apprentice. He grabbed her arms. Riana thought he did this to keep his balance, but when she looked up into his vivid, green eyes his mouth stretched into a smile.

Riana pulled out of his grasp. She'd had enough of people gripping her for one day. "My apologies. I wasn't paying attention," she said.

"The dresses are nearly done. I'm just doing the final fitting," Treyor finally said.

Riana shifted and waited for him to proceed.

"You'll need to get down to your underclothing," Treyor said.. "The dressing room is over there." He motioned to a black curtain, hanging on a brass rod, between two racks of clothing.

Riana went into the little room, closed the curtain on the impish, red-haired boy, and pulled off her gray dress. She itched with anxiety, uncomfortable with the idea of being so exposed to a boy her age.

When she returned, she noticed that the curtains had been drawn and the sign on the front door had been turned so that the 'Open' side faced in. She was relieved the crowds passing by wouldn't witness her being measured in her underclothes.

Riana watched with nervous eyes as Treyor removed the measuring strip from around his neck. The slender piece of cotton was new and all the marks legible. "Arms stretched out," he said.

Riana stretched her arms out, casting a nervous glance around the room to avoid eye contact with Treyor. He wrapped his tape around her middle. He let go and scratched a note onto a small piece of paper before he returned the pencil to its perch behind his ear.

"Mrs. Humphrey did this already. Do we really need to do it again?" Riana complained.

"The Master Seamstress Celeste told me herself to ensure that the measurements from your first were close since you're still growing," he said. "I won't be long and then you can go next door to the bakery for a loaf, if you want."

Riana looked away from him to watch the counter, hoping to see her grandmother return from her visit with Celeste. Many long minutes passed while Treyor pressed, pulled, and stretched the tape to various parts of her body.

"The measurements are all done. You can go get your clothes on now."

Riana nearly ran to the dressing room, swishing the curtain aside a little too violently. It flapped like a grounded crow before it settled into place. Riana yanked the gray dress from the hook, fumbled with the skirts, and pulled it over her head. Through the muffled flap of fabric around her ears, she recognized the distinct rhythm of boots walking across the wood floor.

She pulled the dress over her torso badly, leaving it twisted, and exited the dressing room.

"What is that?" Treyor said. He poked at the chest pocket of her cloak.

"What is what? My cloak?" Riana asked. Had he never seen a cloak before?

To Riana's astonishment, the cloak rustled.

"What—" she started.

Treyor poked the pocket once again. The pocket flapped. Treyor backed up. Riana took several steps toward it, curiosity driving her forward, even as a sinking realization clicked in place. When she'd gone back to get the cloak, she hadn't seen the elemental in her room.

The fire nymph burst from Riana's cloak pocket, flames erupting as soon as she was free of the imprisoning fabric. She flew into the face of the boy, pulling a black thorn-shaped sword from behind her back, the scabbard hidden by her white hair, and brandished it at him. The nymph sang several clipped notes and Riana gasped at their meaning. This creature might be only the size of her opponent's hand, but she still asserted if he poked her once more, she'd stab his eye out and feed it to the antoli.

Treyor—who didn't understand the nymph, it seemed—leaned into the creature. "Are you harboring an elemental?" He turned to fix Riana with an incredulous green-eyed stare.

Riana stared back, equally incredulous, her nerves a throbbing mass sitting squarely in her gut. The queen must have slipped into the pocket when Riana had exited the room.

The fire nymph's flame expanded as she circled Treyor in order to gather his attention to her.

It worked.

Treyor hissed in pain as the nymph touched a shoulder. "Menace," he muttered. He darted to a nearby dress hung on a rack, yanked it from its hangar, and tossed it at the nymph.

"Leave her alone," Riana said. She lunged forward and batted the material away.

"Don't be ridiculous. You can't run around keeping elementals in your cloak pocket. It must be killed. Or would you rather I call the Baron's Guard?" Treyor scooped the dress from the floor and zeroed his attention in on the fire nymph.

"She must not be killed, and you will not kill her, nor will you go running to the Baron's Guard." Riana darted in front of Treyor to block his attack on the nymph. Heat seared the back of her head. Her guts churned and her heart hammered. Her hands trembled, and not because she was scared. She was angry.

"What makes you think so?" Treyor asked.

"I'm not letting you hurt my friend," Riana said.

"Friend?" Treyor asked, so surprised at Riana's pronouncement that he dropped the dress he'd been brandishing to his knees.

The fire nymph saw this as an opportunity and blasted toward him. Warm air washed over Riana as the elemental flew by. Treyor moved quickly, raising the dress just in time for the fire nymph to fly into it. He wrapped her up, making a ball of the dress.

"You'll smother her!" Riana shouted.

"Yes, exactly."

"Let her go," Riana said. She lurched toward him, pulling at his arms to release the dress even as he knelt and pushed the lump of dress and nymph into the floor. He raised himself with the lump firmly held in outstretched fingers. Riana's attempts to remove him were in vain. The boy was much stronger than he looked.

He pounded the dress-wrapped nymph into the ground.

Riana could not bear the thought of finding the nymph's broken body in the mass of smothering material. Anger and desperation raged through her. She would not stand by and let someone hurt a completely innocent creature.

Her nerves sang. An odd sensation of lightness stole through her. As she charged the fire nymph's attacker with outstretched arms, she saw a glow on her skin that made her want to shield her eyes. Gooseflesh raced down her back. Molten need rose within her. He must not hurt the elemental. She zeroed in on his arms and hands, which had turned to instruments of death. She must stop them.

The need flowed from the pit of her stomach, up through her heart and down her arms. "NO!" She screamed and shoved Treyor with everything she had in her, panic ratcheting her voice to an animalistic screech. A blinding light filled the air and a series of cracks reverberated in Riana's ears. The dress-bound nymph dropped softly to the ground.

Treyor fell to his side. Something wet spattered against Riana's face. After a horrific pause of absolute silence, Treyor's scream of agony ripped through the stillness. His hands were bent backward at an impossible angle, white bone jutting out of his wrists as blood trickled down his arms. His fingers were arced and broken until their tips touched his forearms. His mouth stretched wide to reveal every tooth in his head, his eyes closed to the torture.

Riana watched another scream rip out of his throat as his forearms snapped in half with a resounding crunch. More bones broke free from their encasing flesh, blood spurting into the open air. Riana grabbed at the dress, eyes wide, heart pounding.

Footsteps pounded overhead. Riana's gaze jerked to the material-covered nymph. She could not be seen. The footsteps had reached the first landing of stairs. The thump of their approach grew louder. Riana pushed herself away from the counter, skirting the catastrophe of Treyor's broken and bloody body.

She backed away from Treyor, the blood, the exposed bones, his screams ripping out of him over and over. Finding the door, she twisted the knob and fled.

CHAPTER SEVEN

Riana ran over the cobbled streets until she reached the city's end. Passersby followed her movement, some with little noises of irritation or disapproval. Riana ignored them, gently tucked the wadded-up dress and nymph into the crook of her arm, and pelted down the southern road.

By the time she reached the vineyard, her heart was pounding. Her mind raced as quickly as her legs. She fought to piece the incident together. One moment, Treyor had been bent on crushing the fire nymph and the next his arms, hands, and fingers were broken. But there'd been a flash of light as well. Where had that come from?

She entered the vineyard from the southern entrance. She passed through rows of empty vines, the skeletal vegetation whipping by in a blur. She heaved lungfuls of air and pushed herself on, worried about the nymph still wadded up in the material.

Once the trees were solidly around her and she was well beyond the comfort of all other Landsend inhabitants, she dropped to her knees, quickly and gently unfolding the material to release the queen fire nymph.

The nymph immediately sparked to fiery life, drawing close to Riana.

"Are you okay? Are you hurt?"

The nymph shook her head and sang, expressing no, she was fine, and that she was indebted to Riana for saving her life.

"I should have made sure you were still in my room," Riana remarked. "I'm so sorry."

The queen shook her head.

You saved me from the antoli first. The boy is wicked and mean. He deserved to be broken.

Riana shied away from this. She didn't believe anyone deserved to be hurt. Riana shook her head.

"How did that happen?" she asked the nymph.

You awakened your power to protect me.

Snapping zips of electricity tripped up Riana's spine.

"I what?"

Awakened your power. It is time for this. You will see. Things are different since you came to our land. We are more numerous than we have been in five centuries. Now that your power has awakened, it will all be different now.

The queen seemed excited. Riana wanted to vomit. If it was true, if she was Tyrmini, she'd be executed if she didn't turn herself in to the King.

And for what? Her inherent nature. Riana backed into a nearby giant evergreen, finding a perfect round space in the trunk, and curled herself into it. The fire nymph floated down to her knees, fire immediately extinguishing, her skin soft and dusty blue with lines of black like the bark of a tree. Riana's fingers found their way into her hair, twisting at the strange silvery strands in a gesture of self-soothing. Odd. Different. Outcast. Now more than ever she was alone and shunned. Except, she thought as she looked at the fire nymph, for the companionship of elementals.

They'd always known, hadn't they? All the people in town. They'd known she was different and dangerous, and they'd been right. She was dangerous. She'd probably killed Treyor. The thought swelled within her. Her stomach squeezed and she swallowed back bile.

Part of her was proud she'd kept him from killing the fire nymph. She'd kept him from doing that. She sat a little straighter. She'd defended an elemental when no one else would. Her shoulders straightened.

Then the memory of the sound of his bones cracking and splitting through skin and muscle washed over her, and she slumped over and vomited. If her power simply inflicted pain on others, did she really want it? Even if she could be an outlaw, was that the life she wanted to live? Maybe it would be better to give herself up and face the High King's testing...or death. She swallowed around the imaginary sword at her throat.

She couldn't say how long she sat there, thinking, fearing, hoping, dreading her future. The fire nymph stayed with her, occasionally humming. The afternoon sun drifted toward evening when a noise caught her attention.

"Riana!"

"Grandmother?" Riana asked, incredulous. The fire nymph flitted from her knees, looked in the direction of Sela's voice, looked back at Riana, and then, seeming satisfied, flew away into the forest.

"Thank you," Riana called.

The fire nymph turned, placed a hand on her heart, and waved at Riana. Riana mimicked the gesture, gratefulness swelling within her. The nymph turned and disappeared into the trees.

Riana turned from the retreating fire nymph, grateful to her newfound friendship, and ran to her grandmother. She threw herself into her grandmother's arms.

"You came for me," she sobbed. "I thought I was going to have to run away, to hide in the woods for the rest of my life. I'm so scared, Grandmother."

Sela Starliss stroked Riana's hair and waited for her sobs to slow. Riana feared what she would say when she did speak. But the silence stretched out and there was nothing else to cry over.

"What happened to him, Grandmother? Did I—" she couldn't finish the question.

"He's alive, but with a hefty price," her grandmother said.

"What did you do?" Riana asked.

"I bribed him to keep silent and leave Landsend." Her grandmother took a big, deep breath and let it out in a sigh that seemed like resignation.

"With what?" Riana asked. Before her grandmother could answer, the glimmer of golden elixir shimmered in Riana's memory. "But, Grandmother...What about the Baron's portion?"

"I fear there will not be enough for my father," she said.

"Your—"

"Yes, my father. It's time you learned some things, Riana. Let's go home. I have a lot to tell you."

CHAPTER EIGHT

Treyor sat at the bar, flexing his hands, fingers, and arms over and over, marveling at their wholeness. The girl had gotten away, but he would find her. His savior, an old woman—the girl's grandmother—had taunted him as he lay near death's door, blood pumping out of his arms and shock setting in.

"Give me your word and I'll save you."

What a bluff! How would she have explained a dead body appearing during her scheduled time at the seamstress shop. Someone would have guessed at the cause.

Riana Fraely was a Tyrmini.

He should have known. With those odd eyes and strange hair. Clearly, she was different. But with which elements had she wielded her magic? That was the thing Treyor couldn't figure out. There had been no elements conjured or manipulated. He just—broke. The memory of the pain sent a spasm through him. He'd never experienced so much pain, so much fear, so much anger toward the strange girl who'd almost killed him.

He still had shiny lines where the skin had fused back together, forming seams. As if the elixir had stitched him together from the inside out. He reached for his shot glass and poured the liquor down his throat. He winced at the strong drink, shaking his head, and in doing so, missed the dark man who had sidled up to the barstool next to him.

"Hello, stranger, and well met," the man said.

Treyor turned, his eyesight a little blurry. That had been his third drink and he was not accustomed to alcohol. He enjoyed the freedom he felt with the warmth of the alcohol singing in his veins.

"Hello," Treyor said, and his voice cracked. He cleared his throat to recover.

"Young man," the stranger said, "why are you not home with your family at this hour?"

"Got no family," he said. "Burned up." Of course, he could claim his aunt, if he wanted to also explain he was now outcast from her house. He chose not to mention her.

"What is your meaning?" asked the man.

"I mean, they burned up in a house fire."

The man paused, staring intently with dark, glittering eyes roaming over him. Treyor might have imagined it, but he could have sworn the man's gaze lingered over the left inner pocket of his coat. The pocket that held the rest of the elixir—the miraculous drink of healing.

"My condolences," the man said.

Treyor shrugged. He'd set the fire. Condolences were unnecessary.

"What is your name?" Treyor asked.

The man reached out a hand to shake Treyor's. "I am Captain Luther, of the Ogelith Province. May I have your name and call you friend?" Captain Luther's voice drawled and stretched, warm, sweet, gritty. To Treyor, the man's voice rubbed against every one of his nerves.

Treyor reached out a hand and let the man shake it. "Treyor," he supplied. "And I have nothing, sir. Only a few coins to make my way out of this Maker-forsaken town with its Maker-forsaken Tyrmini."

The Captain withdrew his hand and looked seriously at Treyor. "What do you mean, friend?"

Treyor leaned in conspiratorially. "I was attacked today."

"No," the man drawled but didn't really seem impressed. "How did you escape?"

"I. Didn't."

"But you're sitting right here. Sitting' pretty."

"She broke my arms. Snapped them—" he showed him the gleaming seams on his fingers, wrists, even rolled his sleeves up to reveal the jagged lines on his forearms. "I was bleeding out."

The man's gaze drifted back to Treyor's pocket. It spooked him. How did he know there was something there?

"What saved you?" Luther asked.

"I can't say that I recall," Treyor said, hedging his bets that what he held in his pocket, even if he kept it, could fetch him more coins than he had now. Maybe many more coins.

Luther nodded, his dark facial features indistinct in the shadows of the ill-lit bar.

Further down the bar, a man stepped up to the counter and ordered whiskey. The bartender set down a rag and turned to the wall of liquor, picking out one of the many bottles and returning to the counter.

Luther pulled out a pouch. It jingled merrily as he sat it on the bar. He lifted it and dropped it softly over and over, showing Treyor how heavy it was. "Maybe you'd recall with a little...support," he said.

Treyor nodded slowly. "Perhaps." He leaned in closer. "An old woman gave me a drink of something. Some special wine she makes. She told me if I kept silent she would give me the wine and save my life."

"So much for your confidence," Luther said.

Treyor shrugged and reached for the coins. Luther clutched them tightly in his grasp.

"Tell me about this old woman," Luther said.

"Some local big shot. Owner of a winery and vineyard. Apparently, the wine is mysteriously good for this region. Most people can't grow the grapes in the damp weather."

"Starliss," Luther said, stretching out the "s" on the end of the name.

Treyor nodded after signaling to the bartender for another drink. "That's the one," he said.

"And you only got a swig?"

Treyor looked down at the bar and scratched at its wooden surface. He nodded. "Yeah. That's all it took. And look at me." He held out his arms and hands, still marveling.

"Hm," Luther said. He shook the coins, still staring at the inner breast pocket where the bottle of golden elixir was stowed safely.

Treyor's ears burned. The back of his neck prickled.

Luther pushed the pouch of coins slowly across the short space between himself and Treyor, his hand still resting over the top of it.

"Well, then, Treyor. Since you remembered so well, I feel a reward is owed to ya."

Treyor reached his hand toward the coins, but once again the captain pulled the pouch away. Treyor pulled his hand back, feeling like an idiot. His anger flared. He eyed the captain, wanting to stick him with a knife and watch the blood leak out.

To his surprise, the captain grinned at him, then chuckled. Then out and out laughed. "I'd like to see you try," he said, as if he were listening to Treyor's thoughts.

Treyor shook, his fury swelling within him. "You don't know who you're talking to," the teen said.

The captain laughed again. "Oh no, my friend? Well, well, well. A dangerous boy with murder in his eyes and nothing more powerful than an off mind and lack of compassion." He pulled the pouch all the way back and dropped it back into his coat.

"Hey," Treyor said. "I gave you information. You owe me."

Luther leaned in, the smile on his face gone. "I owe you?" Luther stood from the bar, grabbed Treyor by the collar, and slammed his face against the brass railing. Treyor felt bones break for the second time that day.

"Take it outside!" the barkeep shouted.

"Apologies," Luther said genially and dragged Treyor, screaming and clutching his gushing nose, out of the bar and into the darkened alley on the side of the building. He threw the teen against the wall with inhuman strength. Treyor's shoulder popped on impact. He screamed and slid down the wall, screaming again when the popped shoulder hit the cobble alley and popped again.

"You're welcome," Luther said. He leaned over Treyor, grabbed his shirt front, and yanked him to his feet. Thrusting him against the wall he raised him high. Treyor's heels kicked at the wall, feet dangling. He choked against Luther's knuckles pushing into his throat, along with the blood draining down his face from his broken nose.

"Please," he managed. "Stop."

"Oh, but I thought I owed you," Luther said. "I'm simply repaying your kindness. Would you deny my gratitude?"

"What do you want?" Treyor asked, frantic.

"I want you to give me what's in your pocket."

"I don't have anything," Treyor lied.

Luther lowered Treyor and, before his feet could completely touch the ground, he let go. Treyor slid, his feet unable to find purchase, landing hard on his butt against the cobble road. Treyor moaned, clutching his nose as new splinters of pain burst through his head. When he looked up, Captain Luther stood over him, a shadow against more shadows.

Luther held out a hand. Treyor shook his head a little.

"I told you. She only let me have a small drink."

For an answer, the man pulled a knife from his belt. "That's the story you're stickin' to, huh?" He crouched in front of Treyor and pushed the knife's edge to his throat.

Treyor sucked in air as the cool blade touched his neck. His heart hammered in his chest, fear breeding panic. "No. Please," he managed to strangle out.

The dark man held the knife there for a moment, still and watching without a hint of emotion in his eyes. Treyor began to calm, thinking he'd only meant to threaten him. As his breath eased, the man's mouth twitched in a quick grin. The knife sliced through skin, muscle, and cartilage. Shocked, Treyor grabbed his throat as blood gushed out and through his fingers. He choked as blood leaked down into his lungs. He reached for the man for help, but the captain did nothing but observe.

Treyor couldn't believe the man had done it. He'd thought himself the scariest monster around. Murdering his family had come so easy. Torture was second nature. Rape, a treat. And he knew others did not feel the same way as he did. Knew he was different. Special in his ability to kill without feeling.

But this man had matched him.

"Well," the captain drawled, lazy, bored. "Ya gonna just lay there and die or are you gonna do somethin' about it?"

Treyor was dying.

He could feel life slipping out of him as his blood poured down his shirt. He fumbled with one hand, trying to hold the wound closed with the other. His hands were disconnected puppets on unfeeling strings. He searched for the elixir in his pocket, but he couldn't cause himself to grip the bottle from its safe place. Salvation was so close. He didn't want to die.

That was his last thought before darkness enveloped him.

Captain Luther watched the boy die. Once he had breathed his last breath, he loosed the bottle from the dead boy's grip. He held the golden elixir aloft, allowing the moonlight cascading into the alley to catch and reflect off the liquid. It seemed to sparkle, to sway in an independent way. In the dark alley, it almost seemed to shine with its own light.

"So sorry, friend. We have to test this out thorough-like. Can't be handing over fake goods to the High King," he said. He removed the cork from the tear-shaped bottle with his teeth and bent over the impertinent kid. He pulled the cork from his teeth and pinched it between his thumb and forefinger with the hand that held the bottle. On one hand, he hoped the elixir didn't work. He didn't like this kid. He was sick in the head and there were enough of those kinds in the world. On the other hand, if the elixir worked, his work was done and he could finish his mission. Although, returning to the High King sent shivers down his spine too.

No matter the outcome, his business was dark business. He hated himself for the ease with which he could conduct such dirty deeds. But he'd do anything for his daughter. Anything to keep her safe from the High King's grip. The promise of her safety filled him with resolve so intense it transcended dark and light. Whatever it took to protect her, he would do it.

He shook the thought of her out of his mind, casting aside the image of her in a dark prison in the bowels of the High King's castle. He scooped the young man's neck into one of his hands and titled his chin back. "Open wide, kid," he instructed the corpse. He grimaced as he poured the smallest amount he could into the red-head's mouth.

He waited as he re-stoppered the bottle and slid it into the inside pocket of his dirty, wool jacket.

Needles of nerves jangled through his heart and stomach. And he hoped. Not for this murderous boy of a man.

For Fae, he thought.

CHAPTER NINE

"What am I, Grandmother? Am I Tyrmini?"

Grandmother sat straight in her wing-backed chair, peering into the fire. She looked at Riana, and Riana could almost see the secrets floating through her mind.

As soon as her grandmother had gotten her home, Riana had pulled the Maker-forsaken gray dress off of her as if it were dirty from the deeds she'd committed at the seamstress shop. She'd washed herself from head to toe with lavender soap and dressed in a clean sleeping gown. She sat curled up in a thick blanket in front of the fire. She wasn't sure why, but she was chilled down to her bones.

"I don't know," her grandmother said.

Riana regarded her grandmother, a sudden shrill anger gathering in the pit of her stomach. "You. Know. Something," Riana said, unable to keep the anger from her voice. "And you are keeping it from me." She breathed heavily, her heart pounding as if she'd run a race.

Her grandmother hung her head. "I had hoped she would come back by now."

"Who?" Riana asked. "Please. Just tell me what you know."

Her grandmother sat, staring into the fire, then took a deep breath and blew it out. "It's not much. In the days before your birth, two women came to port."

Riana shifted inside the blankets. She'd never been told her origin. She only knew she was abandoned and adopted. She sat silently as her grandmother finally divulged her secret.

"Of course, the one woman—your mother—was clearly about to give birth. She was sickly and weak, emaciated."

Her mother. Sela had seen her mother. Her birth mother.

"What did she look like?" Riana asked.

Her grandmother looked up from the fire to Riana. "Like you in most ways."

"Did she have the same hair and eyes?" Was there family out there to whom she belonged? A place to fit in with all her oddities.

Her grandmother lowered her eyes to the handkerchief she gripped in her lap and shook her head. "No. No, she had brown hair and eyes."

Riana's hope fell.

"Your mother gave birth, barely able to make it through the process before she passed. Poor thing was so weak."

Riana's heart stirred. She'd had a mother. She hadn't been abandoned—at least not by her mother's choice. Her mother had died to give her life.

"Did she say anything before she...died?" Riana asked.

Her grandmother smiled, tears building in her sea blue eyes and slipping down her softly wrinkled cheeks. "I held you up to your mother's face, so she could see you at least once before she slipped away. She gasped in astonishment, and with tears in her eyes, she said, 'Just as beautiful as your Savior. Make sure you return the favor, little one.'"

"What did that mean?" Riana asked. Her heart twisted. Her mother had thought her beautiful. Her mother had loved her. Her mother had done a wonderful thing to give her life. Her mother had sacrificed everything for her daughter. Riana's thoughts zoomed around each other, emotions ratcheting inside her at the revelations.

Her grandmother shook her head. "I don't know. The woman who accompanied her promised she would return for you one day when you neared womanhood. I had hoped she would be back by now. Who knows if she even survived?"

"Grandmother, that's not very hopeful. How on Tyrinth am I going to understand what I am?"

Her grandmother—at least the woman who was in every sense of the word her grandmother—reached out to her. Her body followed her hands, moving her to crouching where she gently, carefully, placed her hands on Riana's blanket-covered knees.

"Whether you are Tyrmini or something else entirely, I swear to you I will protect you with everything I am. I'm so sorry you had to discover your power in such a way," she said. "You've such a big heart, Riana. You saved that little fire nymph, didn't you? First from the antoli and then from Treyor?"

"He was going to squish her. He wanted to kill the creature. He even threatened to call the Baron's Guard on me for harboring an elemental unless I let him kill her."

Riana paused, looking down at her hands, which still felt stained with spatters of Treyor's blood although she had washed them thoroughly.

She yanked her head up to her grandmother. "I swear, Grandmother, I didn't mean to hurt him. I just didn't want him to hurt the nymph. I just shouted no, and then there was this weird flash of light, and when I could see properly, he was broken and breaking. I saw his arms break themselves, Grandmother. I saw them snap. There was so much blood..." Riana trailed off. She felt sick again and saw stars swimming around in her vision.

"Take a deep breath, Riana," Grandmother said.

The admonishment was far away. Riana was suddenly too hot. Sweat beaded and ran from her forehead onto her face, down her back, and slicked her torso. The world grew fuzzy. Before she knew it, she was lying on her back, pillowed against the blanket. Her grandmother left and was back, pressing a cool, damp rag to her forehead.

"Just take nice, slow, deep breaths," she said. "There you go. The moment is over. You're okay."

Riana calmed herself, letting the air she inhaled soothe her panic.

"You're safe, Riana," her grandmother crooned.

Riana thought that might be a lie, but she wasn't able to say so out loud.

CHAPTER TEN

Riana woke to the sounds of pots and pans scraping, followed by the rich smell of bacon. The aromas lifted her out of bed. She pulled the velvet robe around her, pulling her silver hair over the collar, and pushed her feet into her house shoes. She stumbled down the hall, yesterday's bruises waking pain. She paused in the hallway, considering if she wanted to just go back to bed, but decided food sounded like a good idea.

Once she stood on the threshold between hallway, kitchen, and living area, she was filled with the comfort of home. The kitchen and living area were one large room, with the kitchen on the back of the house and the living area on the side nearest the road. The floors, walls, and ceilings were all wood. Sunlight filtered in from sets of windows on all three walls. Their house had two fireplaces. One in the kitchen, which had been built higher in the wall to facilitate ease of cooking, and the other in the living area. Both fires crackled this morning, making the open area warm and cozy.

Her grandmother stood in front of the kitchen fire, stoking the flame under a black pot that hung from the rack. With a thick pad, she lifted the lid from the pot, inhaled deeply, then set the lid back in place.

"Good morning, dear," her grandmother said.

Riana shuffled to the table where a place was set for each of them. The sausage and bacon were already on the table, as well as butter, jelly, and jarred tomatoes.

Her grandmother pulled the pan from the hook and placed it on the table. Returning to the fire, she pulled the small logs away from each other to encourage the fire to peter out.

"You have good timing. Everything has just finished." She pulled the lid from the pot to reveal thick, light yellow pound cake. Steam rose off the cake and Riana's mouth watered.

"That smells amazing," Riana said. Her grandmother was a fine cook but didn't typically go to the trouble, preferring simple meals.

She cut the cake into six portions while Riana opened the jar of tomatoes. Once they'd helped their plates, they dug into the meal. Riana lost herself in the flavors of the food. She didn't speak while she savored rich bacon combined with tart tomatoes. When she was done with the savory parts of the meal, she drizzled honey over the cake and sunk her fork into the soft treat. She could taste the flowers the bees had used to make the honey. She pictured sunshine and open fields, fragrant in a cool spring breeze. The cake was still warm and melted in her mouth.

When she sat back and sipped her tea, her grandmother wiped her mouth and smiled in her direction. "How do you feel this morning?"

Riana felt like a shard of glass had just punctured the lovely glow of her meal. She set the tea aside and measured the words she planned to say. She'd thought about it as she laid awake in the night after waking from a nightmare in which she'd accidentally and gruesomely broken her grandmother's legs.

"Treyor is really gone?" she asked.

Her grandmother nodded.

"And no one will know what happened?" she asked.

She shook her head again.

A hot hand of warning wrapped around Riana's insides and squeezed.

Silence stretched between them.

"Are you afraid of me, Grandmother?" Riana asked, after flashes of her nightmare tumbled into her brain.

Her grandmother looked shocked at first, then smoothed her features. "Because you're dangerous?"

"Yes. I almost killed him," Riana said.

"He almost killed the fire nymph. If you'd killed him, it would have been his fault, not yours."

"Easy for you to say," Riana blurted.

"Yes," her grandmother said and hung her head, "you're right. I'm not the one who wielded the power you have."

Riana pulled her legs up into her chair, wrapping her arms around them and looking at her grandmother over her knees. "It will never happen again."

"Riana, please don't shut it down because you're scared. There are probably really beautiful things you're capable of."

Riana shuddered. "Grandmother, I'm dangerous."

"And the only way you'll be able to control whatever this is, is by learning about it."

"I don't want anything to do with it," Riana said, her voice sharp.

"You may not have a choice, my dear." Her grandmother paused while Riana's breathing ratcheted wildly. When she calmed, her grandmother continued. "I'll help you."

Riana looked up at her, wanting beyond anything for her grandmother to drop it and pretend it hadn't happened.

"Sixteen years ago, there were no elemental sightings. Today, there are several a week. They are drawn to you, listen to you, even attempt to protect you. You can't deny your nature, Riana. For years, your power has manifested through your connection to the elementals. Yes, something bad happened, but you can't throw out all of it because of a mishap triggered by a dangerous situation."

"Grandmother, you're harboring a Tyrmini. Or at least— something..." she tried to say magical, but couldn't bring herself to attribute the property to herself. Her throat clenched in her fear. "Something forbidden," she finally managed. "Whatever I am, I'll be executed if I'm discovered. And you right along with me. I'm putting you in danger just by being here. Why would you risk your life for me? I'm not even your own flesh and blood. I'm just an orphan."

Her grandmother had tears slipping down her soft wrinkled cheeks as if Riana had slapped her. Riana stared at her, unwilling to turn away and unwilling to let the question go unanswered.

"I love you, Riana," her grandmother said, but Riana could feel the other truth underneath her statement.

"No," Riana said. "That's not the reason you do what you do."

Her grandmother met her gaze with steely eyes still sparkling with tears.

"You're right," she said, "that's not the *only* reason." She closed her mouth and rapped her knuckles softly against the wood table next to the empty plates sticky with food and dirty utensils. She inhaled deeply, lifted her chin and spoke. "When I was your age, my best friend Kaely was murdered because she was Tyrmini."

Riana let that sink in. "And this is your way of making up for it?"

Her grandmother fixed her with a hard stare. "Riana, I want to keep you safe from her fate, not make up for what happened in the past."

Riana didn't believe her.

The next day, life went back to normal. Riana and her grandmother agreed it was for the best. And with her new apprenticeship came a new schedule. Riana began her day at school, then transitioned to the vineyard midday. She was grateful for the distraction of school but dreaded being around her grandmother in the afternoon. She didn't want to talk anymore about what was happening with her, or about elementals, or Tyrmini who had been murdered as was set by the law. She didn't want to know and she didn't want to relive the awful moments of the days before. She wanted to go on with life, being as normal as she could be. If she just worked hard enough, maybe she could fit into the community. But even her dogged determination couldn't sway the part of her that said she'd always be an outsider.

She stuffed aside the piece of her that was curious to understand her nature and her origin and ground her way down the road toward the schoolhouse. Treyor was gone. Her explosion of power was covered up. All she needed to do was focus on the tasks at hand.

Elynda met her at the back of the schoolhouse. "Are you okay? You look a little wild around the eyes," she whispered.

Riana hadn't ever considered whether she would tell her best friend about what had happened, rather *when* she would tell her. Yet, faced with the prospect, she had a sudden change of logic. If she divulged her truth to Elynda, would Elynda turn on her? She peered into the kind, fierce face of her friend, words lingering in her mouth unspoken.

Would telling Elynda put Elynda in danger? Would *not* telling Elynda put her in danger?

She couldn't be sure. And the bell was ringing anyway. She chose evasion.

"Rough night," Riana said.

"Oh?" Elynda asked as she and Riana moved down the aisle of desks and slipped into the two they had occupied for years. "Did you get fitted for the Baron's Ball? Is your dress gorgeous?"

Riana recoiled. Sometimes her friend had an uncanny ability to pick up on situations before she knew about them. Riana measured her words carefully. "Yes," she said. "Second measurements are all done."

"Second measurements?" Elynda asked, black eyebrows crunched over vivid green eyes.

"Mmm," Riana confirmed, unable to bring any further words out on the topic.

Riana pulled her quill out, set it on the desk and reached for paper. She bumped the quill which sent it skittering off the side of the desk. It bounced its way under her chair. Riana spied it on the floor behind her. She reached over the chair, kicking out her leg to stretch the necessary distance to pick up her quill.

Pain splintered through her foot. Riana yelped, her head swiveled to the source of the pain. Donny Derringer was standing on her, leaning into her leg with the weight of his body. Anger swept through Riana like wildfire. Her eyes flashed in sudden, vivid light. In the instant she felt the power working its way through her, she pulled back on invisible reins. She said a silent command for it to cease as flashes of Treyor's body breaking smashed into her vision of Donny.

Heat traveled from the crown of her head and down her arms and legs, where it sparked against Donny's foot. At her insistence, the power snapped back into her body like a loosed rubber band. A soft rasp echoed around her. Donny stumbled back, his face an open question. Caught off balance, he fell into the desks behind him. A girl screamed as Donny fell into her. He rolled off the desk, landing in a heap on the wood floor. His eyes rolled around in their sockets until at last they landed on Riana.

She barely contained a growl, biting her lip against a noise rising from the depths of her. Even though no noise escaped her, her face must have communicated every emotion rolling through her in uncontrollable waves. Yet, she contained it.

Donny pulled himself away, scrambled to his feet, and made his way to his desk with nervous backward glances.

She hadn't let the power out, but had he seen or felt something?

Riana rolled her shoulders and breathed deeply, working to calm herself.

"Are you okay?" Elynda asked as she handed her the fallen quill.

Riana fought back tears. Her leg really hurt.

"I'm fine," she said through gritted teeth.

"No, you're not, Riana. You're shaking."

Riana clamped down against a sudden shiver, fighting the clatter of her teeth. She couldn't respond. She wrapped her arms around herself, hoping to distill the sudden cold sweeping through her.

"Riana, you're in shock," Elynda said. She pulled herself out of her desk and ran to the front of the room where Mrs. Tomlin was toiling over many papers. Elynda leaned over and whispered in the teacher's ear, then cast a glance at Riana.

Riana's vision narrowed, her breath ratcheting up in rhythm. She gulped, her sensitive throat tissue sticking together on sudden dryness.

Donny Derringer looked back at her, his face curious.

Elynda and Mrs. Tomlin ran down the aisle to Riana, pulling her from her chair against uncooperative muscles. With Elynda and Mrs. Tomlin on either side of her, they rushed her out of the schoolhouse. They sat her down on the porch.

"Riana, take slow, deep breaths. Nice and slow," Elynda instructed.

Mrs. Tomlin rubbed Riana's back. "Oh, dear, oh, dear, oh, dear," she soothed. "Was it Donny again? Oh, dear, I'm so sorry. His parents will hear from me, dear. What a bully."

Riana gulped on the fresh air, salted by the sea and fogged with morning mist. But all she saw were flashes of Treyor's arms snapping, pouring blood, and breaking yet again. She squeezed her eyes against the visions, but that just intensified them.

"Riana," Elynda said, "remember that time we were at the vineyard? It was your eighth birthday, and you begged your grandmother to let us have a picnic by ourselves. We walked and walked, trying to get to the field she'd told us we could use. One they weren't working that day."

Riana let Elynda's soothing voice wash over her, recalling that day.

"Mom made us cupcakes. And your grandmother had packed us cordial. Dad had given us salted ham and somehow your grandmother had gotten us the really good bread and butter she usually kept for high-paying customers."

Riana took one big, calming breath at the memory of that day. She had so looked forward to her picnic.

"Our parents had given us so much great food that the picnic basket was heavy, so we decided to carry it together and let the basket drag in the dirt. We just pulled it. We thought we were clever. We even felt like the further we went the easier the basket was to carry."

Riana's breathing returned to normal as she smiled.

Mrs. Tomlin listened intently.

"We made it to the picnic spot. We spread the blanket. We set the basket on the blanket. Then we opened the basket."

"And everything was gone," Riana said.

"And everything was gone," Elynda said at the same time.

"What happened to the food?" Mrs. Tomlin asked.

Riana and Elynda looked at each other. Elynda nodded to Riana to finish.

"We drug the basket for so long it ripped and all the food fell out, little bit by little bit," Riana said. She breathed deeply. Her heartrate had returned to normal. She'd stopped shaking except for a small tremor in her hands.

"Everything except one cupcake and the cordial," Elynda finished.

"So we split the cupcake and drank the cordial. By the time we walked back, the ants had gotten to the food. Even that lovely bread and butter."

"Grandmother doesn't know," Elynda said and put a finger over her mouth toward Mrs. Tomly.

Riana nodded. "Not even to this day."

Elynda grasped Riana's hand and patted it. "Better?"

"Yes," she said. "How did you know what to do?"

Elynda shrugged. "I was just trying to get your mind off whatever was bothering you. That's all."

"It worked."

"Yes, what a stroke of genius, Elynda," Mrs. Tomlin said. "Well, then, my dears, if you're ready, we should get back to class."

CHAPTER ELEVEN

R iana walked to the vineyard from the school. When she arrived, the sun was past midpoint in the sky. A few vineyard workers were out amidst the fields. They stalked through the naked vines, brown and gray clothing against brown and gray foliage. It was the season of preparing the plants for their upcoming growth.

Riana inhaled deeply. The Tyrinth smelled good, all soaked in ocean mist. The forest edging the vineyard beckoned her, but Riana was an apprentice now and she had work to do. She straightened her spine and finished the walk to the winery, set in the hill and waiting, like home always does.

Her grandmother was in her office. As Riana entered, she startled.

"Oh! It's you," she said, smiling away her nervous reaction. She had a hand on the potted miniature evergreen and another held a small pendant dangling on a silver chain around her neck. She sat upright, pulling her hand from the tiny tree and quickly tucking the pendent into her shirt. "I'll have to get used to you coming so early."

"Hello, Grandmother," Riana said, pausing as she puzzled through her grandmother's startled reaction. "What will we be working on today?"

"I'll be showing you a private reserve section of the winery," she told her as she rose from her large oak desk.

"I know where the private reserve is, Grandmother."

"The *other* private reserve, Riana." Her grandmother raised her eyebrows high. "Now, come on. The cellar manager is out today. She doesn't know about it and neither should anyone else."

A surge of bewilderment bubbled in Riana's gut. "Grandmother, don't you find it exhausting keeping so many secrets?"

Grandmother turned to her, her face a solemn mask of age and wisdom. "Sometimes, my dear. The skill is one you too must acquire."

Riana shrank back as if she'd been struck. A clot formed in her throat. When she swallowed, it paced its way to her stomach and burned. Her most awful secret was only a day old and it maimed her in such a way she wasn't sure she could recover.

Her grandmother picked two of four identical lanterns lined neatly on a wall shelf. Setting them on the desk, she pulled matches from her skirt pocket and scraped a match across the striking surface. Once the wick was lit on both lanterns, she stuffed the matchbox back into her skirt pocket. She handed a lantern to Riana and led her out of the office and through the cellar entrance. The Tyrinth swallowed them. Mounted lanterns along the brick walls cast yellow pools onto the dirt floor and resting barrels. Riana inhaled the soft scent of soil and rock and oak. The further they descended the cooler the air became.

The narrow, barrel-crowded hall opened to a cavernous workroom. This was where the wine was bottled once it had aged appropriately in the barrels. Two large candelabra dominated the brick-covered ceiling, throwing flickering circles of yellow light onto the floor. Wine racks filled the perimeter of the room with handwritten labels at their ends, identifying the type of wine and the season and year in which it had been bottled. Dotting the open floor were worktables, some with crates of empty wine bottles, burlap sacks of cork, and sealing wax.

The air was always very still in the cellar, but today the underground felt more like a tomb where even the dead were afraid to whisper. Her grandmother crossed the open working area, leading them to the door on the opposite end. She pulled the heavy iron handle, and the oak door groaned against her efforts, as if it couldn't be bothered to perform its function. Riana wondered when the door had last been used. It was generally ignored by the staff, and there were even some who had superstitions that the racks beyond the door were haunted.

The ledge of the door was a step up, marking the two areas that had been built at separate times.

Despite her mood, Riana couldn't help a shrill of excitement seeing the area again. She'd seldom been allowed there, and it held a certain mystery only born in the imagination of a child denied exploration.

She stepped up and through the door. A cold wall of air met her exposed face and neck. It was pitch black. Her grandmother halted her with a hand on her shoulder, then fumbled with her lantern, pulling a small stick from one of her dress pockets.

"Here," Riana said and held the lantern while her grandmother opened its door and set the stick aflame from the burning wick. Once the wood caught fire, she moved to a mounted candelabra near the door. This area hadn't been upgraded to lanterns, it seemed. Three modest white candles took turns coming to life. Their glow was hardly enough to make a dent in the waiting darkness.

Grandmother hurried to another set of candles and lit them, then rushed to a third set before dousing the flame threatening to burn her fingers. She took two more lighting sticks from her pocket, handed one to Riana, and set the other alight on the newly lit candles.

"Be a darling, Little Miss, and help me out," her grandmother said. She hadn't called Riana that pet name in a long time, and Riana was comforted by the familiar title.

Riana took the stick, set it aflame, and cast about for more candles. As set after set of candles were lit, a little more of the room revealed its secrets.

Cobwebs shrouded old but sturdy A-frame racks of wine. A giddy sense of discovery shrilled through Riana. She'd neither seen nor tasted any of the wines in this room. She immediately went to the first of ten racks, holding her lantern next to its label and reading the information recorded there.

"Grandmother! This wine is a century old," Riana said.

"Yes, this is the historic section, if you will," her grandmother said. She smiled as she pulled a corkscrew from another pocket and went to the third row of racks. Without pausing to review the collection, she plucked an ancient looking and slightly misshapen bottle, grasped it between her knees, and went to work removing the wax and cork. "Riana, go back to the other room and fetch us two glasses."

Riana turned, careful with her footing in the dim room, and crossed over the threshold and to the shelf holding tasting glasses. "Red or white, Grandmother?" she yelled, facing the neatly lined glass.

Her grandmother's voice floated toward her confirming the former.

Riana pulled two glasses with rounder, wider bowls on the stems and returned to her grandmother in the darker room. Her grandmother was standing near an oak barrel, one of many they used as tables. Riana set the glasses down on the top of the barrel. Her grandmother tipped the bottle and poured the first sample, then the next. She set the bottle on the barrel. Riana put her nose into the glass, inhaling deep reds, hints of licorice, a touch of clove, and the warmth of oak. Sela and Riana both swirled the glasses, expertly airing the wine. Riana stuck her nose in the glass again—and wrinkled it.

"Grandmother," she started, but her grandmother interrupted her.

"Taste it first and then we'll discuss." She raised her glass to her lips and sipped.

Riana followed suit. Her grandmother watched her, sea blue eyes patient and knowing.

"It's so tasteless. It's nothing like what we produce now." Riana was stunned. She knew the vintage varied from year to year, but this was as if the wine had been made from an entirely different fruit.

"Very good," her grandmother said. "The wine is different now because the fruit has been imbued with Kaely's magic. The very Tyrinth here is still blessed by her short life."

Riana gaped. Kaely had grown things. Riana had nearly murdered someone. She tried swallowing her shame, but it left a lump in her throat.

"Let us move further into the cellar," her grandmother said.

"Further? There's more?" Riana said. She looked around the room at the racks of ancient bottles collecting dust. Past the resting wines, the candlelight barely reached the perimeter walls. "Where?" Riana asked.

"Take your lantern," her grandmother said. She moved to the large oak door, reached out over the threshold, and pulled it shut. It complained just as heavily as it had upon opening. When the door slid into the threshold, Riana had a distinct moment of claustrophobia. She snagged her lantern from the dirt floor and followed the bobbing lamp her grandmother held.

At the end of the wine racks, her grandmother turned left, squeezing between the wine bottles and the brick wall. Riana followed her, pulling her skirts away from bottles. They would be filthy by the time they emerged.

Her grandmother grunted as she knelt onto the floor at the end of the row. "I'm a little too old for this," she said through gritted teeth. More grunting followed as she pulled at a spot in the wall.

Riana held her lantern aloft, unable to see what her grandmother was pulling at in the darkness of the room.

"Riana, there is a reason I left this room dark," her grandmother said. She heaved once more, and as if by magic, a door appeared in the wall.

"Where did that come from?" Riana asked, stunned as she peered into a cramped entrance to yet another room.

Her grandmother crawled on her hands and knees, uttering quiet oaths against old age. After she passed through the entrance, Riana pushed herself through.

Riana's spine tickled, little hairs on the back of her neck rising in the darkness of the new room. Her grandmother was already lighting candles in the cramped space. This was not just another holding place for ancient wines. Riana felt a stone drop into her stomach as she took in the chamber of forbidden things.

CHAPTER TWELVE

"Grandmother," Riana whispered. She moved on numb feet over the dirt floor to the first shelf on the right. She reached trembling fingers out to a framed painting of an antoli, a creature Riana had seen for the first time just days ago. Next to the painting, books lined the shelves. She read the spines.

Anatomy of Fire Nymphs

The Great Battle of Tagorbi

Water Elementals

Air Creatures of the Sylvanean Plains

Policies from the High King for Creature Control

Riana stopped reading and swiveled toward her grandmother. Behind her grandmother were more shelves lined with odd instruments, bottles of seeds, herbs and other dried things, and jars with odd substances stored inside. The containers were each labeled in fading script with such things as: Oroncopella thorns: alleviates rashes; Fulicity venom: polishes teeth—very potent; Marsh weed: reduces swelling; Fire nymph tree bark: cleanses poisons, clears skin, purifies infection, and many other applications.

On one shelf a glass case was filled with samples of fire nymph wings, collected, pinned, and labeled. Another shelf was lined with seven tear-shaped bottles of glimmering golden liquid.

Riana's stomach squeezed in on itself. The crown of her head prickled while her throat and ears burned. She swallowed. "Grandmother, if anyone were to find this, you'd be hung."

"Yes, my dear, I've known that for three times the years you've been alive," her grandmother said nonchalantly. She gestured to the golden elixir on the shelf over her left shoulder. "This is somewhat of an assurance for our safety, even if by some small chance someone were to discover my little room of secrets."

"Why did you bring me here?" Riana asked. "Why now?" Her heart pounded in her chest. The only thing she could think of was how much in her life guaranteed an early death.

"I thought that would be obvious." Her grandmother blinked at her, a puzzled expression pulling at the corners of her mouth and hitching one eyebrow higher than the other.

"Well, it's not," Riana said and crossed her arms over her middle.

"It's clear from yesterday that you have some power. The things in here may help you understand what it is." Her grandmother gestured around the room at the shelves of books, paintings, scrolls, jars, and odd implements.

"I don't need to understand it, Grandmother," she said. "I just need to hide it. To keep it secret."

"And how will you do that if you don't understand the nature of it?"

"I'll just ignore it," she said, but there was a niggling in the back of her head that caused her to doubt her ability to ignore something so big.

"Riana, you really must embrace this. It is what you are—"

"Grandmother, how can you say that? I can't embrace it. If I embrace power that can maim and murder, I'll become a monster. Or be hung. One or the other. There is no room for the power *and* my survival."

"Don't stay in the fear, Riana. Maybe if you embraced this, things wouldn't turn out the way they've always turned out."

Riana's mouth hung open. "Grandmother, elementals are hunted. Tyrmini are slaughtered. For hundreds of years. It's just the way things are. What on Tyrinth is going to change that?"

"I don't know," her grandmother said, casting her gaze to the floor, her shoulders drooping. Riana could see the memories floating through her grandmother's fine, sad features. She looked back up at her adopted granddaughter, stiffened her chin, straightened her shoulders. "Maybe *you* could."

The silence hung in the still air of the cramped cellar of forbidden things. To Riana, the walls seemed to close in more tightly. Before she suffocated on her fear, she forced herself to speak.

"May I be excused?" Riana asked, without verbalizing her doubt of her grandmother's sanity.

"Very well." Her grandmother's jaw ground one way and then the other. "But, you know where this place is now and you may come here whenever you please."

Riana turned, knelt, and pushed her lantern back through the hole of the entrance.

"Riana, before you go," her grandmother said.

Riana turned back to her, still on her hands and knees, ready to escape. Her grandmother plucked a small version of the teardrop-shaped bottles from the shelf. She crossed the space between them in three strides and held it out to her.

"Keep this close and hidden. But only use it if you are on death's doorstep, and then only a small drop."

Riana looked at the bottle, questioning whether she would take it or not. She looked up at her grandmother's face, ready to refuse. But the stern pleading in her grandmother's sea blue eyes changed her mind. She took the bottle, her hand brushing her grandmother's, and placed it deep in an inner pocket of her skirt that closed with a button. Even when her grandmother had their clothing tailored, she considered how she would conceal her many secrets.

Riana crawled out of the secret room, into the candle-soft light of the ancient vintages. The elixir in her pocket added an extra weight to her skirts and pulled at her.

Secrets are heavy burdens, Riana thought and made her way as quickly as possible out of the cellar and into daylight.

CHAPTER THIRTEEN

As much as Riana despised keeping so many secrets, she was a dedicated observer of elementals, and she hoped that would never be discovered. She wondered about her little fire nymph queen and whether she was safe and well.

Riana's boots crunched over the leaf litter and pine needles. She'd meandered to a section of the woods she hadn't traversed in a while, further southwest, closer to town as well as the Dreavynan Sea. The air was more salted here and the rhythmic swell and hush of the waves filled her ears. There was madrone interspersed with the giant evergreens the TyrMinHai was most known for. The green trunks of the madrone were showing under the peeling red outer bark.

Riana inhaled deeply, soaking in the scent of pine and loam and ocean. It was as though the clean air stripped away all the hurt of the last day and a half, leaving her free, clean, clear. She followed an animal trail into the forest. The trees were large and widely interspersed so Riana could see far into the forest. The giants gathered around her like kindly guardians. Riana recalled days as a child when she'd sat at their roots, talking to them as well as listening to their stories. Oh, did they have stories to tell!

She leaned into one of the giant trees, pressing a hand onto its rough bark. She sighed in relief, sensing the life energy flowing through it. It seemed to Riana that it cast her in a green nimbus, washing away the negativity that clung to her before filling her up with positivity once again. What did people do without trees, Riana thought, then shuddered at the idea.

She hummed a little as she wandered into the forest, occasionally climbing over giant fallen trees upon which baby trees had rooted and fed from the nutrients the log provided. She stopped to peer at some fantastically large mushrooms, freshly bloomed and vibrant with red dust on the caps. When she followed the sounds of water, she found a stream trickling over roots and stones. She sat on a moss-covered boulder and watched the water's progress.

She was perfectly at peace here in her woods. Woods her grandmother owned and that she would one day own. Woods that had belonged, to no one's challenge, to the Starliss family for generations out of time. No one else wanted to claim them. They were wild, and wild things were feared.

Riana breathed in deeply, drawing her legs to her chest and resting her cheek on her knees. When she heard a twig break, she twisted her body to the left to see what was behind her. She reached for her notepad, hoping to catch a glimpse of something new. She saw nothing. Disappointment filled her as she turned and peered into the water.

A cool absence of light roused her from her reverie. She turned to the other side, expecting to see a new cloud blocking the sunlight filtering through the treetops. Instead she saw the ugly face of Treyor.

She gasped, pulled herself from the boulder and retreated backward.

He laughed.

To Riana's horror, the boy whom she'd nearly killed had dried blood down the front of his white shirt. On his neck was a nearly black, wide swath of crusted blood. His nose looked to have been broken at one point as well. The blackened stains of more blood on his nose and upper lip deepened the sense of mania indicated by his wide grin. From this distance, Riana could smell the decaying blood and retched on it.

Even though there was dried blood everywhere on Treyor, Riana could see no wounds. His eyes were clear. His skin glowed pink with health. There was no cut on his throat either, despite the mucky horizontal line over his flesh.

"Wha...what happened to you?" Riana asked, backing further away from him.

"First you nearly killed me. Then I was fully murdered. But I'm here to even the score on at least one front."

Treyor advanced toward her, a wicked gleaming knife in his hand. Riana's heart banged at the door of her ribcage. She took two more steps backward before she bumped into the cradling curve of a giant pine. She felt at the bark, somehow reassured by the presence of the tree. Yet she was still cornered by a dangerous boy. And people thought creatures were dangerous.

Treyor was on her before she could track his movement. At this close range the stench of old blood, sweat, and urine overpowered her. He growled at her, lifted the knife, and plunged it toward her chest.

"Do you know what it's like to have all of your fingers break at once?" he asked, words cutting through between grunts as he slashed at her.

Riana shouted as she raised a hand to block his movement. He was so strong, just as he had been at the seamstress's shop; maybe stronger. Riana fought back the urge to go searching for that deeper power to protect herself. She shoved against him as he crowded over her. Gaining purchase with both of her hands on his wiry arm, she pushed against the downward-aimed knife with everything she had in her, teeth gritted, a hungry fight to survive welling up within her.

Treyor barked a laugh, pulled away to release Riana's grip on him, and backhanded her with his other hand. The blow was so hard it sent her spinning away from the tree. She stumbled over the tree's roots and fell to the forest floor. Her cheek exploded in pain and her eye instantly swelled. She looked up at him through the eye that wasn't swollen.

He looked appraisingly at the hand and arm he'd used as a weapon against her.

"I have to say, your grandmother's special drink sure is something. I've never been so strong. It's a shame the rest got stolen from me. Got any more?" There was a feverish need in his face. Even though he was apparently strong, there was something taut about his features. The veins on his neck stood out; his forearm muscles were tight. It was as though he were a pulled bowstring ready to be loosed.

"No," she lied.

He cocked one side of his mouth into a grimace made gruesome by the old blood moustache he wore. He looked down at her.

"You're lying," he said and advanced toward her.

Riana rolled, pushed herself onto her hands and made to lunge away. Treyor jumped, a ferocious cry escaping his mouth. Riana tucked her arms into herself, trying desperately to guard her vital organs at the very least. He fell onto her, pinning her legs to the ground and holding her arms pinned to her body. She yelped but the sound fell short with the lack of air in her lungs.

He ravaged through her skirts until at last he came up with the tiny bottle of elixir. He held it aloft, like a god he intended to worship. "Looks like it's my lucky day. I get the girl and the gold."

"Help," she managed. "Please, someone help me." Tears slipped from her eyes as she wiggled with no effect under Treyor's strength.

He looked down at her with wild green eyes. "What? No zapping light? No breaking of my bones? Where did all your power go?"

Riana struggled against him, turning her face left and right, hoping someone would come along, but no one came out here. This was the TyrMinHai. It was full of dangerous creatures that no one wanted to encounter.

Riana inhaled sharply.

No one wanted to encounter the elementals.

If only...

She pushed against Treyor even as he lashed out at her. She screamed when his knife found purchase in her shoulder and dragged through the flesh. She drew up the memory of the first time she'd met the queen fire nymph just two nights ago. She turned her scream of fear and pain into a note. His next blow landed in her hair on the ground so close to her face she could feel the coolness of the blade against her skin.

She turned her next shout into another note, and before he could aim another blow, she sang out a third.

He slashed his knife through the bodice of her dress, the tip sliced through the skin of her belly. He swung again, and the knife carved through her forearms. A gush of scarlet splatted across her face. She blinked away the blood in her eyes, fighting against the burn to see where Treyor aimed the next strike.

She couldn't see.

Her arms flailed, but she had no idea if she could keep him at bay. Hot lines of pain seared her arms again and again. It was only a matter of time before he would land a killing blow. She screamed out in desperation. One more achingly warm blossom of pain erupted and then the weight of Treyor was gone.

She pushed herself up, rubbing madly to remove the blood in her eyes. The acrid odor of her life essence assaulted her senses. With gritty red vision she searched around for her attacker.

Treyor was surrounded by fire nymphs. A floating ring of screeching fiery creatures wheeled around him. In one hand Treyor held the elixir and in the other he wielded the knife, stained red with Riana's blood. He slashed out at them, but they dodged and weaved through the attacks, countering his moves by touching fire to his clothes. He yelped in pain and put out the flames, only to have more ignite in a different spot.

Riana watched in grateful horror as the fire nymphs lit the murderous boy aflame. He ran from them and they followed. Deeper and deeper into the forest. Further away from the reach of anyone who could save him. A bottle of elixir stolen away.

CHAPTER FOURTEEN

Riana's arms wept scarlet. Blood dripped in a steady stream onto her blue skirts. Her head swam as if it were disconnected from her body. She'd hung around her healing friend enough to know she needed to staunch the flow of blood. Of course, if she had the elixir, it would be as easy as taking a sip. But after seeing the crazed need in Treyor's eyes, she was grateful he'd taken it with him.

She pushed herself back until she rested against the tree's trunk. She gulped in air, trying to calm herself and fight away nausea from the sight of so much blood. A cold sweat prickled her hairline and neck. She pulled the outer blood-soaked skirt away from the white petticoats. Luckily, Treyor had slashed enough of the material to make tearing a portion possible, but even so, the cut muscles of her arms protested at the work and made more blood come rushing out.

Once she had a few good strips of fabric, she wrapped them gently around her arms. They were red within moments, but not dripping. Her stomach was bleeding, but she felt the wound was only flesh deep. Her left eye was swollen shut and her head throbbed.

When she'd left the vineyard, she'd walked a good mile before entering the forest. What she'd normally cross in ten minutes or so seemed like an eternity in the state she was in. She wondered if she could make it back without passing out from blood loss.

"Only one way to find out," she said out loud to herself. She pushed herself up from the ground, looking in the direction Treyor had been chased by the fire nymphs to make sure he wouldn't return. Sunlight filtered through a thin layer of clouds. Here and there Riana saw small fires in the leaf litter and on trees. The mist-soaked forest prevented most of the fire from taking root. Fire nymphs the color of cobalt flitted from flame to flame, extinguishing any lasting fire. Riana wondered if the troop of fire fighters were a part of the group who had attacked Treyor, and if seeing them put out the flames meant that Treyor had gotten away from them. Or if they'd finished the job.

Riana pushed out the thoughts of Treyor being burned alive in favor of exerting enough energy to get back to the winery. Using the tree for support, she pulled herself into a tottering standing position, leaning heavily against the trunk. Every move made the injuries on her arm scream in pain, and new wetness seeped into the makeshift bandages. The material of her dress rubbed harshly at the cut on her stomach, making her woozy at the thought of it pulling the wound wider.

The forest around her shimmied in her vision. Misty cool air wrapped around her like a mother's embrace. She inhaled the scent of pine and sea, hoping to clear her head. The world whipped around her in sudden vertigo. She leaned her whole body into the tree, unwilling to give up the progress she'd made to get to a standing position.

She placed a hand on the trunk and silently thanked it for the support. The tree vibrated beneath her, and because Riana was on the verge of syncope, she could have sworn it whispered "You're welcome" and then "Help is on the way" and also "Rest." Just as she questioned whether the tree had communicated with her, she slumped down to the curving roots and passed out.

The forest observed her.

Her arms were bleeding badly. The cuts were more serious than she could recognize amid her shock. The forest watched the pale girl turn paler, her energy dwindling. For eons, the trees stood silent and rooted, nonpartisan to the affairs of humans. Yet they remembered their origins.

Long ago, they had been created and tended by the loving care of the original elemental-wielders and elemental dragons. Their consciousness, which had floated without purpose, had been invited into the trees, the grass, the dirt, the rocks. They comingled with entities of water and air, forming a fast union. Even fire had its place to destroy diseased portions of their body and releasing precious seeds for new growth. Their consciousness retreated from the unhealthy portions to spring forth into new growth. They were one. All trees individual, yet all the same. In the old days, those possessing sacred elemental wisdom knew this, and before taking any of their body, they asked first. With the proper warning, they pulled their consciousness from the trees the people needed, and the trees were removed without injury or insult.

Today's people had lost the knowledge that the forest was alive.

Except this one. She knew. She was like Kaely. She took comfort once again in their presence and understood they appreciated kindness. It had been centuries. They whispered among each other as they watched the child grow. She was different. They could see it in her energy body and even in her physical body. She had magic, like their creators. Her presence in the forest had enlivened the population of elemental creatures the forest harbored.

Creatures living and thriving amid their trunks and limbs brought the forest immense joy. They'd been sleeping for so long until she came. Having her light around awakened them from their long slumber. They soaked in her energy, feeding her doses of their own, creating a positive exchange that helped them each thrive.

She loved them. And they loved her back.

CHAPTER FIFTEEN

"His need for more elixir is an indication of his failing health," Sela said.

Captain Steph took the tear-shaped bottle in his hands with reverence, fear, and maybe even disgust. "This is nothing more than a drug. Do you think she knew that when she fashioned it?"

"She fashioned the fruit for the fire nymphs. It was never meant for human consumption. We were desperate. If I could turn back the clock and change things, I would." Sela eyed the bottle of elixir with wonder and heartache.

"But then our Baron would be long dead," Steph noted.

"And Kaely would be alive."

"Not so. It would have only been a matter of time before the High King sent his twisted guards to eliminate her."

"Or recruit her," Sela said. "Sick bastard."

"Careful, Sela," Steph said, casting a gaze to the ceiling. "They say he has eyes and ears everywhere."

"Not in my office, he doesn't," Sela said, pulling herself into a straight line. "I'll say anything I like about him here in my private space." Sela reached a hand to the tiny tree on her desk. She fingered the pot, tracing the grooves and lines absently.

"Yes, well, you'll understand if I don't stick around while you insult the High King," Steph said. "Thank you, Ms. Starliss, for the elixir. I'll take your leave to deliver it to the Baron."

"One more thing, Steph," Sela said, pulling her gaze from the tree. "I have tried to tell the Baron he must cut back on the amount he's consuming, but he won't listen to me."

"He's addicted, Sela."

"He's addicted to a limited resource," Sela said, pinching the bridge of her nose and closing her eyes. She breathed deeply to soothe the frustration rising within her.

"What?"

"There's only one tree that produces the fruit. Just one. And it cannot produce enough fruit to keep up with the amount the Baron has been drinking."

"How low are we?"

"He'll be out in the matter of a month. I can't produce more until the tree bears fruit again, which won't be for another six months." Of course, the Baron would have had two more bottles, but Sela had used one to bribe the boy at the seamstress shop and another to give to Riana in case of emergency. She'd had a niggling intuition that now that Riana's power had manifested, the potential for danger would increase.

"What happens when he runs out of the elixir?"

"He goes through the all-too natural process of dying, as we all do," she said, exasperated. "Except he'll have an immense amount of... discomfort due to withdrawals." She pulled the miniature tree toward her. Something about it had caught her attention.

The little evergreen was a perfect tiny version of the trees in the TyrMinHai. Kaely had made it for Sela when she'd started her apprenticeship at the vineyard so she wouldn't feel so lonely in the office. Kaely used the tree to send messages, letting Sela know where she was in the forest so Sela could come out and meet her. The tiny tree was connected to all the trees in the TyrMinHai. Kaely would ask the trees to relay the message, and they sent it to this miniature.

But, of course, the tree was silent, ever since Kaely had been killed.

"That doesn't sound pleasant," Steph said.

Sela looked up at him from the shimmering pine needles. "Which is why I've been advising him to cut back."

"Okay, I'll speak with him about it."

"It doesn't matter to me whether he makes the elixir last or he slurps it down in one gulp and waits for death. He can do whatever he likes with it. It's his curse." She looked back at the tree, certain this time that it was vibrating.

"What a hard woman you are, Sela Starliss," Steph said.

"Excuse me?" she looked up at him. "The man you've sworn fealty to has done nothing but exploit my tie to him, exploit the creation of a young girl whom he murdered! Perhaps you're the one who's hard, if you can stomach such injustices."

"The girl was a Tyrmini, Sela," Steph said.

Tyrmini. As if that was the only identity she had. Just a dangerous wielder of elemental magic. Kaely was more than that. She was kind, compassionate, giving, and a genius. She helped people with the plants she grew. She was a natural healer, being able to pinpoint a person's problem and prescribe them plants and herbs that would treat and cure their illness. She gave everything to help the people—and creatures— around her. Everything. Even her life. Yet just the one label weighed more than all the beauty she bore.

Sela's throat constricted at the thought of her lost friend. It wasn't just that she missed her. What happened to Kaely was a representation of what could happen to Riana. And to all the countless Tyrmini who'd swung from the gallows in the town center. And she just couldn't bear to watch it happen again. It disgusted her. She was scared for her granddaughter and what lie ahead for her. Steph's words rang a chord within Sela.

Would Riana be stripped down to the label Tyrmini?

Sela's stomach squeezed in warning. Anger blossomed as she resolved with everything in her to keep her granddaughter safe from Kaely's fate. She pushed herself away from the desk and rose out of the chair. She rounded Steph and pulled the door open. "Good day, Steph."

Steph grimaced at her, his jaw grinding together. He shoved the precious elixir into an inner pocket of his navy officer's jacket. He tipped his hat to Sela and left. She was happy to see his retreating figure.

She slumped back into her wooden desk chair and pressed her fingertips into her brow bone. She fought back tears building in her eyes. A soft rustle tickled her hearing. She looked toward the door, readying herself for a verbal confrontation with Steph, thinking he'd returned to make some point about the magnanimity of the Baron, but no one was there.

Thinking she'd imagined it, she turned back to her desk and to the work she still had left to do. The little tree in the pot shimmied and swayed, as if waving its arms to capture her attention. She lurched toward the tree, confusion spreading through her. The tree had not spoken to her in fifty years. For a split second, Sela had the familiar excitement of when Kaely had used the trees to communicate with her. That hope popped like a flimsy soap bubble when her logic caught up.

She leaned close to the tree, her heart pumping faster. A stone of worry dropped in her stomach. There was only one magical person in the TyrMinHai who could possibly send a message through the trees.

Whispery words creaked out of the small tree. Like an old person who didn't often use their voice.

The girl. Hurt. Come fast! Where the madrones grow.

"No!" Sela said, shoving herself so quickly out of her chair it screeched backward over the wooden floor.

She ran out of the office, her old bones protesting the effort. She pulled the reins of her horse from the post and hastily hitched her to the cart, fighting the worry while she was dealing with the animal. Once the horse was in place, she climbed into the cart and whistled for the horse to make haste. The mare twitched its ears but bolted forward.

The sky outside was too gray, the clouds closing on Sela. She twitched the reins, and the mare galloped down the dirt road. Memories flooded through her of the last time the tree had sent her a message. And the last time she'd seen her best friend.

CHAPTER SIXTEEN

Kaely, Fifty Years Earlier

S ela's forward momentum jerked to a halt as she raced for Kaely. Arrows flew at a coalescing collection of vines that twisted and stretched toward the red moon bulging against the jagged horizon of forest. In her sixteen years of being alive, Sela Starliss had never seen the moon so imposing. As if it would swoop down on them and stop the horror. But, it didn't. It simply watched.

The Baron's Guard had come for her, claiming that Kaely needed her help. Why it wasn't Kaely's father who had come she hadn't been able to piece together. There had been no time to argue. Not when it came to her best friend.

Sela had climbed into the cart and allowed the guard to race them to the north end of Landsend. Her mind had whirred; worry painting images of illness or injury. She had anticipated a drive to Healer's Hall and was surprised when the cart stopped at an open field of her family's vineyard.

The arrows snapped from the archers' bowstrings. The steel heads met a wall of leaves and branches and skittered to the ground. Soldiers advanced. Vines leapt from the column of vegetation to grasp them in a tangle of thorns. Twisting around their bodies, some soldiers hacked at the imprisoning creepers, fighting desperately to free themselves. Some lost all composure and simply screamed, raising their faces to the night sky and invoking the love of the Maker.

Sela's breath hitched as she turned her sea blue gaze to another throng of soldiers. Globes of fire darted in and out of the crowd garbed in navy uniforms. Sela watched a man slice at a pulsing red light that bore down on him. The fire nymph extinguished to blue before it fell into the tall grasses of the field. Sela pulled against the ironclad grip that held her arm in place. Why was Kaely fighting? Why was she revealing herself and the elementals? Even at the tender age of sixteen summers, she knew the price.

"Kaely!" Sela screamed. Angry hazel eyes framed in leaves snapped onto Sela before softening to surprise. The man holding her yanked. Sela fell backward into the guard's torso. Something cool and sharp pressed against her neck. She coughed against the pressure.

"What are you doing?" she managed around the choking presence of the blade. The Baron of Landsend strode forward on his mount. The horse's eyes rolled as he tossed his mane. The Baron fought against the animal's fear with expert precision.

"Call off your demon elementals or your friend dies," the Baron said, his voice even and unforced. Sela's mouth fell open as the shock of the Baron's words brushed her logic. Sela's presence was a brilliant piece of strategy for the Baron. Nothing more.

"What?" Sela cried. "You would kill me?" An invisible hand squeezed her insides. Kaely never paused. She raised a green-laden arm. It stretched out, gathering the elementals into an embrace of foliage. The hush of the leaves and cracking of growing limbs vied with the fire nymphs' crystalline protests. Loop after loop, the plant grew taller and thicker into a cylindrical cage. The nymphs banged at their prison with tiny, flaming fists.

Kaely untwisted her body from the entangling growth. Soldiers uncoiled from the gripping thorns. The last one to escape was a thick man. He stumbled forward as he wept in fear. His face was smeared with scratches, blood, and dirt. His clothes were thrashed and hung with gaping holes that revealed angry red cuts.

Sela had never seen Kaely use her Tyrmini abilities against a living soul. Always, she used her elemental power of Tyrinth and Water to help someone: to grow a rare herb that alleviated a symptom or draw the essence out of a plant to heal a hurt; to fashion a shelter for an injured elemental...to create a fruit whose juices could heal breaks and major wounds. Sela let the bitter regret fill her mouth like poison.

Kaely lowered herself, her bare feet touched the ground as she raised her hands in surrender. The plants snaked away from her, retreating to the looming forest. Once the cover of green was gone, Kaely was left standing in nothing but white cotton bloomers and a button-up white chemise. Sela could only guess that they had brought her out of the house after she had already started undressing for bed.

"Please," Sela's voice scraped against her throat. The knife pressed into her skin; the sting preceding a wet trickle. The coppery odor pierced the cool night air. She looked at the Baron across the open field. Soldiers gathered in a haphazard arc, their swords and bows drawn, squared off against her best friend and Tyrmini, Kaely. "I beg you. For the love of the Maker...she saved your life! Don't do this. Don't do this to her. Don't do this to me!" Sela's voice rose, the rawness burned with every syllable.

Kaely kept her bare arms raised and her round hazel eyes wide as they darted from Sela to the golden-haired Baron mounted, healthy, and hunting down Sela's best friend and his once-savior.

"Let her go. I promise, I won't run," Kaely's voice trembled.

"Not until it's over," Baron Tarbyrwin's voice leached into the night, adding shadow to shade. He shifted in his saddle, his fine golden hair glinting even in the dark of night. He sat atop his horse with perfect posture, the dark cape of his station hanging off his shoulders, undulating with his shifting mount. The horse tossed its brown head, prancing further away from Kaely. "Bind her hands."

The thick man who had been trapped earlier sidled toward Kaely, his arms outstretched, a rope held in his shaking, meaty paws. Kaely moved closer to him, but the man's hands jerked up to cover his face in defense, a shrill yelp erupting from his gut. Kaely stopped; her hazel eyes peered through a tangle of long, dark hair as she waited for the man's cautious steps to resume. Her thin, pink lips pressed together and turned down at the corners; her nostrils flaring. Her breath expanded and shrank her heaving chest. Sela thought she looked twenty years older than the day before, when they had roamed the vineyard grounds together, carefree and unworried. Kaely's moon-kissed olive skin shone where her cotton undergarments didn't cover.

Sela shifted in the grip of the guard. One arm clamped across her chest and shoulders pressed her body into his while the other hand pushed the knife against her throat. His breath hitched with fear. The smell of his body odor was as suffocating as his grip on her. The brass buttons of his navy coat dug into Sela's back. He shuffled through the tall grasses, so she did too.

"Don't do it, Kaely! Don't you—" the blade strangled off her next words. The fresh cut burned while the blood running down her neck tickled the sensitive skin.

"Don't hurt her!" Kaely shouted. She held out her hands to the approaching guard. "Here. Tie me." Trembling, he attacked Kaely's wrists with the rope and tied a quick knot. When she was bound, he walked a little straighter. He circled to stand behind her, then kicked the back of Kaely's knees with a grunt. Sela inhaled sharply as her friend crumpled to the ground.

A slender man approached, the grass whispering against his leather boots. His navy uniform was less tattered, his breath slow and calm. Sela was sure the man holding her squeezed her tighter because she couldn't breathe as she looked at the executioner. Tall and slender, pale of skin, pale of hair, and eyes black like the oncoming night. For the space of several heartbeats, nothing moved: not a person, not a fire nymph, not even the wind. The guard stood above Kaely. Kaely stared into the ground from her hands and knees. The man lifted a wickedly curved and thick sword. Kaely's clear voice cut through the air.

"You should know," she began. The man paused, his brass buttons gleaming like coals against the red moonlight. "After you kill me, there'll be nothing to stop them." She tossed her head over her shoulder in the direction of the forest. The man's black eyes flicked to the Baron. Baron Tarbyrwin paused, reigned in his dancing horse, and then nodded once.

Sela screamed, her voice shredding her throat. "No!" Steel glinted. Kaely's head thumped and rolled forward in wave upon wave of dark hair. Blood spurted from her neck. A forest of elementals erupted onto the open field. The man holding Sela's throat lurched away. Sela sank to her knees, hearing her own screams as if they came from someone else. A cloud of fire swept past her, roaring and screeching. The air blew hot against Sela's cheeks. For a moment, the darkness was awash in red. After they passed, she blinked in the contrasting darkness through a veil of tears. She crawled to the head and body of her best friend.

"No, no, no..." her head shook as she muttered a chant to make reality change. "No, no, no." A roar split the air around Sela. The air around her grew still before it exploded with a gust of wind. In a split second an antoli appeared with a swirl of white mist. Sela looked up at the massive white beast that towered above her and her dead friend. From her kneeling position in the dying grass she was eye level with its dingy white foreleg. Craning her neck, not sure if she should move or sit silently, she watched the eyeless creature turn its large, pink nose to the corpse of her best friend. The antoli sniffed low and loud, as if it were sucking air through water. It raised its enormous head and howled around a mouthful of curved, needlelike teeth. The air rent with the sorrow of the beast, rumbling into Sela's chest. Sela rocked back, pulling her knees to her chest, ducking her head to make herself small.

Peering over her knees, she watched it take a single long stride as its enormous nose sniffed the air around its jutting lower jaw and row of yellowing teeth. The air squeezed around Sela. Like the wind in a storm, the beast disappeared. It reemerged near the retreating executioner. The long, dingy, silver hair on its body shifted with its exit through the air. A mighty swipe of a long, white leg knocked the man down. One short scream escaped the man's mouth before it was cut off with a muffled crunch and snap.

Giant thuds resounded through the Tyrinth, and Sela looked up from the bloody mess of her friend to see a berubula launch itself on shiny, brown legs through the air. The giant toad-like creature aimed for the Baron. Sela willed the creature's success in its advance on her friend's murderer. Stopping short of its target, the giant pink tongue shot out from its mouth. Catching on the Baron's mount, the horse shrieked as its trajectory hurled backward. Baron Tarbywin leapt from his mount. The wail when he landed convinced Sela that he'd likely broken an arm or leg. A grim smile quirked the corners of her mouth. The horse was gobbled into the waiting cave that was the berubula's mouth.

While it swallowed, the Baron found his legs, turned, and hobbled away. Another rider scooped the scrambling Baron onto his horse. A nearby mounted archer pulled three arrows, aiming for the berubula's opening mouth. The archer loosed the arrows. With a gurgling grunt, the giant beast shook its slimy head, fell sideways, and relaxed in a mass of glistening skin.

Sela looked away from the berubula and watched the fire nymphs chase the Baron's Guard. Some of the men escaped. Others were ignited by the nymphs' touch. Their screams were almost as torturous as the smell of burning flesh. In a matter of minutes, the guards either lie dead and smoldering or were chased away. The Baron regrettably escaped.

Under the burgeoning glow of the harvest moons, Sela turned, looking at the open stare of her friend. Her stomach clenched. Her vision was lost in a swell of hot tears. Her head throbbed as she wailed. "I'm so sorry, my friend!" she sobbed. She closed Kaely's vacant eyes and smoothed away the strands of her chestnut hair.

Fire nymphs gathered around her; the bobbing flames borne on iridescent wings circled Kaely. Sela backed away from the growing heat. The coalescing golden cloud pressed onto her fallen friend. Sela watched the nymphs kiss Kaely's hair, skin, and nightclothes. As the blaze grew higher, the cloud of nymphs spun, first slowly, then faster. As the pace quickened, their cries rose. Higher and higher, their piercing wails reverberated against the red rays of a blood moon. Sela covered her ears, collapsing into her skirts in the tall grasses. Kaely's makeshift funeral pyre reflected in Sela's overrunning sea blue gaze.

CHAPTER SEVENTEEN

Sela brushed away the memories even while fear rose that she was headed to a similar scene. When the madrone trees came into view, she yanked the reins, slowed the horse, and pulled the cart to the grass on the side of the road. She climbed out of the cart, careful to pull her skirts aside, and dashed into the woods as quickly as her worn body would allow.

When the madrones faded away and the evergreens loomed, she stopped at the first tree and placed a hand gently on its rough bark. She shivered at the feel of its energy. She was no Tyrmini, but the trees felt alive today. More alive than they'd felt since Kaely had died.

"Where is she?" she asked the tree.

The trees around her groaned, trunks moving as if by strong winds. She looked up, mouth falling open as she realized the tree bent itself, as if to point.

"Thank you," she told the tree.

Hurry, it said.

She dashed over leaf litter and pinecones, feeling the way the forest floor sprang against her boots. When she reached the next giant, it shimmied and moaned and pointed with the top of its tall body. Sela moved forward, following a wide path, noticing everything and nothing as she scanned the forest for her granddaughter.

She almost missed her. She expected her to be a little closer to the ground.

The trees whispered to her, *Here!*

Sela halted, casting her frantic gaze around to locate Riana. And then she saw it. She stumbled back, her eyes scanning up higher and higher until she looked face to face with the greatest Tyrinth creature of all the legends. Not even Kaely had summoned the presence of this beast. Not in all the time she had spent in the forest, growing it.

Sela's eyes grew round as her mouth hung open. She trembled as the Tagorbi, dragon of Tyrinth, lowered its head to Sela, moving one of its massive clawed feet to reveal Riana nestled in a bed of moss and surrounded by fire nymphs. Riana was silent, eyes closed, unmoving, and very, very pale.

Sela had imagined seeing this dragon before. She and Kaely had played in the woods and pretended it would appear to them. She had never imagined it was so immense. It hulked amid the forest like a small mountain. Sela surmised it lived underground and rising had gently lifted this portion of the forest where it resided on Tagorbi's shelled back. The edges of the shell showed glimmering hints of rock and gems. Sela stared, stunned, as she tried to make sense of the animal's seemingly cobbled together body, wondering how it kept its form.

The creature regarded Sela with eyes of twinkling jade and emerald, long sweeping eyelashes of ferns framing stone-like eyes. Upon its brow grew berry bushes that had flowered with buds of white. As if it understood the questions running around in Sela's head, it spoke to her.

"I *am* the Tyrinth," it said. Its voice growled and vibrated in deep notes, warm like cedarwood, strong like the mountains, rich like soil. Sela shuddered at its power, lowering herself to kneel on the forest floor and allow her shaking knees a rest. "I am not separate from it. I simply take this form now so that you may identify me as who I am."

"Why are you here?" she asked.

Tagorbi slowly swiveled its enormous head to the inert form of Riana. The fire nymphs were laying plant leaves over Riana's arms. Her dress had been cut open to reveal a nasty wound they touched with tentative fingers, conferring with each other before several of them flitted away, up to the face of Tagorbi. Tagorbi blinked giant eyelids and bowed its head slightly. The fire nymphs pulled several of the fern leaves from its eyes and flitted back to Riana.

"I am here because it is time to restore balance," it said.

"What does that have to do with Riana?" Sela asked.

"The girl is the only one granted the power to make the change."

"And what is the power she has? If she's Tyrmini, she'll be found and killed."

"She is not Tyrmini. And yet, she is. She is different, with power that is not detected by the twisted means of the one forcing imbalance."

"She doesn't want anything to do with the power. She fears it."

"Only she can choose. If she does not choose to embrace her power, we all will perish."

"How do I help her see?" Sela asked.

"Soon, she will understand, little by little. Her compassion will win out. I must go now. I have blessed her with what little power I can, but she must still be tended until she is well again. Refusal to use her power has caused a deep hurt within her. She will heal when she wields it once again."

Tagorbi lowered itself foot by foot, as if melting into the Tyrinth. Its body began to disassemble, losing the form of a shelled dragon.

"Wait, I can't do this alone. How can she gain the wisdom she needs to grow? What's she supposed to do now?" Sela asked, frantic to get as many answers as possible from the creature of legend.

"I must go. I am unlike the girl. I can be seen by the dragon's eye."

"What is the dragon's eye? What do you mean?"

Tagorbi didn't answer, but closed its eyes as it drifted further into the Tyrinth. The forest settled back into itself, but there was a sheen of vibrant green shimmering in the air. Sela could feel the magic snapping at her senses. The energy enlivened her in a way that took ten years off her aged body.

She sprang forward over roots and bramble toward Riana. Fire nymphs zipped toward her, halting her forward momentum with a wall of fiery protection. They hissed at her in warning. She held her hands up in surrender.

"It's okay. I'm her grandmother. I'm here to help."

That didn't seem to help. They advanced on her, brandishing small black spears and baring their sharp teeth. Their eyes were black and fearsome in the glow of their flames. She took a step back.

"Please," she said. "That's my granddaughter. I need to help her."

Beautiful, songlike speech issued from a fire nymph near Riana. The nymphs preventing her approach extinguished their orange and yellow flames back to blue, softening their expressions as they looked at their queen. Sela continued forward, the fire nymphs escorting her toward Riana.

The queen they'd taken care of two days ago was vibrant blue, her long silver hair streaming down her back between her transparent, multi-colored wings. She turned toward Sela, her wide, dark eyes made more feminine with feathered white eyelashes. She beckoned Sela forward from where she knelt on Riana's chest, peering down at the girl.

Sela was shocked to see Riana's eye was swollen, as if she'd been hit in the face. Her arms were entirely covered in green leaves, and Sela shuddered to think what the nymphs were treating. Riana's pale face was splattered with dry blood, and her dress was covered in darkening red. Sela couldn't hold back tears as she bent closer to her granddaughter, brushing her pale face.

Sela wished she wasn't such an old lady, but she was grateful for Riana's slender form. Still, Riana was almost fully grown. Sela positioned herself behind Riana and scooped her up under the arms and around her middle. It wasn't ideal, but she would have to drag her out. As she reached her arms beneath her granddaughter, her hands touched vines or roots. She removed her hands and looked closer.

"Bless it in the Maker's light," she said. Tagorbi seemed to have considered Sela's need to transport the girl and had provided a means. She followed the roping plant life to find it looped up, far past Riana's head. She pulled the braided vines away from the bed of moss upon which Riana rested. The natural-made rope had green tips that still seemed alive. Under Riana was a lattice of intertwining vines that formed a pallet. At the top left corner there was another end of green vines that matched the rope Sela held.

"Clever dragon," she said. She stood with the rope in her hand, then wrapped it over her middle. She bent down to attach the two green ends but was interrupted by the wooshing of sudden wind. She looked up and found herself face to face with an antoli. Fire nymphs scattered, a buzz of panicked frenzy breaking through the throng. The antoli sniffed the air where the fire nymphs had just been, then zeroed in on Riana. Its low hum resonated Sela's worry.

"Yes, she's badly hurt," Sela said. Riana had told her about the encounter and knew the creature meant her no harm. Still, the curving length of its needle-like teeth jutting up from its lower jaw was enough to stir a healthy amount of respect for the predator.

Sela looked down at the rope, carefully fashioned by an ancient god dragon of Tyrinth, and then back to the antoli. "Were you summoned, I wonder?" she asked the beast out loud.

The antoli sniffed at Sela and purred in content, as if to answer in the affirmative.

"Can you pull Riana to the edge of the forest for me?" she asked.

It purred again, the noise vibrating deeply in its throat as it snuffed and chomped its mouth in her direction.

Sela stood, unwound the vines from around her middle, and made space for the antoli. It stood in front of the elemental-made litter and waited like a patient horse. Sela wrapped the rope of vines carefully around the chest and shoulders of the creature and touched the two green ends together, fascinated by how they grew to from a strong bond. The vines further shifted to form a collar around the antoli's shoulders, then cinched itself tighter to lift the head of the litter just enough to create less drag and keep Riana's head and shoulders from bouncing against the rough forest floor.

Sela led the way.

Chapter Eighteen

onny Derringer was on his way home from his training with the Baron's Guard. Muscles he didn't know he had screamed for his attention. The sergeant had berated him regularly while the officers sniggered at their new comrade. Donny was unaccustomed to so much physical activity. He wondered if it had been this difficult for his brother, Jack.

Donny fought against the pulling sensation that stretched from his chest to his stomach. It had been two months since his brother's death. He dreaded going home. He even dreaded going to training, but at least the physical excursion kept him so busy he had no time to think about his brother. When he wasn't occupied, the nightmares of his death plagued him.

Shadow wolves hadn't been seen in a century. And then one showed up, right on their property. The thing had taken a pig. Lured it into the shadows but didn't eat it, not really. No, it bit the pig, then when the pig lay in a waking nightmare of illusions, squealing as if it had suffered real injury, the wolf basked in the fear rolling off the poor creature.

Donny hated seeing the part of the pig's life where it ended. His dad called him a wuss and soft. Hearing that pig's squeals had sent both he and his brother running. It was almost the worst sound he'd ever heard. The worst sound being the sound of his brother's screams of agony after the wolf had bitten him.

His brother had been much braver than he could ever be. He'd gone into the shadows and tried saving the pig. Donny would have left the animal to squeal until it died to keep the shadow wolf away.

That thing was as scary as Widdawah's throne.

His brother's death was a gruesome sight to behold. The wolf had tortured his brother and then fed off Donny's fear too. Donny could still feel the taint of fear coating his insides like tar from pipe smoke. And he was still nervous of dark corners and the shade of trees.

He shivered as he stepped out onto North Road, grateful for the sunshine, even if it was overcast. He cast a nervous glance over to the looming TyrMinHai. So much darkness under those trees. He subconsciously sidled over to the further side of the road, boots scuffing in the rocks as his eyes peered into the forest. He shifted his gaze back to the destination ahead, but something caught his attention.

He did a quick double-take, then stopped dead in his tracks. He shuffled back several steps. His heart hammered away in his chest. Mrs. Starliss's white hair glinted in the afternoon sun. Donny breathed a sigh of relief that the snatch of white he'd seen was her hair and not an antoli, like he first thought.

Then his heart flipped. Mrs. Starliss was struggling to get an inert Riana into a cart. Riana had odd leafy bandages wrapped over her arms and her dress was torn open. One eye was swollen shut as well. Worry needled its way through his middle.

"Mrs. Starliss," he hailed and then trotted to her aid. He looked around once more, making sure they were alone, not wanting to give away his secret.

Mrs. Starliss's white head whipped up. "Donny Derringer," she said, not in a kindly way.

Donny knew he deserved that with the number of times he'd tried making Riana's life more awful. He ducked his head as chagrin filled him. He swallowed down his pride and horror and faced Sela Starliss. He wondered if he'd ever be brave enough to treat Riana the way he wanted to treat her.

"She looks hurt," Donny said, working his voice into something that sounded like he didn't care much but felt responsible to help.

"Yes, she's been badly injured. Attacked and cut to ribbons," Sela said, struggling to pull Riana from the grass to the cart.

"Here, let me help." Donny moved toward her. He whipped the hair back off of his sweaty forehead.

Sela looked up at him with steely sea-blue eyes that dissected his insides. Donny stopped in his forward movement and squirmed under her gaze. Finally, she released him. "That would be very kind of you," she conceded.

Donny bent over and scooped Riana up from her grandmother's awkward hold. She was light enough in his arms. A bright warmth swelled inside his chest. As always, he fought against the emotion he kept hidden through a series of unkind tactics whenever he got close to her. Something about Riana got to him in a way no one else ever had. And he didn't like the loss of control he had in her presence. After he'd been old enough to recognize what the feeling was, it was too late to change his treatment toward her. And she would never accept him as anything more than her personal bully.

His emotions were so close to the surface since his brother's death, the familiar reaction he had in Riana's presence overwhelmed him. His head buzzed with the closeness of her, and he worried at the paleness of her skin and the way her eye was swollen shut. He pulled her close into his chest, relishing the way she felt against him. All the while, trying to emote careless apathy.

And then a new emotion rang through him.

"Who did this to her?" he asked through gritted teeth. He was losing his careful control on his displayed emotions. He walked toward the cart with Mrs. Starliss beside him. He watched the way Riana's hair swung, caught the cloudy light and reflected back at him. She was so different. She was so beautiful.

"I don't know," Sela said. "I found her this way, and she was already unconscious."

Donny came to the cart and looked at Riana, then back to the cart. "You taking her to the Healer's Hall?"

"Yes," Sela said.

He imagined laying her in the back of the cart and then imagined the jostling she'd endure. Even if she was unconscious, he couldn't bear the thought of her not being carefully transported. He stood for a long moment in the road, holding Riana's limp form. Something wet and warm was soaking into his tunic. He looked down at where Riana's arm rested against his middle. A spot of blood expanded in the fabric from under the leaves. He made up his mind and climbed into the cart.

"I'll hold her," he said and that was that.

Sela stared at him with her mouth hanging open.

"C'mon," he urged. "She's bleeding all over me." He didn't mean to yell, but he had.

Sela shook herself out of the shock and climbed into the cart, ignoring his outburst. She snapped the reins and let the mare carry the cart south on Coast Road.

Donny watched Riana as they jostled along. She was so pale, and she barely breathed. At one point, he worried she was dead. He worried she was dead and he was carrying her corpse and would never be able to make up for all the times he'd scared her, hurt her, and made fun of her. She was so fragile, and he was so big. He was strong enough to lift her with no problem. His arms encompassed her with ease. And yet, he'd used all those things against her.

His brother would have been ashamed of him. He'd told Donny to cut it out. He'd warned him he'd regret it someday. And he did. If Riana woke up right now, with Donny holding her like this, what would she think? She'd be scared. Scared of Donny. And all Donny wanted was to be close to her and feel the odd, warm feeling that always filled him while he was in her presence.

Shame filled him as the cart carried them closer to Healer's Hall and closer to the end of his time holding her.

"Was she out in the woods?" Donny asked Sela after she'd started driving.

"Near them, yes," Sela said. There was something a little too wild in her eyes, but he supposed that was because she cared for Riana and was probably really worried about her.

"What was she doing out there?"

"She often walks the perimeter between the woods and the vineyard. It's good for her to know the property, especially now that she is my apprentice."

"Oh," Donny said, figuring that made good sense. "And then someone came out here and just attacked her?" He looked down at her, puzzled at the situation.

"It would seem so," Mrs. Starliss replied.

"Who would do that?" Donny asked. Donny looked at Riana

Sela didn't respond, instead looking at Donny with raised eyebrows.

Donny cringed. "I—I know I haven't been nice to your granddaughter," he said.

Sela glanced between the road ahead and then back to him, waiting for him to continue.

Donny fought the urge to belch out his declaration of love for Riana. Everything was so messy inside him. He missed his brother, he was ashamed of how he bullied Riana, he cared for Riana, and he was uncomfortable with that. He feared elementals, and yet he'd be fighting them as a Baron's Guard. And now there was some nameless, faceless person going around cutting up young women. It was too much.

Donny knew he'd been wrong all those years, and he couldn't say why. So he settled for something else. "Mrs. Starliss," he began. "I promise I won't pick on Riana any longer. It was stupid and childish of me. My brother would be ashamed. I'm sorry."

"Oh, my dear," Mrs. Starliss said, "that's a very nice thing to say, but you should say that to Riana. If you can't say it, you should definitely show it. I'm going to keep you at your word, Donny Derringer."

Donny swallowed against the stone of commitment lodged in his throat. He adjusted Riana in his arms. His muscles burned from the exertion of holding her. She never stirred. She never knew how tenderly he held her. Still, she would see a different Donny from here on out.

CHAPTER NINETEEN

Riana propped herself up in bed, grateful that after a week of healing she could finally do it herself without straining the wounds on her arms. The stitches still felt foreign in her skin. She fought a wave of dizziness as she pushed her body to an upright position. According to Elynda, it would be a couple of weeks before her body made enough blood to replace what she'd lost. She'd lost a lot, thanks to Treyor.

She wondered if he was truly dead. Her nightmares were full of him returning and finishing what he'd begun. She also dreamed of strange things she couldn't make sense of. A dragon made of a mountain, halls of darkness leading to a caged dragon, storms that rained fire instead of water.

Riana pressed her fingers into her forehead and waited for the world to stop spinning and the flashing images of her last dream to fade. She couldn't get the white dragon out of her head. It was as if once it had been implanted there it took root and grew.

The dragon's face was beautiful, white, almost feminine. Its eye—it only had one—was so similar to Riana's eyes, it shook her to the very core of her being. Her insides quivered as the image danced in front of her closed eyes.

When she looked up, her grandmother entered her room, a tray laden with food that steamed and instantly filled the space with the aroma of bacon and potatoes and cracked pepper. Riana inhaled, and her stomach growled in response. She was finally getting her appetite back, and she was ravenous.

She ate the food as her grandmother watched, seeming pleased with the amount she gobbled down. When she finally laid her fork and knife aside and sighed in contentment, her grandmother spoke.

"How are you feeling today?" she asked.

Riana nodded. "Much improved. Thank you, Grandmother."

"That's excellent to hear," her grandmother said. She took the tray from Riana and laid it on the dresser, then returned to the bed. "I have some things I must tell you now that your health returns."

Riana wiggled down under the covers some more, resting her head against the pillows. She wasn't sure she was ready to hear what her grandmother had to say, but she was certain there was no escaping, if her grandmother's steely gaze was any indication. She could feel trapped by her grandmother's intensity, but she didn't have enough energy to fight the oncoming conversation. So she gave in and relaxed.

Grandmother Sela plucked at her emerald dress until she located a pocket and pulled out a handkerchief. It was white with green stitching on the edges. She wiped at her nose then clutched the material in her left hand, wrapping her right hand over the left.

"I'm certain if you weren't who you are, you would have died at Treyor's hands." Her voice was calm, but there was still a tremor to it.

Riana blinked slowly. She knew the knife wounds had been very deep. When the healers had started their work, there were some odd things that seemed to have happened. Elynda said it looked as though the arteries, the big tubes in her arms that pumped blood to various parts of her body, had been cut then stitched back together. They had to stitch the muscle together first, then stitched the skin together. She would have scars for the rest of her life, but she had not died from blood loss, and why remained a mystery.

"What do you mean, Grandmother? 'If I weren't who I am.' Who am I?" Riana felt the question vibrate deep in her body and soul. *Who am I?* she repeated in her mind, as if calling out to some greater power that would have the answer. On one hand, she was desperate to find the answer. On the other hand, she shied away from the question, sensing a bigness she wasn't sure she could handle. She pulled the covers up and rested her throbbing arms over her middle.

It had been a week since the incident. She'd stayed in the hospital for several days, receiving care from her friend, Elynda, her mother, Mrs. Heilbee, and several other healers. Elynda seemed to vacillate between giddy joy to care for her best friend and utter worry that her best friend was at Healer's Hall. The story had omitted fire nymphs and golden elixir. All the healers knew was that Riana had been attacked by a young man from out of town. He was crazy. He'd attacked her once and then stalked her out into the woods and attacked her again. In the story Grandmother Sela told, Riana had been rescued by the happening of her grandmother on the two during the attack.

Riana knew different. She'd called for the fire nymph queen, who had come with her legion of fellow fire nymphs. The tiny and fearsome army had chased the murderous boy deep into the forest. Riana was grateful beyond words that the queen had answered her call.

Did she hope Treyor was dead? The question made her shudder. Who was she?

"That's still a mystery," her grandmother said. "It seems you are so important that the ancient elemental dragons are conspiring for your safety."

CHAPTER TWENTY

Two weeks came and went, and Riana finally felt well enough to return to normal life—and school. As she approached the schoolhouse, Riana gauged how close Donny was to the entrance and whether she wanted to get near enough to him to risk an encounter. She still remembered the last time she'd seen him, and the pulled tendons and bruises she'd sustained.

Riana approached from behind the school. She peeked at the entrance, then Donny Derringer in turns. Donny stood near the porch on the front lawn of the schoolyard, looking out at the road, as if waiting for someone's approach. Riana was looking at the back of his head. Donny raised a hand and brushed through his hair. He seemed to be rooted to the spot. Riana dithered, not sure if she should wait and watch or try to sneak around him.

"He won't bother you anymore," Elynda said, startling Riana out of her covert planning session.

"Elynda," Riana half yelled. "You snuck up on me." Riana clasped her hand to her chest. "And what do you mean?"

"Didn't your grandmother tell you?"

"Tell me what?"

"Oh," Elynda began. "Maybe I shouldn't say anything." She twisted her hands around the strap of her lunch bag, her emerald eyes downcast to the hems of her blue and white dress.

"Too late," Riana said. "Tell all."

Elynda yanked her gaze up to Riana, then over her shoulder to Donny, then back again. "Very well," she said. "Although, your grandmother could be cross with me if she finds out I've said something."

"I won't tell her," Riana said. "You should know that by now."

There were so many secrets between Elynda and Riana it could put even her grandmother to shame. They hid nothing from each other. At least, they hadn't. Riana still hadn't got the nerves to tell Elynda her new secret.

"Donny saw Mrs. Starliss trying to heave you into the cart the day you got attacked. He came up and not only helped you in, but held you as Mrs. Starliss drove you to Healer's Hall. Mrs. Starliss told Mother that he'd confessed his shame at treating you poorly and vowed to abstain from his bullying. Mrs. Starliss even said she thought he felt a fondness for you."

"Fondness for me?" Riana asked incredulously and loudly.

Elynda's gaze jerked past her. Riana turned, annoyance seeping into every fiber of her being. Donny looked over at them from his spot on the porch. He didn't smile, but he nodded.

"What are you talking about? Donny Derringer has haunted my steps since I was a small child. How does that translate to feelings of fondness?" Riana had lowered her voice but couldn't help the disbelief that drenched her words.

"I don't know, except Mother said when boys have feelings they don't understand, they sometimes funnel the energy into meanness. She said it's because boys aren't always raised to accept their emotions. Which is a crying shame. She had a lot to say about it, actually..." Elynda trailed off, her eyes searching the limbs of the nearby oak before they found Riana again. "So, she wasn't surprised to hear Donny cared for you. Also, I saw him carrying you into Healers Hall. He held you like you were the most precious thing alive. I was so stunned Mother had to pinch me."

Riana's scalp was itchy with tingles at this new revelation. A molten anger bubbled within her, the incredulity of it all made her hurt in more ways than she could express.

"So," she said, the dangerous note in her voice more pronounced than she meant it to be. "He treats me poorly because he cares for me?"

"Don't be cross, Riana. I didn't say it; Mother did."

"I'm not cross," she said, straightening her shoulders. The twinge and pull of the lacerations across her arms and stomach gave a nasty ring to the anger pulsing through her.

"You're not?" Elynda asked, suddenly seeming to not trust her friend's words.

"Not at all," Riana said. "And just to prove it..." She pivoted and crossed the school's front yard.

Donny pulled himself away from the spot he'd rooted himself to and moved closer to Riana. "Riana," he said. His hazel eyes had gone wide as he watched her approach and moved for the close conversation. He looked relieved, excited, eager. And then Riana got near enough even he could read her features.

Riana's ears thrummed. She gripped her hands into fists.

He was ten feet away when she halted, her stance wide and immovable. She crossed her arms, but that hurt, so she dropped them to her side again.

"I suppose I ought to be grateful to you," she spat.

Donny halted mid-step toward her and leaned back, as if blown by a gust of wind.

"Do you think one act of kindness can undo a lifetime of bullying?"

"Riana, I need to say something," Donny began, but looked over his shoulder. His friends were hanging over the porch railing, mouths gaping.

Riana closed the space between them and looked up at her bully turned savior. "No, you don't need to say a thing. Because nothing you can say can make up for what you've done to me. Nothing!"

"I should never have hurt you. I was wrong," Donny said.

Before he could go on, she continued. "Yes! You were wrong. You have no heart, Donny Derringer. None. You think it's not enough to be orphaned as an infant? You think it's peaches and cream to grow up with silver hair and multicolored eyes and get called a freak for it? You've got no idea. And you never wanted to know. All you wanted was to make me feel like less of a person than you. As if that weren't already a struggle. No words could possibly make up for the hurt you've caused me. So don't even try."

To Riana's stunned horror, Donny dropped to his knees. She stepped away from him, her lip curling in disgust. She wasn't sure which she disliked more: a Donny who bullied her, or a Donny who was deferential to her.

"I know. So, I'm going to show you, Riana Starliss. I'm going to show you if it's the last thing I do." He planted his hands into the muddy grass and bowed his head to her. "Even if you never forgive me, I'll somehow find a way to make it up to you."

His friends were laughing now. Laughing and pointing.

Riana crossed her arms again and this time, let the pain swell. "Don't get your hopes up," she said and walked past his prostrate form.

After school, Riana and Elynda walked along the road. It was a Friday and they both had the day off from their apprentice jobs. They planned to spend the afternoon and evening together, walking to Lighthouse Hill and then to the Heilbee home for dinner and a sleepover. Riana was ecstatic to be out of the house. Three weeks cooped up and mostly in bed had grown a moldering cabin fever in her.

They crunched down the rock road, Riana giddy from the fresh air and sunshine. She didn't care that her muscles were already aching, she was enjoying the outdoors too much to complain.

"I have a snack for when we get to the Hill," Elynda said.

"Oh? What sort?" Riana was a little winded already.

Elynda turned back toward Riana. "Brownies," she whispered.

Riana brightened further. Chocolate sounded amazing. "Your mom is the best cook. I don't know how she manages it all. Healing people, managing a household, cooking..."

"Oh, Dad does as much as Mom. They make sure they share the responsibility. And they make us help too."

Riana nodded, thinking back about the times she'd seen Elynda's father darning socks or assisting in peeling vegetables or cleaning. Her own adopted father had tended the shop but never lifted a finger for household chores. Her grandmother had blamed him for driving her daughter to an early grave, more from the heartache of marrying a man who couldn't show his love than anything else.

"That's the way it should be," Riana decided.

Elynda nodded. "That's what Mother says. Dad agrees. He adores her."

Riana wondered if she'd ever find someone like Mr. Heilbee was to Mrs. Heilbee. Then she decided she'd probably grow old and be a spinster. If she even lived to be that old.

"What are you thinking about?" Elynda asked.

Riana wrestled with the ugly truth. Her truth.

"All these events lately. I'm just not sure what to make of them. And Elynda, you're the only one I can talk to." Riana hurried ahead to get in step with her best friend, then gripped Elynda's hand as if holding onto a lifeline.

"Riana," she said and pulled close to her. "You can always count on me. We have to do this together."

Riana sobbed, sudden sorrow and confusion boiling to the surface and making her situation real in the extreme. She tried finding words to express all the feelings she had mashed up inside her. She opened her mouth to speak but was interrupted by a strange new noise. She snapped her mouth shut and halted, straining to hear the noise again.

Elynda stopped walking as well. "Are you okay? Are you in pain?"

"No, I thought I heard something. Listen," Riana said. She faced Elynda, and they looked into each other's eyes as they listened through the crashing tide and cry of seagulls.

The foreign noise broke across the open field leading up to the lighthouse. Elynda and Riana turned in the direction the noise had come from. It was unlike anything Riana had ever heard. In the distance, a little splash of sea green shimmered then disappeared. The Dreavynan Sea roared and hushed over their left shoulders.

"What was that?" Elynda asked, gripping Riana's arm.

"No idea, but it sounded like an animal."

"Or an elemental," Elynda said, clearly afraid.

"You think?" Riana said and took two steps toward the field, curiosity leading the way.

"Wait, Riana," Elynda said and pulled her back. "You're in no shape to go traipsing after a creature. What if it's hungry?"

Riana looked at her and laughed. "Elynda," she said. "They're not going to eat us. What if it needs help?" What if it's a creature I haven't met yet, she thought. The squealing chirp broke across the air again. Riana turned from her friend to the direction of the noise, trying to pinpoint its location, stepping closer to the field.

Elynda tried pulling her back, but despite her current weakness, Riana's curiosity overwhelmed her fragility and she won the tug of war.

"Don't be a baby, Elynda," Riana said without turning toward her friend.

Elynda squealed through pressed lips, but followed so close to Riana that she nearly tripped on her. They left the rock road and swished into the tall grasses, following the direction of the sounds. There also seemed to be an odor coming from the same direction. Riana cupped a hand over her nose and choked back bile.

"I think the noise is coming from there, and I'm certain the smell is getting stronger," Elynda said through little gasping breaths.

Riana agreed with her. The knee-high yellow grass clung to their clothing as they passed over the rolling terrain. An oak tree in the middle of the field marked the sight of their destination. In the background, the white lighthouse of Landsend stood tall and elegant. As she walked, she grimaced at the sound of the grass against their legs. Whatever it was, she didn't want to startle it. She looked at Elynda's nervous face and second-guessed her decision to investigate.

She halted and whispered to Elynda, "Why don't you stay here? Just in case it's dangerous?"

"What?" Elynda whispered back, looking taken back. "I'm not letting you face something dangerous on your own. And besides, we're nearly there now."

Riana frowned but said nothing more. The whimpering chirp of the animal grew quiet. Searching the ground for signs, Riana spotted a skinny trail of bent grass and followed it. Riana could feel the placement of Elynda's feet close behind her as she took step after careful step toward the sound and stench where the little trail led.

The bent grass of the trail widened, forming a large indentation. Riana stopped. Elynda's foot came down on Riana's boot heel. Riana lost her footing and stumbled as her foot pulled from the boot. Elynda yelped as she fell onto Riana. With a thud, the girls landed in a heap.

The dry grass pricked at Riana's palms, the smell of the stalks wafting up from the chilled Tyrinth. The healing lacerations on her arms stung. Elynda was on top of her, her weight pinning her to the ground. Riana raised her head. Large, dark eyes greeted her. The fur of the animal glistened in the gray sunshine like kelp in water. The animal chirruped around small, pointed eyeteeth and sidled away on clawed web feet, closer to something the same sea colors. Riana lie frozen under Elynda, trying hard not to breathe or make a sudden movement.

Elynda barely breathed into her ear, "What is it, Riana?"

The creature regarded them past a small, rounded black nose that wiggled back and forth in the air between them. The markings on the creature's face were beautiful, like dark streams of water had made lines from its rounded, dog-like snout around its onyx eyes, lining its eyebrows, and finally fading into two high ridges of fluffy fur on either side of the top of its head.

"I'm not sure," Riana said, but she knew where she could look to find out. A lump of lead dropped into her belly. Going down to the hidden cellar meant she was accepting what she was. She wrestled with curiosity and her own fear of being discovered.

The elemental fidgeted its small ears from being completely curled in and flat to its temples, to flared out and erect. They were round and on the small side with long, feathery tufts that extended up and fell in single green strands.

"I'm sure it's a water elemental, though. And that looks like it was probably its mother," Riana said. She smiled at the creature and clicked at it. "Hi, little one." The animal turned its head sideways.

"Oh! So sweet!" Elynda gasped. The little creature curled up next to the bloated body of the other creature and closed his eyes. His whiskers waggled as his body quivered. He drew his long, slender tail around him. "Wait," Elynda said. "What's wrong with him?"

"I don't know," Riana said.

The tip of the creature's nose where the fur started and the black, glistening flesh ended began to turn the faintest shade of yellow. The grass was yellow. Was he trying to camouflage himself?

As soon as the color began to creep up past the lines of his eyebrows, it went very wrong. Where the tip of his nose had turned yellow, it began to turn green and then it leaked brown. Elynda slid from the top of Riana, and the two girls laid in the grass watching as the creature tried in earnest to hide from their sight.

Gray, black, blue, and even purple, the fur on the animal's head shifted in quicker and quicker succession until at last it chirped in exasperation. He curled up against his mother, rubbing his face on the fur of her belly, his lungs heaving.

"Poor little guy," Riana frowned. "He doesn't have anyone to teach him anymore." She knew how that felt. A band around her heart squeezed. There was no telling how long it had been since a creature like this could be found on Tyrinth. Riana wondered what other creatures were crawling back into the here and now through the ages of lore and history?

Riana knelt under the watchful gaze of the sea creature. She held out her hand, wondering what its fur felt like. It ducked its head under the concealment of its shiny, sea green tail. Riana backed away and waited.

136

She reached again, and the elemental stretched its tentative nose out of the comfort of the dead body and sniffed her hand. Its tongue darted out and gave a little lick that tickled her fingers. She grinned at him and then nodded to Elynda to come closer.

Elynda crawled on her hands and knees until she was side by side with Riana. It shied away for a moment before sniffing Elynda's outstretched fingers, butting his head against the palm of her hand. Elynda smiled at Riana as she petted the animal's sea green fur.

"Ah, his fur is so silky!"

Riana looked at the bloated figure of the bigger creature. Its facial markings were marred by the presence of maggots. Its eyes gaped with rot over its open mouth. Riana covered her mouth, trying not to vomit. There was a jagged, blackened wound around the sea green neck of the animal that spilled out maggots and pus.

Riana looked from the body of the mother to the sea. "The seashore is pretty close. I guess these creatures come to land to have their babies," Riana said.

Elynda had sat down cross-legged on the ground, and the creature had crawled into her lap. It wiggled into just the right place, curled its tail around itself, and closed its eyes. Elynda stroked its fur, tracing the lines that started at the nose and finished at the end of its long, furry tail.

Elynda looked up from the elemental pup. "Riana, what are we going to do?"

"Hey!" a voice rang with anger.

Riana jerked her head in the direction of the road from whence they came. Her heart dropped into her stomach. This would be her end. She'd been caught, and by none other than her school bully, Donny Derringer.

CHAPTER TWENTY-ONE

Donny couldn't help himself. Something had started to grow within him after he'd held Riana so close to him. The smell of her wouldn't leave his nose. The feel of her wouldn't leave his arms. She had been so delicate and fragile. He was overwhelmed by a need to protect her.

After school, he'd hung back, watching to see which way she and Elynda would go. Then he followed. He needed to be near her. Like he needed to drink water and breathe. Friday was a day off for apprentices, so he had the leisure of nothing else to do. He was sure to hang back far enough they wouldn't be alerted by the sound of his clumsy footsteps or his hulking mass in broad daylight. He already figured where they were going. He knew Riana loved the old lighthouse and she and Elynda hung out there regularly. He wasn't concerned when they escaped his sight.

He trudged along down the road leading to the lighthouse. His dad's mood had grown fouler since Donny had taken an apprenticeship with the Baron's Guard rather than with him. And it had already been foul since his brother's death, preceded by his brother's apprenticeship and assignment in the Baron's Guard. His father often exploded in angry tantrums. Donny saw the wear in new lines on his father's face and less hair on his father's head. Death takes a toll on a family.

If it wasn't for those damn elementals...

His shoulders inched to his ears as his arms swung to and fro with the rhythm of his gait. Feeling the tension in his neck, he forced a straight posture to prevent another headache. Because when the headaches started, the memories came. He just couldn't handle seeing the death of his brother again.

He took a few deep breaths and squished his mind up so it would go blank. Once he'd accomplished that, he moved forward at a quicker pace, craving the sight of Riana. They were so far ahead that he'd totally lost sight of them, even after picking up the pace. They should have been around here somewhere. He stopped in the middle of the road and looked over the fields leading up to the lighthouse. The grass was dead still, long and yellow, but not so long he'd miss seeing at least the tops of their heads—especially Elynda's raven black hair.

He wondered if they'd gone down to the beach already and he'd missed them. He waffled between heading down the beach or heading toward the lighthouse, weighing if he wanted to stay hidden from them or if he wanted them to see him. Riana had been none-too-happy to see him earlier, apology ready or not. If she saw him, would she assume he was there to pick on her?

He hung his head. Of course she would.

He scuffed his toe in the light dirt and white rocks while he dithered about what to do next. Maybe he'd just go home. He could help his dad bring in the pigs and feed them. Maybe that would help his mood, and he wouldn't be so angry at dinner time. That's what his brother would have wanted him to do, he decided.

He turned to leave and head home when a flash of black caught his attention. A little tweeting sound, something like a bird but not quite, broke through the constant ebb and flow of the ocean waves. He did a double-take and saw Elynda's head just breaking the line of the grass. He'd spent a decade looking at the back of that head, so he was sure it belonged to her. He searched in the vicinity for Riana when at last the silver strands of her colorless hair breached the grass line.

He simply stared for a long moment, soaking in the sight of her, somehow breathing easier. They were facing the lighthouse, so their backs were turned to Donny as he peered over the field from his position on the road. He wondered what they were doing, then he decided they must be having a picnic or something. A breeze washed over him and an awful stench came with it. He plugged his nose, eyes watering.

He was sure the smell was coming from that direction. Why would they picnic in a place that smelled so awful?

Donny strained forward to see if he could make out what they were doing in the tall grass, trying to see if they were in any distress. Riana was looking out over the ocean, her face concerned and serious. There was something sort of beautiful about the determination he saw there. Like this morning when she'd been so angry with him. It showed something about her he hadn't quite seen before—fierceness. When Riana had been unconscious and he'd held her in his arms, she'd been as fragile as a bird with broken wings. Today, she'd been like a wolf, all canines and growls. Seeing the two different sides of her had only grown his fascination with her.

Elynda shifted and something colorful caught Donny's eye. A jolt of fear sent his heart racing while his guts twisted.

"Hey!" he shouted and ran at the same time.

Elynda and Riana whipped their heads around in his direction; one multicolored gaze and one bright green peeking above the swaying grass. Riana shot up from her seat and ran toward Donny. Elynda was doing something, still crouched, but Donny couldn't see because the oncoming Riana was blocking his view.

"Donny," she said, "what are you doing out here?"

"Is that an elemental?" he asked without bothering to answer her question.

"What? What are you talking about?" Riana evaded.

"I saw something from the road as I was walking past."

Riana looked over her shoulder at her best friend who had stood and was now walking toward them.

"What did you see?" she asked.

"I saw a shift of color. It was sea green and blue. And there's been reports of amatsus in this area burrowing and nesting in people's fields and yards, eating the vegetables out of their gardens."

"What's an amatsu?" Riana asked.

"It's a sea creature that also comes on land. An air breather. Warm blooded and covered in fur. They're difficult to find because they can camouflage to their surroundings. But their natural color is the color of the sea. It's also believed these guys are responsible for helping the rogue Tyrmini Serena flood Landsend five-hundred years ago. They're dangerous."

The girls glanced at each other.

"And you think you saw one out here?" Elynda asked.

"Just now!" Donny shouted and Riana flinched but didn't retreat. Even that small movement of fear triggered a lump to form in his throat. "Sorry," he said and swallowed the lump down. "I'm sure it was nothing. Sorry I bothered you." He turned and began walking through the tall grass, the swish, swish, swish accompanying the sea's constant song.

A small chirp punctuated the other sounds and Donny whirled.

"What was that?" he asked.

Riana had knelt when he'd turned his back and was fussing with the hem of her skirts.

Elynda covered a hand over her mouth and made a small noise. "Sorry. Hiccups."

"Something's going on here," Donny said and turned back to the girls.

"I'm sure I don't know what you mean," said Riana, finally standing. The chirp sounded again, but it didn't come from Elynda. It came from Riana's feet.

Donny charged forward, knocking Riana to the ground and grabbed blindly through the grass at the source of the noise. The little sea green creature recoiled, but Donny scooped the animal up as it tried to flee.

"Let it go, Donny!" Riana screamed.

Elynda pulled at his arm, which did nothing to break the grip he had on the amatsu's scruff.

"Got you," Donny said. He reached around for his knife which he held in a belted scabbard on his left hip. He was going to relish ridding the world of one more elemental, and this one before it could grow and cause more damage.

The knife came free with a satisfying rasp of blade on leather. The amatsu struggled weakly against his grip. It chirped wildly, crying out in fear. Riana shouted something at him, which was lost amidst the animal's cries, the sound of the ocean, and a new wind that had sprung up from seemingly nowhere.

The cacophony of noises pulled at Donny's anger. The world was a better place without elementals, and he would start his campaign with this creature. He only thought for a moment of exactly how he would deliver the killing strike. The Baron's Guard had found these creatures were not particularly difficult to kill; a straightforward slice through the neck severed the artery, which would empty it of its blood while the heart still pumped until the brain caught up and stopped sending the signal. Easy peasy.

He was dimly aware of Riana clinging to his pants and begging. He worried about this, wondering why she was concerned about a dirty elemental, but decided it was less important than the issue at hand.

He raised the knife, angled it around the weakly struggling creature's neck, and bunched his muscles to make the cut. As he did, he wondered what he would do with the carcass. He'd heard the pelts would fetch a pretty price on the market, but maybe he'd keep this one as a memento of his first elemental kill. He liked that plan.

This is for you, brother, he thought and pulled the knife.

CHAPTER TWENTY-TWO

R iana tried hiding the creature, but it had no fear of the hulking Donny Derringer. Donny found and snatched the elemental so quickly, Riana had no time to react and conceal the creature further. She watched in horror as Donny held the amatsu aloft and pulled his knife from his belt.

She shouted at Donny, falling to her knees and begging. Her stomach squeezed and morphed into a solid steel ball which rang with each of her pleadings. "It's just a baby," she said. "It's innocent and hasn't harmed anyone."

Elynda pulled at Donny's arm, adding her shouts to those of Riana's and the insistent ear-piercing shrieks of the amatsu. Donny was untouched by any of this, his strength of body so intense he simply ignored all as he positioned his knife against the amatsu's neck, ready to deal out death.

Riana's blood boiled. Donny Derringer, the boy who'd used his brute strength against her his whole life. Donny Derringer, who'd laughed at her when he'd pummeled and bruised her. Donny Derringer, who'd spat at her, berated her, and isolated her. She would not be ignored.

Liquid sunshine burned through her veins, forcing her to rise to a standing position. She stopped pleading as the power within her filled her to bursting. She didn't want to harm him. She just wanted him to stop. She squeezed her eyes closed as the internal battle for control waged within her. The bigness of the power within seemed uncontrollable, but somehow she had to contain it.

A separate aching need to turn the violence Donny meant for the elemental back onto him rose within her. No, she told it. I will not harm him. I only want to protect the elemental. I just need enough strength to get him to stop. So he'll listen to me.

The power within her pulsed like a heart. Just a little, she thought, just enough for extra strength. I don't want to hurt anyone.

The light of the power building in her squeezed her heart. She only wanted to protect the creature. Her hands glowed an ethereal white light. Just enough to keep him from killing the creature.

Her hands sparked and shone. She reached forward as Donny bunched his muscles around the blade's handle. He made a minute movement to pull the blade, and Riana placed her hand around his wrist.

His arm halted. His gaze yanked to hers; his hazel eyes wide. First his mouth hung open, then he closed it and sneered at her, his face crumpling into hard lines, baring gritted teeth.

"Riana Starliss. Let go of me now," he commanded.

"I will not," she said, fighting against her anger. The light cascaded off her hand, wound around Donny's arm, spread over his shoulder, and spilled down his chest, torso, and legs. It danced in semi-transparent white light that glittered and glowed like sea mist in the sunshine.

With her free arm, she scooped the amatsu into her, willing Donny to release the creature. He groaned as his hand relaxed against his will. Riana was careful to pull the animal away from the blade so it didn't fall into the knife. The pup landed in a heap in her arms against her chest. She let a small rasp of relief escape her mouth as the warmth of the creature pressed into her.

The power wrapped Donny in a cloaking embrace of light as Riana dropped her hand from his wrist. She backed away from the Baron's Guard in training, unsure how long the power would last after she wasn't touching him anymore.

Elynda scurried over to her, wrapping her arms around Riana's waist and placing a shielding hand over the pup who chirped and cried, butting its head against Riana's chest, then Elynda's hand, then Riana's chin.

Donny's head was free of the encompassing light while his body was still frozen in a position to kill.

"You're a Tyrmini," he accused.

"You're a killer," she accused back.

"Elementals are dangerous. One killed my brother."

Riana held out the amatsu. "This creature did not kill your brother. Maybe the creature that did kill your brother was just trying to defend itself."

"Maybe I don't care! He was my brother. And that thing tortured him! It didn't just defend itself. It fed on his fears and pain. I saw it, Riana. It was evil."

Riana hung her head. She couldn't say and she didn't know. Maybe there were elementals out there who did horrible things to people. Donny and everyone else would be afraid of that. They would do what they could to protect themselves. But slaughtering them to extinction? That was wrong.

"I'm so sorry you lost your brother. Losing someone you love is awful," Riana said.

"What do you know? You don't even have any real family," he said.

Despite the years of having her status as an orphan flung in her face, it still stung when someone pointed it out. As if losing her mother at the age of eight didn't count because they hadn't shared the same blood.

"I'm sorry," he said. "I shouldn't have said that. I know your mom dying was hard. And I really am sorry I've bullied you all these years. That was wrong of me."

"You want to make up for all those years of bullying?" Riana asked, not looking at him.

Donny was silent for so long she finally caught his gaze in hers, suspending him as he hung helplessly in the embrace of some unidentified power. He finally, slowly nodded.

"Then help me," she whispered with such intensity her throat burned.

Donny looked at her incredulously. "Help you? You're a Tyrmini. If I help you, I put my own life at risk."

"If you don't help me, if you report me, I'll be put to death. So either you kill me or you help me."

Donny screwed up his face and thought hard about it. It looked like it hurt.

Riana held her breath and stroked the fur of the amatsu, her heart hammering at her rib cage. She wondered what it would be like to die, to be hung. She looked down at the amatsu as it began to purr, looking up at Riana with wide, trusting eyes. Her own life—all by itself—was one thing, but she couldn't bear the thought of being able to make a difference and just giving up on innocent elementals without a fight. Win or fail, she had to try.

"If I help you, will you let me out of this thing that's holding me?" Donny asked.

Riana let out the breath she'd been holding. She nodded stiffly against taut neck muscles and hoped she really could release him.

"I'll help you," he said. Simple words, but beneath them was a raw desperation Riana had never heard in Donny. It sounded like there was much deeper stuff to him than she'd ever guessed.

"For the years of torture you've put me through, I will release you on condition you help me survive and help me keep elementals safe."

There were tears standing in Donny's eyes as his jaw ground from one side to the next. He was giving up a lot in helping her. Riana hoped she was worth it.

CHAPTER TWENTY-THREE

Riana handed the amatsu pup to Elynda and stood in front of Donny. She was just wondering how she would consciously release Donny from his restraining hold when the light surrounding him faded until it disappeared. Surprised but trying not to show it to Donny—this was her leverage over him at the moment—she stepped away as if she were in full control. She nodded at him in satisfaction to cement the ruse.

Donny dropped his arms, the knife still gripped in his hand. Riana eyed him nervously as he stood looking between her and the amatsu and Elynda.

"We're probably all going to be put to death for this," he said.

Riana cast a look around the fields and nearby road. The ocean roared and hushed. The air was damp and sweet with the sea. Sunshine glowed through a thin blanket of cloud cover. There was not another soul in sight.

"Not unless we're caught," she said, and vowed she wouldn't be.

"Riana, what do we do with the pup?" Elynda asked.

Donny shuffled forward to look at the creature he'd moments ago been bent on killing. Elynda leaned away from Donny, wrapping her arms tighter around the little creature. Donny ignored this.

"Does he have teeth yet?" Donny asked, stepping back.

Riana guessed he wasn't volunteering to check. She bent over the creature snuggled in Elynda's arms and gently lifted its upper lip. It squirmed away, but she'd caught a glimpse of sharp canines.

"Yes," Riana said, looking to Donny.

"Well, then it should be able to eat fish if we toss it back into the sea."

"*Toss* it back into the sea?" Elynda asked.

Donny rolled his eyes. "Oh, I'm sorry, was that insensitive? Release. We'll release it back to the sea. And hope some fisherman doesn't come right along and kill it." He said this last part under his breath.

"Does that happen often?" Riana asked.

"Lately? Yeah." Donny looked at her incredulously. "Don't you ever go down to the pier?"

"What do you mean?"

"I mean, if you'd get out of the vineyard every now and then and out into town, you'd see there are a couple of fishermen who sell amatsu pelts."

"Pelts?" Elynda asked, her voice quavering and her green eyes wide. She held the amatsu pup a little tighter.

"Pelts. As in the fur and hide of the animal," Donny explained.

Riana's stomach rolled.

"So the sea isn't safe?" Elynda asked.

Riana thought hard. The creature needed the sea to survive. Did they risk someone hunting and killing the pup? What about all the other amatsus?

"It doesn't matter. You either let him go into the sea and risk him getting fished out, or you leave him out here in the field and he'll die from lack of food. Or whatever got its mom." Donny looked around Elynda and Riana, face crumpled as he surveyed the carcass of the mother amatsu.

Riana took the amatsu from Elynda and snuggled the pup to her chest. She really hated the two equally horrendous choices she had available. It seemed like she was always being told it was this bad consequence or another bad consequence. Anger rippled up her spine.

"Maybe those aren't the only choices available," she said.

CHAPTER TWENTY-FOUR

Riana marched through the grasses with the little amatsu in her arms, hidden under the folds of her gray cloak. Elynda and Donny watched, unmoving.

"Where are you going? The Dreavynan is that way," Donny pointed out.

"I know," Riana said, but continued east. Grass swished behind her, and she knew Donny and Elynda were following even if they didn't know where she was going. She knew and she hoped it worked.

When they passed the schoolhouse, Elynda caught up to her and pulled at her arm. "Riana, where are we going?" Frustration laced her words.

"To the safest place I know for elementals," Riana said. After another half mile, she turned off the road and proceeded down an animal trail—or maybe just a Riana trail; she'd traveled this way so many times after school she had little memory of whether the trail had been there prior to her walking it.

"We're not seriously going into the TyrMinHai," Donny said.

"Yes. Why not?" Riana asked.

"Because it's full of elementals!"

"Exactly," Riana said and kept walking.

After they broke through the tree line, Riana began to see flits of blue light in the trees. She climbed over fallen trees and meandered through tree circles and over toadstools. Donny crashed through the forest behind her, grunting and pulling at foliage that clung to his clothes. Elynda hardly made a sound as she stepped in Riana's shadow.

The amatsu slept. Riana's arms burned from the effort of holding the creature.

"How far is this safe place? We've been walking forever," Donny complained.

More blue light flashed in the high tree limbs. Riana wondered if her companions had spotted the elementals. She stopped for a moment and listened. "Hear that?" she asked the other two.

"Hear what?" Donny asked.

"Listen," Elynda hissed at him.

Riana had heard the welcome trickle of water many yards ago, but she knew she would. No one knew these woods better than she did.

"Is that water?" Donny finally asked.

"Yes," Riana said. She moved forward, increasing her pace in anticipation of seeing her destination. The trees began to thin out. Riana slowed her pace as glimpses of sunlight glinted off water. One more tree line left and they'd arrive.

Blue lights darted in around them, down from the trees above, and halted their forward momentum. Her little queen friend hovered directly in front of Riana, her light fiery golden in contrast to the other nymphs' blue flames. Her wide, dark eyes were steely in a look of stern displeasure. The queen sang several notes that undulated and tripped through the air, punctuated with short hisses and clicks. Riana was sure she'd never seen her so upset. When the queen cast her eyes past Riana and to Donny, she understood why.

"It's okay," Riana said, stroking the fur of the amatsu who had roused at the sound of the fire nymph's voice.

The amatsu chirped its distress. Elynda tripped through the dirt and tree litter, protectively wrapping a hand over Riana's arm and the amatsu.

The queen paid it nor Elynda any mind.

"He is now a friend," Riana said. "He even helped me when that other boy attacked me."

Donny stood frozen as a group of fire nymphs drew close to him. He'd made the mistake of putting a hand on his knife.

"You idiot," Riana hissed at him. "Get your hand off your hilt."

Donny slowly loosened his grip, raising his hands into the air to show their emptiness.

Riana regarded her childhood bully, and her annoyance with him ebbed. He was genuinely afraid of the fire nymphs. And maybe that was okay. He'd spent far too many years doling out fear. Maybe a little turnabout was fair play.

Riana traded off the amatsu to Elynda, then moved swiftly toward Donny. She pulled the knife from its sheath and tossed it several yards away.

"Hey," Donny said, "that was my brother's."

"You'll get it back when we're done here," Riana said. Except several of the blue fire retinue, as Riana was coming to think of them, picked up the knife and flew off into the deep parts of the forest with it.

Donny watched, open-mouthed. "They just took—" he started to say, but then several of the blue nymphs flew close to him, brandishing black thorny swords igniting in orange and gold flame and chittering menacingly. The look of horror and fear fixed itself back onto Donny's face.

"Please," Riana said to the queen, "he really is a friend. He helped me and he helped this little guy." That was stretching it, but in the end he'd sworn his fealty to Riana and the creatures.

"I promise," Donny said shakily. "I won't harm any of you." His arms were back in the air, and Riana noted how they trembled. She wondered if she'd ever get over the sense of satisfaction at seeing him afraid, while at the very same moment feeling sorry for him. How could a person hold such disparate feelings in one heart?

The queen sang many staccato notes and fell silent. Riana opened herself up to what the little nymph meant. "I guess you have to take my word for it."

The queen regarded her as she hovered in the air, a tiny ball of flame and anger. Then she pointed at the amatsu and issued another question.

"Yes, we're trying to keep him safe."

The queen nodded, sang one small note, motioned Riana forward and turned. She still didn't seem totally convinced, but she appeared to have agreed to allow them to pass.

The blue fire retinue backed away from Donny. Donny shakily lowered his hands, looking at Riana with wide eyes. Elynda struggled with the wriggling amatsu, who chirped and nuzzled at Elynda in fear. The creature seemed to be picking up the anxiety of the situation.

Riana led the way, following the fire nymph queen. The air grew chillier, scented by a sudden blast of ocean salt. They passed through the last line of moss-covered trees and emerged at the grassy bank of a slough.

"Is this a river?" asked Donny.

"No, it's a slough," Riana said, really pleased with herself. "It's slow moving and shallow, which will be perfect for the amatsu until he gets a bit bigger and can swim downstream." And hopefully, stay far enough away from the fishermen.

Elynda plopped down on a clump of particularly green grass and put the amatsu in her lap. The water meandered past them while the amatsu leaned over Elynda's knees to peek into the water.

The fire nymphs peered out at them through the cover of the trees. The queen turned to Riana, nodded, gave one last mistrusting look at Donny, and flew off.

"You've got a lot to learn about how to act around elementals," Riana told Donny.

"Now that you're not killing them," Elynda said, not looking up from the water creature. The amatsu put a tentative webbed foot onto the bank of the slough, sniffing at the air. As soon as his paw touched the grass, a ripple of green went up his fur, inking over his default sea green pelt.

Donny and Riana gathered close to Elynda and the amatsu. "I don't know if this is going to work," Donny noted.

"Why?" Elynda asked, looking up at him.

"Amatsus are ocean creatures. I don't know if the slough will appeal to him."

The amatsu dove into the water, hardly disturbing the surface with his entrance. He swam under the water, stopped. Silt from the slough bed clouded the water, then the amatsu popped through the water's surface with a shrimp in its front paws. Little canines tore at the white flesh and thin shell while the amatsu paddled in place.

"He seems fine," Riana noted. The amatsu discarded the uneaten shell and legs of the shrimp and dove again through the water. Within moments, he returned with a small fish, which he gobbled, chirping occasionally around bites.

"I stand corrected," Donny said.

CHAPTER TWENTY-FIVE

Riana and Elynda explored the stretches of the TyrMinHai slough banks over the next several weeks. The amatsu thrived in the slough, eventually venturing further west and into deeper waters, but returning occasionally when Riana and Elynda came to check on him. He seemed to have built an on-land nest of sorts just off the bank where they'd originally introduced him to his new home. He wasn't always there, but occasionally they found him nestled in the grassy indent on the bank in the late afternoon, napping through the brightest part of the day.

Riana found need to take wine inventory often, and from there, enter the hidden room of outlawed elemental information. She'd even been able to spirit Elynda in there a time or two. But communications with Donny were kept to school lunch hours.

"What's the news with the Baron's Guard?" Riana asked. The big oak in the front schoolyard was budding yellow-green hints of leaves-to-be. Clouds chased sunshine in the blue sky overhead as the wind swelled and ebbed, like the waves of the sea.

Donny tore at the young sprigs of grass while he chewed at a hunk of bread and slab of ham. Riana bit into the cold-stored apple her grandmother had given her. Elynda watched the clouds overhead, chewing her own sandwich of nut butter and preserves.

Donny swallowed. "There's been sightings of a creature near the Sully farm."

"Sully?" Riana asked and looked around at the classmates littering the schoolyard. "Do they have any children our age?"

Donny scrunched up his face, holding up a finger as he finished chewing a bite. Once he swallowed he said, "Yes, but too young to be Tyrmini. She's just a toddler still."

Riana mulled this over. If suspicions were rising about elementals and Tyrmini, would the general populous get overly zealous and suspect the child as being Tyrmini?

"The Baron's Guard isn't even looking at the child as being dangerous. But Sully is still nervous, and he's asked for help getting rid of the elemental. He says it hides in the mud and is eating his chickens. He's not even sure what it looks like. All he sees is the mouth and a giant tongue shooting out to catch the chickens when they get too close."

"Seems like a pretty sweet set up," Riana said.

"Except for the chickens," Elynda said quietly.

"Probably not for much longer. Sully is setting a trap for it tonight."

"Well, stop him," Riana said.

"Riana, I can't just tell Sully to not protect his chickens. That's his livelihood," Donny said.

Riana backed down. She couldn't blame Sully really. Riana was more worried about Sully's child though.

"In the last month, he's lost a hundred chickens," Donny said.

"Oh, that's a lot," Elynda said. "Poor chickens."

Riana swallowed her bite of apple and nodded slowly, a plan coming into place. "Okay, well, we just have to find it a new place to live," she said.

Donny choked, pounded his chest with one meaty fist and swallowed. He took a swig from his canteen, wiped tears from his face, and looked at Riana. "How's that?"

"I don't know," Riana said, slumping back into the trunk of the oak tree, the apple in her hand falling to her lap.

"Maybe we just have to lure it out. Like with bait or something," Elynda said. "Then lead it to somewhere in the TyrMinHai.

Riana sat back up. "Good idea, Elynda. What should we use for bait?"

"Well, it seems to like chickens..." Donny said, shrugging.

"But how do we get enough chickens to bait it out?" Riana asked.

The trio looked at each other. "I only have a few for eggs," Elynda said.

"All we have are grapes and fruit," Riana noted.

"Gerty and Wil would be missed at our house," Donny said.

"Are those the names of your chickens?" Riana asked, dumbstruck. She didn't picture him as the sort who would name his chickens.

"Chicken and rooster," Donny said and took another bite out of his thick slice of brown bread and hunk of ham. He chewed and looked away, watching the other kids scattered around the schoolyard, eating or playing.

"So chickens are out," Riana said, disappointment slopping into her guts.

They all took simultaneous bites of their lunch and chewed in silence.

Donny looked down at his food as he chewed. "I wonder how it would feel about pork," he wondered aloud.

Riana and Elynda looked at him. "How many pigs do you think you could get off the farm?"

"Well, we'd have to use younger pigs to keep their size smaller, so two or three?" he said.

"Great," Riana said. "We'll meet you tonight at midnight near the Sully farm."

"Wait, wait," Donny started. "That's hardly a plan. What happens after we arrive at Sully's farm with the piglets? I'm pretty sure Sully won't take kindly to us trespassing onto this property."

"Well, then, we'll have to take care to not alert Mr. Sully to our presence." Riana stood up and brushed herself off, tossing her apple core over the fence hemming in the schoolyard.

"Right," Donny said. "Sure. Easy peasy. But then what?" He shoved the rest of his food into his mouth and packed away the material sack it'd come out of.

"We simply find the creature, lure it out with the piglets, and lead it into the TyrMinHai to a muddy place. I know just the one."

"Riana, as sweet as you are on creatures, you do realize they are dangerous," Donny said.

"I suppose for some that may be true," she said.

"But not for you?" he asked.

"Riana has a way with creatures. You saw her with the amatsu," Elynda said.

"If that's true, then Elynda, you have a way with creatures too," Donny said.

Elynda blushed. "Thank you," she said.

"I didn't mean it as a compliment," Donny bit back.

Elynda frowned and opened her mouth, but Mrs. Tomly appeared on the school porch and rang the bell to gather the students for their afternoon studies.

"Right," Riana said. "I'll see you all at midnight. This will be fun!"

Donny huffed and muttered something about the sanity of girls.

Donny, Elynda, and Riana all went their separate ways to their apprenticeships. When Riana arrived at the vineyard, she quickly disappeared into the cellar, checked to see if she was being watched, and then slipped into the Old Wine room. With the sparest of light, she hunkered down at the secret entrance and crawled her way through.

Once she was inside, she lit the collection of lanterns she'd secreted down and made a beeline for the books lining the wall shelves. Donny didn't know what sort of creature they would be dealing with tonight. Riana hoped she could find it in the *Catalogue of Creatures*. Or maybe the *Tyrinth Elementals* book. She pulled the catalogue off the shelf and situated herself into the ancient wooden chair.

The flame from the nearest lantern flickered. She looked up from the book in her lap. The fuel in the lantern was running low. As she swung her eyes back to her work, her gaze caught on the shelves her grandmother used to store the elixir. They were empty. Just weeks before there had been seven. Now there were none.

Riana wondered if that meant the Baron had drank it all at last and now would pass away. She also wondered what that would mean for her grandmother. Would the Baron dole out some retribution?

She reached for a lace sleeve and fussed with it while she worried, hoping her grandmother was okay. Eventually, she let her gaze fall from the empty shelves, the flickering lamp, and the rows of dried things captured in colored jars, and turned again to the book.

She flipped through the sketches and descriptions. She'd made it past Amatsu—water creature—Algolance—air creature—and Azurynth—fire creature—and moved on to the B section. She was about to close the book and retrieve the Tyrinth-specific tome when she landed on Berubula.

This toad-like creature was giant, slimy, and fascinating. It lured its prey by creating a purple bubble filled with a scent that was alluring to the specific animal or creature it hunted. So chickens maybe smelled grain and fire nymphs smelled Kaely's fruit, Riana guessed. When the prey got within range, the berubula captured it with a shot of its long, sticky tongue.

Furthermore, the berubula was a creature of water and Tyrinth, and had the ability to move swiftly through muddy terrain. It also set mud traps, drawing in water to its domicile to make the mud thick and deep. When prey wandered into its terrain, it got stuck and was held prisoner until the berubula was ready to feed.

The text further went on to describe how to locate a berubula bog, as they called it. The scent would be sweet and earthy and often resemble a person's favorite odor. The mud would be thick and difficult to navigate. It would have a nearby food source because it was a lazy creature that wanted to do as little work as possible to feed and maintain health. It was also highly territorial and had several defense mechanisms to keep other predators away. In that way, the berubula was a creature that would be good for farmers, as long as they had enough livestock to keep the berubula happy. Although for all the predators you might keep away, the berubula could eat their share of livestock and then some.

Berubulas had large appetites and the more they fed, the larger they got. The larger they got, the less likely the berubula would ever move.

Riana's heart sank. Would the berubula care about a few piglets enough to get it away from Sully's chickens?

Riana read on that if a berubula had been planted for more than three moons, its latch on the land was almost impossible to break. She wondered if it was lazy to begin with, would she be able to get it out of the mud and moving toward the TyrMinHai?

Riana looked at the picture depicting a berubula in its muddy home. The thought of feeding piglets to any creature made her stomach squirm. She might have affected confidence to Donny and Elynda, but she couldn't feel more nervous.

The way Riana saw it, though, even a muddy, chicken-eating toad deserved a chance to live in peace. She snapped the book closed and ran a hand through her messy, silver hair. She got up and looked through other books. Maybe there was more information on them in a different book. Riana wanted to make this relocation mission as easy as possible. Perhaps there were hints on what would lure the creature out more.

Tucking the catalogue back in its place, she pulled the book specific to Tyrinth-based elementals. Dust sifted off the tattered covers. She sneezed.

She wiped her nose with her handkerchief as she plopped back into the chair and leaned toward the lantern propped on the shelf. She flipped through the pages until she found the berubula, this time spelled barubula, in the middle section of Tyrinth-water elementals. There was a map at the beginning of each creature's section denoting the regions in which the creatures lived.

Riana looked at the map. "This doesn't make sense," she said to the book. The author clearly missed the northwest region of Aelos as berubula territory. She shrugged it off and moved to the next section, entitled "Habits and Habitats."

Riana skimmed the section, reading through similar information as the last book. Mostly carnivorous. Fed during the night when they could, but if their food source was more active during the day, they would feed then. Favorite foods varied from region to region, but included rats, ferrets, weasels, and most especially, mud crabs.

Riana sat straight in the chair. Maybe they wouldn't need the piglets after all. She jumped up, crossed the room, and shoved the book back between its fellows. After dousing the extra lamps, she took the last lamp and knelt onto the floor. She listened intently before climbing through. Once she was on the other side, she carefully replaced the door, marveling how it slid so smoothly into place that it looked like any other section of the wall.

She was making a mental list of the things she would need to capture the crabs, accounting for the time it would take and how fresh they would need to be to solicit the interest of the berubula. She passed through the aisles of darkened and forgotten wines and reached for the handle to the door when she recognized her grandmother's voice on the other side. She sounded annoyed. Riana almost pulled the door open when the other voice caught her attention. She paused with her hand on the handle.

"You're telling me..." the other voice drawled and dripped. Riana had never heard an accent like it before. "...that the golden elixir spoken of so softly is just a figment of imagination?"

"I'm afraid so," her grandmother said and tittered. "Our dessert wine is delicious, and it's certainly good for the soul, but it doesn't have any magical healing properties. I'm so sorry to disappoint you." This wasn't the first time her grandmother had someone come by with the outrageous claim of magical elixir. It had happened at least twice before, from Riana's recollection. Now she knew it wasn't just imaginative rumor at work. She wondered how the story had gotten out.

"Well, of course it's a tale," he started. "And if your wine is so good it inspires legend, I simply must taste it," the other voice said, then neither of them spoke. There was something about this other voice that made Riana's skin crawl.

The silence on the other side of the door caused a ripple to chase down Riana's arms and up her neck. Perhaps her grandmother was feeling the same way about this new visitor and potential customer. She held the door handle with an iron grip. The moment of silence passed and Sela Starliss responded.

"*Imaginations walk on vines,*
Feed on velvet, silken fruit.
While sunshine leaks through clouds and pine,
Fantasy warms to bud and bloom.
Fancies grow from bottled dreams
Of purple, red, and clearest gold.
Starliss wine inspires dreams,
Wishful hopes we can't help hold."

Grandmother Sela quoted the old poem while Riana mouthed the words. Of course, now she knew there was more to what the poet had written than she could have guessed before the last several weeks. "Starliss Vineyard has a reputation for inspiring fancy, sir. I assure you, it's nothing more than spun yarn after imbibing." The man seemed to listen, then pause to consider.

"I've a proposition for ya," the man said. "I'm coming back here tomorrow at the setting sun. And then you can give me samples of your best—and I mean your very best—wine. The kind that captures the muse of poets."

"We'd be happy to accommodate you for a tasting," her grandmother said.

"Aw, surely, darlin'. You surely will. And if you can't please my palette, you're surely not pleasin' the palette of the High King. So, y'all be sure to serve your best, ya listening?"

Riana's gut clenched as anxiety squeezed her. Her heart thrummed in triplets. The High King, she thought. Maybe the elixir isn't all they've heard about. What if they're here for me? What if someone's reported me?

"I. Am. Listening," Her grandmother confirmed. "Now, if you've finished here and you do not intend on purchasing wine tonight, I'll show you gentlemen to the door. It's this way," directed her grandmother.

Riana shivered at her grandmother's tone.

"Well, the hospitality runs short. Pray the wine doesn't."

"I assure you, the wine is spectacularly classier than anyone currently in the winery this evening."

Riana wanted to gasp at her grandmother's disrespect, but dared not make any noise.

"Very well, Mrs. Starliss. Have it your way. On the morrow, we'll be the judge of your *wine*."

Footsteps echoed off the stone. Riana strained to hear the sounds fading over the insistent throb of her own heartbeat in her ears. When she was certain the High King's emissary had gone, she carefully pulled the door free of the jamb, peeked around the corner to ensure it was empty, then hurried out.

She looked around for her grandmother, but she was gone as well. Tomorrow, the High King's emissary would return. Would it be for the elixir or for Riana? Panic swelled inside her. Either way, the outcome couldn't be good for the Starliss household, could it? Riana's mind churned out gory scenarios for both herself and her grandmother.

Your secrets are getting you in trouble, Grandmother, she thought, and then was filled with utter disgust that Riana was one of the secrets that could get her grandmother executed. She was harboring a Tyrmini, wasn't she? Or something, anyway, if not Tyrmini.

Riana stood in the cellar, surrounded by muffled quiet, dust, and rows upon rows of racked wine bottles and stacked barrels, all aging. The oil lamps hissed, casting a steady yellow glow to combat the innate darkness of the cavernous under-Tyrinth tomb for wines.

The wine was far from dead, though. In the stillness, the seeming sleep, the yeast was hard at work producing alcohol from the sugars in the juices. What once was a light-eating fruit had been cultivated, coaxed, maybe even cajoled into a liquid that was imprisoned in the darkness of a bottle, and the darkness of this cellar. And there it still grew, still was on its journey of transformation.

Riana couldn't help feeling a correlation as she kept her silence about what she was. If she was hiding in the dark, there was still a transformation underway, she felt. Something hidden inside the imprisonment of darkness. If the product was disturbed too early, it wouldn't be strong enough.

Riana wasn't strong enough. And she hoped if her grandmother was in danger, she would grow strong enough, quickly enough, to keep her as safe as she'd kept Riana.

CHAPTER TWENTY-SIX

"Goodnight, Grandmother," Riana said.

Her grandmother was toiling over documents at their kitchen table in a pool of lantern light. She held her pince-nez to her sea-blue eyes and squinted in the poor light before looking up, silver eyebrows pinched in concentration.

"Oh, yes, yes," she said. "Yes, goodnight, my dear." Her face softened as Riana hugged her. "I love you," she said.

"I love you too, Grandmother," Riana said, worrying about her grandmother and the man who'd visited her today, praying her grandmother really could keep the secret a little while longer.

Riana tiptoed down the hall with her finger lamp and into her room, trying to push away the guilt building in her gut for what she was about to do.

She laid down in bed and waited. True to her habits, Sela Starliss's footsteps sounded off. The floorboards groaned. Riana listened with eyes closed as her bedroom door creaked open. She waited, the soft light of her grandmother's lamp casting an orange glow through her eyelids. Her grandmother's breath whistled three times while she surveyed Riana's supposedly sleeping form. Riana feigned deep, slow breaths; all the while antsy for her grandmother to move on.

At last Sela pulled her granddaughter's bedroom door closed with a rasp. Riana waited for the floor to signal Grandmother had made it to her room. She held her breath for a moment, listening as her grandmother shifted around her room, changing into her nightgown, pulling pins from her hair, turning down the covers.

Riana wiggled under the usually comforting covers, which had turned constraining in her moments of impatient waiting. The springs to her grandmother's bed creaked. Riana waited, hoping this night would be one of swift sleep for her grandmother. After what felt like an eternity, soft wheezing snores echoed through the walls.

Riana threw back the covers. She'd gone to bed in her clothes, a pair of pants and a long tunic. If she pulled her hair into a cap, she'd probably look like a boy. She ruined the effect with her cloak, which was gray and stitched with flowers. It was the warmest outer clothing she owned. After pulling soft riding boots up over her pant legs, she tiptoed to the door. She shook her hands in the air to dispel her nerves before she reached for the knob. With excruciating slowness, she twisted, wincing at the click of the latch.

She paused, listening. There was a long, quiet moment. Riana held the knob, heart pounding. Then her grandmother snored, and Riana exhaled. She pulled at the door. It rasped, as it usually did, but her grandmother went on snoring.

Every step down the hall was an experiment in fear. If she were caught here, the chances of getting back to bed and back under the covers were nil. When she made it to the front door, she hardly believed her luck. She checked the clock hanging above the mantel; it was ten. She had two hours to catch crabs before meeting Donny and Elynda. She prayed she'd be able to find the crabs easily as she closed the door behind her and headed out into the moonlit night.

First stop—the muddy banks of the slough in the TyrMinHai.

CHAPTER TWENTY-SEVEN

Riana had never been so muddy in all her life. She stood spattered and drenched, her boots and arms thickly coated. Riana could see a figure walking down the road under the waxing moon. The form was accompanied by the soft squeak of piglets. When she turned the other direction, another form approached. Elynda and Donny were both on time.

"I hope you appreciate this. These piglets were meant for fall's slaughter. Dad's gonna lose it," Donny said.

"Riana, are you sure about this? Did you find anything out about the berubula and where it needs to go?" Elynda closed the gap before she caught sight of Riana. "What happened to you?"

"We may not need the piglets after all," Riana said. "You're welcome," she added, turning to Donny and smirking with muddy arms crossed over her muddy cloak.

Riana stepped aside to reveal a basket full of mud crabs. She was proud of her haul. It turned out mud crabs were most active in the night. While it was a messy business of slogging through the boggish banks of the slough, catching the critters was easy as pie. She simply plucked them up as she'd waded through the mud and stuffed them in the basket.

"Ooooo..." Elynda said, shuffling back from the basket of crabs.

"You've been busy tonight," Donny noted.

"Yes, I have been. And we've got a lot more work to do. Let's go," Riana said.

Donny led the piglets back to the pen on his property, which was on the way to the Sully farm. Riana and Elynda each carried one side of the crab basket. It wasn't very heavy, but it was awkward and banged into their legs. Riana was sure she'd have bruises under her wonderfully comfortable leathers by morning.

When they finally reached the Sully farm, they were sweaty and sore. The basket made a lot of noise, so they entered a field of Sully's by climbing a fence and wading through the grass. Cows were standing and sleeping under the moonlit sky. Riana thanked her lucky stars it wasn't raining.

They trudged closer and closer to the homestead. When they squished in sudden mud, Riana called out to Donny and Elynda. "Stop here," she said. "It should be somewhere close now."

Donny brought up their rear and peered over the two girls, and crabs, to the blue-lined horizon ahead. Disrupting the even flow of the landscape was the barn and Sully residence. The chicken coops could be made out at this proximity. The chicken yard was fenced in, but Riana could see how the berubula would be able to get to as many chickens as it liked through the slats in the fences.

Riana scouted around the bog, looking for the perimeter, and searching for the boggiest center and the home for the berubula. When she found the squishiest parts, she noted there seemed to be a small collection of reeds growing close together, as if on an island. She returned to Donny and Elynda, carefully skirting the thick mud pool.

"Okay, let's take the crabs over that direction. I think if we just set one free onto the mud, the berubula may be enticed out. Donny, have you got the rope?"

"Yes," he affirmed and touched the rope at his side.

"Okay, hopefully it doesn't come to that. I can't imagine the creature will want to be dragged to the TyrMinHai forest."

"I hope it doesn't fight us," Elynda squeaked.

"It'll be fine," Riana said, beaming at Elynda, even though inside she felt the very same way.

"I do not think this is going to work," Donny said.

"Well, thanks for your positive attitude." Riana rolled her eyes, snatched the basket of crabs, and proceeded to the far side of the bog.

"You're welcome," Donny said.

Riana looked over her shoulder and glared at him, although she was sure the glare was cut short by the night's darkness. As she turned back, she noticed the reeds in the center of the bog vibrated, as if blown by an unseen wind. Water in front of the reeds boiled lazily, bubbles breaking the surface and popping. The crabs in the basket shook the cage with erratic movement. They crawled up the side of the basket, they pushed clawed arms out of the wooden slats, they snapped at Riana's cloak.

Riana stopped inches from the edge of the muddy shore of Boggy Pond, as she was coming to think of it. She set the cage on the ground next to her, watching the crabs crawl over each other, fighting to get to the top of the basket or to the side of the basket. Out. They seemed to want out. And Riana was just wondering how they knew they needed to escape when she was struck by the most delicious odor of baking bread.

Elynda sidled up to her. "Riana, do you smell that?"

Riana inhaled deeply, relishing the odor of yeast and hot wheat. She could almost smell butter melting on a piping hot slice of thick brown bread. "I love the smell of bread," she confirmed. Riana looked down at the crabs. They were fighting to get out and into the pond.

"No," Elynda said, "it's not bread, it's chocolate cookies."

"No," Donny said, right next to them. Riana jumped. She wasn't sure when he'd gotten so close. "That's fried pies. Mmm...Holy Maker, those are my favorite! I didn't know Mrs. Sully made them."

Riana looked at the two of them. Then back to the house across Boggy Pond. Then at Boggy Pond and those vibrating reeds. The crabs and the reeds seemed to want to meet, Riana thought.

Donny pushed his way past Riana and stepped squarely into the marshy mess of soil and water. The mud in the center of the pond boiled, the reeds rising higher as the mud slopped away off a dome-like shape. A pair of shiny neon green eyes broke the surface, just barely visible as glinting reflections in the moon's light. Its eyelids were ridges of muddy brown. The giant creature opened its mouth, neon green tongue lighting up the void.

"No!" Riana launched herself at Donny, jumping awkwardly over the ratcheting basket of crabs. Donny turned just in time to catch Riana's diving jump. With his arms wrapped around her, Riana and Donny went down in a heap of tangled cloaks and boots.

Neon green lit up the space near them as the tongue shot out, extending over the muddy pond. Riana ducked her head into Donny's chest, her face flat against him as she watched the berubula hunt. She had a mere moment to fear the berubula was hunting them when the tongue whizzed past her boots and latched onto the crab cage.

Elynda screamed, stumbled, and fell to the ground in her attempt to distance herself from the hunting green tongue. She crab-crawled backward as the berubula yanked its head back to reel in its dinner. But those were the only crabs Riana had.

"Stop," she shouted, her hand reaching out toward the basket. White light shot away from her, enveloping the basket in a net of ethereal threads. The berubula's eyes widened as its meal stayed in place, along with its tongue. "Do you know how long it took me to get all those crabs? No. You're not going to eat them all right here. It's moving day, buddy."

Riana tried pushing herself off Donny and failed. She looked down at him in frustration to find his face serious and flushed as he stared back at her.

"Help?" she asked.

Donny's eyebrows squeezed down over his hazel eyes, his mouth snapping closed. He put his big, meaty hands around Riana's waist and lifted her up. His hands were warm against Riana's stomach and rib cage. She was shocked at the gentleness with which he handled her. Not like the many times he'd used those hands to torment her. The juxtaposition of those memories to his current care sent a wave of confusion over Riana. She pushed the feelings aside as she achieved an angle that made standing easier.

She scrambled to her feet, praying she could hold the power to keep the berubula from eating the bait. At least until she got it moved. With white light cascading off her arm, she reached for the basket.

"Riana, no. What if it takes you with it?" Elynda warned.

"It's alright. I think I can hold it. And I've got it just where I want it."

Riana lifted the basket and walked away from the pond a few feet. The tongue extended. The berubula sat wide-mouthed and wide-eyed in its muddy home. It yanked its head to pull the cage back, and Riana too, but Riana held firm. She looked down at her boots and noticed the white light had slithered down her legs from her hips and had rooted itself into the ground. Feeling more confident, she walked a few feet more, the sticky green appendage stretching thinner. The berubula grunted, air loosed from its wide nostrils, but it shifted forward. Muddy brown legs pulled out of the muck and made a halting step toward Riana.

"Yes," Riana said. "Come on, guys, we're going to lead it back like this."

Donny stood from the muck and made his way over to Riana. She shied away from his proximity. He looked at the white light that swirled and wrapped around the cage in a net of encasing energy. Riana wondered what he was thinking, what he would do. She couldn't tell if he was afraid or angry or maybe disgusted.

"It's really beautiful," he said, his eyes seeming to light up.

Elynda sidled up next to her. "It is," she said.

The berubula barked out a croak. The three jumped.

"Alright, let's get moving so this thing doesn't wake the Sully's."

Riana guessed the muddy pond where she'd harvested the crabs was two miles from the Sully stead. She prayed to the Maker this would work. She took several steps away from the pond and was rewarded by the slurping movements of the truculent berubula as it made its way out of its home.

Riana, Elynda, and Donny moved through the Sully field, passing sleeping cows snoring under the shifting moonlight. Riana walked through the tall, fragrant grasses, the crab cage held firmly in her hand and in the essence of light roping around the cage and supporting her every step. The berubula balked, yanking at the cage and the light that had trapped him. His neon green eyes glared in frustrated annoyance at Riana.

The berubula stopped. Riana pulled, sending enough energy down the creature's tongue to illuminate its cavernous mouth. The creature belched out its dismay and took a halting step forward. The berubula stopped for a moment, and Riana thought she would have to tug the creature again to get it moving.

She wrapped a hand around the coil of energy cascading out of her hands. The creature's hind legs tensed. A sweeping alarm of fear rang through her body. Her heart hammered into overtime.

"Oh, sh—" she started.

The berubula launched itself toward them. Its mouth was wide. Saliva spilled over the jawbone through a row of teeth ridges. The neon tongue shortened with its ever-approaching trajectory. Its slimy, brown skin glinted under the moon and starlight, but most of its bodily features were lost to shadow.

Elynda screamed. Donny shouted. Riana fell to her knees and crouched behind the flimsy wooden cage of scrambling mud crabs. Riana glumly realized how ridiculous it was to get eaten by the creature whose life she was trying to save. Giggling mania swept through her, jangling her nerves and lighting the white cords of energy with rings of gold light.

Riana waited, the second before impact stretching out to an eternity in which she contemplated the purpose of life, or lack thereof. She considered what it would feel like to give her life over to an elemental creature. She wondered if it would hurt. If the berubula would kill her first before it swallowed her, or if her death would be a slow thing of acidy digestion.

She decided creatures really were dangerous, although still undeserving of the hatred spoon-fed to every man, woman, and child for centuries. It really wasn't their fault. The berubula was just working out its own survival. She really couldn't blame it.

Although...

She really didn't want to die just yet.

Feeling ambivalent, she crouched and waited. A heavy thud reverberated through the ground beneath her, rattling her body so her bones threatened to fall apart. When enough time had elapsed, she realized she'd closed her eyes and was not consumed. Something wet splattered against the hand that held the crab cage. Her eyelids fluttered open.

Hot, moist breath washed over her. She stared through the cage at an undulating surface of whitish green, speckled in brown spots. Her eyes roamed slowly up from the belly of the berubula to its folds of neck, to its partially open mouth.

A strand of saliva dribbled onto her hand.

CHAPTER TWENTY-EIGHT

A neon green tongue roped out of the berubula's mouth, still attached to the crab cage, still wrapped in threads of living light. One green-rimmed eye slowly closed, sinking into its head. Riana could see the bulge of the eye descend past the upper surface of the berubula's mouth. The eye lifted again, eyelid opening, eyeball rolling back in place. The other stayed trained on Riana.

Riana stared up at the creature, unwilling to move or even to breathe. Riana surveyed the waiting mouth of the berubula, lined in rows of comb-like teeth. She gulped. Two glands on either side of the berubula's tongue swelled, growing larger and larger, expanding out to form perfect spheres of what looked like water. Riana stared, fascinated as the elemental drew on its first element.

"Riana," Donny warned. "You need to run."

But she couldn't. She was rooted in place, transfixed by horror and fascination at the power and magic of this creature of myth. She wondered what it planned on doing with the water, or whatever substance it was, that welled in its mouth. The liquid filled its orifice, defying gravity as it created a wall along the edges of its mouth, which had stretched all the wider.

Then as she still stared, the minutest shift in the berubula's posture signaled its next move. Riana threw up an arm as the head of the berubula crashed toward her and the cage of crabs.

"Riana!" Elynda screamed.

Power flew out of Riana. She could feel its searing touch, like stars born through her skin. The berubula grunted, the cage yanked out of her hand, pulling violently against her grasp. She had a moment of panicked concern for the creature, but the power was indiscriminate in its need to protect her. She feared the worst as she looked up, ready to see a bloody mess of elemental.

Regret filled her as she cast her gaze up. The berubula's green tongue whipped back into its mouth. The crab cage rolled away. The berubula shuffled back, away from the blinding white that had burst into the space between them. Riana marveled at the magic she observed. It was not just a blast of light. The power that had exploded from her was fashioned in the shape of a white dragon. Riana held out her hand, tendrils of white and rainbow energy connecting herself to the dragon.

She had a sense of homecoming, a realization of self, a yearling understanding of the energy cast in front of her. As if fueled by this realization, the dragon before her expanded out, uncoiling its tail and wings. The wings shielded her from the berubula.

The creature went wide-eyed, then slowly bent its head, shying away from the power between them. At last the creature's head touched the dirt, closed its eyes, and belched its obeisance.

"I am not your enemy," Riana said, and her voice was no longer just her own. There was another presence within that spoke through her, using her voice like a megaphone. A part of her was perfectly comfortable with this other entity. Another was screaming about the insanity of the situation. "I am not your meal," she continued. "I am not your master. I am your mother."

The berubula croaked in regret.

"I am here as your protector. I have revived you and your kind. Respect me as the source of energy that gives you life and heed my counsel," Riana and the voice of the dragon continued. As Riana spoke the words, the mouth of the dragon moved along with her. Following some demand made by the presence within her, Riana stood. She raised both hands and blew light onto the berubula's head. The energy funneled into the creature's head. It blinked rapidly, breath wheezing; brown, glistening body trembling.

When the last bits of energy soaked into the creature, it raised its head to Riana. Riana instinctually knew there was no more need for the manifested dragon. She lowered her hands, calling back the energy. It flew into the air, its white and rainbow light glittering against the night sky. It arced high above them, circled backward, pulling in its wings, and dove into Riana's head.

For a moment, Riana's arms were splayed wide, muscles gone rigid with sudden fullness. As her body absorbed the light back into itself, a last whisper shivered through her.

I am Magloryn.

Something deep inside her felt alive in a way Riana had never experienced. As if a missing piece of her slid into place. She could almost feel its weight in the center of her body and somehow knew now that she had been reunited with it, it could never be taken from her.

Riana stamped her feet into the ground and watched silvery threads of energy skitter away in the grass and dirt, jumping over itself before descending into the Tyrinth. She flicked her arms away from her and dissipated more of the lingering power. In front of her the berubula stared at her, waiting.

Elynda ran toward her, grasping her arm, then pulling her into an embrace. "Are you okay?"

Donny approached more slowly, his head shaking to match his pace. "This just gets weirder and weirder."

Riana looked at him over Elynda's shoulder and wondered how much weird Donny could take before he broke down and betrayed her.

CHAPTER TWENTY-NINE

In all the seven hells he'd circled, he'd never seen such a power.

Captain Luther ducked behind a large tree, hiding from the blinding light of the girl's erupting power.

"Holy Maker, whose names sit salty on the lips of the High King," he said, his voice a whisper.

He'd been following her since he caught a glimpse of her near that damnable vineyard. When she ducked into the woods, he'd followed. When she'd captured the crabs, he'd watched by the light of the waxing moon. When she'd met up with her friends, he'd spied on them, following far behind so as not to alert them to his presence.

And stunned by their dumb, blind luck, he watched as they'd snagged a berubula and tugged him right out of his habitat. What a berubula was doing this far north, he didn't understand. Most berubula had been hunted to extinction, and the ones that were left were in the deep swamps of *his* homeland. Down where the weather was hot, the mud was thick, and the critters were dangerous—especially the elemental ones.

When he heard why they were dislodging the creature out of the mud, he nearly fell over. They weren't hunting the creature, as he'd thought at first. They were *saving* it! And they were succeeding. At least up until this point.

He watched as the girl—it had to be that girl the boy had claimed had broken his arms with some blinding light—shifted slightly away from the giant water and Tyrinth elemental. The berubula made the most minute movement, then smashed his head toward the girl. Luther was just thanking his lucky stars the berubula was going to take care of the girl so he wouldn't have to, and then that mysterious light had burst out of her.

No, such a thing he'd never witnessed. And he'd witnessed it all. At least that's what he'd thought. But now here was some purely un-elemental power being wielded by a girl who never showed up in the dragon's eye.

The very dragon who he knew to be locked in a dungeon as deep as humans could dig beneath the High King's castle. Maimed, forgotten, tortured, starved, and nearly powerless. Nearly. Which is exactly what the High King wanted. He wanted the creature just surviving so it could power the eye which he used to find and destroy Tyrmini.

Or employ them.

Maybe the girl wasn't a Tyrmini, but an apparition arose out of the girl and protected her from being dinner for a berubula. That apparition was none other than the captured dragon.

He watched in awe as the dragon-shaped light spread its wings wide and guarded the strange girl with the silver hair. Silver hair that was uncannily like the sorry feathered hide of the dragon prisoner.

It looked like he'd have to involve himself after all. The girl was saying something to the creature, but he was too far off to hear. He waited for the little group to carry on with their mission and followed. He wanted to involve as few people as possible. Best to let this carry out, let the other kiddies go home, and then he'd meet the strange girl with the power of...what sort of power was it, he wondered. No combination of the elements made light, did it?

He scratched his head as the dragon form rose into the air then plunged back into the girl. Maybe that's all it was. Maybe it was just light. He shrugged and pushed himself away from the tree.

It didn't matter so much. Soon the mysterious power would be dead, along with the girl.

CHAPTER THIRTY

"I'm okay," she said to Elynda.

"Riana, what was that?"

"I'm not sure," she said, but inside the name of the dragon wouldn't quit whispering through her. *I am Magloryn. Magloryn. I am Magloryn.*

"Looks like it showed the berubula some manners," Donny said.

The berubula nudged the wooden cage of crabs, which had rolled toward it. The berubula looked up at Riana, as if asking for permission. It was Elynda who responded first.

"Aw, he's hungry, Riana. Can we give him a snack now?" she asked.

"Sure," Riana said. "I guess he's earned it. For not eating me and all."

Donny chortled. "Good creature for not eating somebody," he said.

Elynda retrieved the cage under the watchful gaze of the berubula. Riana helped her open it, then retrieved one of the crabs.

"Sorry, fella," Riana said to the crab, then tossed the crustacean toward the berubula. The sticky neon green tongue shot out of the creature's mouth, stuck violently to the crab, and then reeled back into the berubula's mouth. It munched on the crab. Its eyelids melted half closed. The reed-like antennae on its back quivered in delight.

"Donny, why don't you give it one," Riana said.

"No way," Donny said.

"Come on. I think it will help."

"Help what?" Donny asked incredulously.

"Help build a relationship so it doesn't try to eat you behind my back," Riana retorted, growing irritated.

Donny glared at her.

"I liked it better when I was bullying you instead of the other way around," he said.

Riana's anger flared. "Turnabout is fair. You've got years of this coming to make up for the torture you put me through. And I'm just trying to help you. But if you'd rather take your chances, that's fine with me. Let it eat you. I don't care." Riana crossed her arms and glared back at Donny.

He mumbled something about leaving her at the edge of the road that day but crossed the short space between them and reached in for a crab. He was too slow, and one snapped his outstretched finger.

"Ow!" he complained.

Riana giggled.

"Are you okay?" Elynda asked half-heartedly.

Donny looked at her flatly, glanced at Riana, shook the hair out of his face, and glowered. "I'm fine."

He reached in again and snatched a crab more quickly. In one swift movement, he tossed the crab toward the berubula, who zeroed in and caught it with a giant flick of its monstrous tongue. It purred in contentment, a low rumble from the back of its throat vibrating through the ground beneath them.

"Elynda, you're next."

Elynda applied a deft hand to capture one of the crabs and flung it neatly into the air. Riana was always surprised at Elynda's strength, which contrasted so absolutely with her demure demeanor.

Once the creature had eaten two crabs from each of them, Riana turned to it and spoke.

"Now, it's time to settle into your new home. Follow me."

The berubula's antennae wriggled, hushing and clacking against themselves.

"Great," Riana said. "Hopefully that means consent."

She picked up the basket with the remaining crabs and headed into the growing line of trees of the TyrMinHai. The berubula followed by waiting for the space between them to widen, then launching itself forward on its powerful back legs. Elynda and Donny were careful to stay in step with Riana. Every time the creature bounded forward, Elynda let out a little squeak of terror.

Once they arrived at the muddy section of the slough, further east from the portion where the amatsu had made its home, the berubula settled into the mud with what Riana thought was a sigh of relief. She tossed it the rest of the crabs, which it made quick work of before burying itself into the water and Tyrinth of the TyrMinHai.

Riana watched the creature settle in, feeling comforted by the success of the evening, yet, overwhelmed by the revelations and subsequent questions. She swayed on the spot. It had been a busy night during her normal sleeping hours. She watched as bubbles rippled through the mud, the berubula's antennae swaying gently until they hushed to a stop. Donny stood beside her, glancing her way every now and then.

"Thanks for your help," she said.

He shrugged.

Elynda sidled up next to her and pulled Riana's hand into hers. They stood observing the mud under the light of the waxing moon.

"I'm glad you were with me tonight," Riana said.

"We've got a lot to talk about," Elynda said.

"We do?"

"Yes, of course," Elynda said. She peered into Riana's eyes with her own emerald stare. "Like what this power is you have and why it manifests as a dragon."

"Yes, there is that," Riana understated.

I am Magloryn. Magloryn. I am Magloryn. The name that meant to embed itself into Riana's memories circled and swirled through her.

But who was Magloryn?

CHAPTER THIRTY-ONE

The kiddies had traveled back through the trees and onto the road before they finally said farewell to each other. Luther waited patiently, not particularly pleased with what he'd have to do next.

The girl with the silver hair departed from the other two and headed, not back to her home, but toward the vineyard.

"Well, isn't this handy?" he said to the moon.

The moon didn't answer back.

He followed the girl, quiet as a shadow.

She was silent as she moved with purpose down the night road. When she reached the vineyard, she jogged past the main entrance and sidled past the sloping, soil-covered eastern exterior. She was just about to pull the door open, when he allowed himself to make his first noise.

The scuff of his boots in the dirt was enough to capture the girl's attention, as he'd meant it to.

She started and wheeled around, her mud-caked cloak flapping tiredly. Her eyes were wide, her skin and wild hair illuminated like a lamp against the dark night. As Luther approached, Riana took several steps back.

"I don't believe I've had the pleasure of meeting you, ma'am," he said and tipped his tricorne hat.

"I don't think this would classify as a pleasure. What business do you have at the vineyard at this time of night?" Riana said.

Luther thought the girl was as full of fake confidence as her grandmother had been. "One may ask you the very same question, my unique friend."

"I am no friend of yours," she noted.

"Very well," he said, raising his hands in a placating gesture of surrender. "I saw you along the road and approached to offer my escort to your home."

"Is that so?" Riana said and crossed her arms.

Luther pulled at his stubbled chin as if in thought. A breeze lifted the air between them and filled his nose with the scent of the sea. Somewhere in the distance, a night bird sang out. There wasn't another human soul around. He didn't relish what he had to do. Not a lot anyway. Especially since the girl had to be the same age as his own princess. His princess who was as locked up as that almost-dead dragon. And for her, he would do anything. So he relished what he would do next for the opportunity to report his good behavior to the High King, and hopefully gain his favor enough to let his sweet girl sign on as a soldier, rather than be put to death.

"No," Luther said. "You're right. You've caught me." He chuckled, the low rumble seemed to unnerve the girl—which Luther thought was just fine. He had wielded fear long enough that the weapon had become comfortable. He wondered what had become of the man who had fathered such a sweet girl, and quickly pushed the thought away. Soft, kind men hung in the gallows when they were outed as Tyrmini.

Luther shuffled closer to the girl as he fingered the knife at his belt. He wouldn't belabor this execution. There was no need for it. He could get some information from the girl before he killed her, though. "Well, now," he said, considering. "It's true I did see you on the road."

"But?" the girl asked. She seemed to be growing brighter by the second.

Luther wondered if she'd give him trouble. "But I don't mean to see you safely home. Not unless that's a euphemism for—something else."

Real horror passed through the girl's eyes, and Luther could swear they shifted from steel gray to green to violet but couldn't say for sure in the near darkness. He was glad she was finally recognizing the levity of her situation, and he hoped to use it.

He pulled the knife from its scabbard and noted the gorgeous way it melded into the night, into his skin, nearly disappearing save for the wicked way it winked in the moon's light.

"What is it you want from me?" she asked, and the captain of the High King's retinue of Tyrmini guards stopped dead in his tracks as violet light winked like lightning just around the girl's body.

"It is a real shame I have to execute you. I have never seen a creature quite like you. And I've seen them all, Sugar."

She turned and ran, silver hair whipping away from her as she headed into the rows of vines. Luther sighed. Now he'd have to drag the body back so Grammy-dearest could find the corpse.

He strolled past the winery and headed toward the vines. He watched her run for a moment, then bent to his beloved knife.

"Won't you sing for me, my sweet?" he whispered to the blade. It hummed in response as he connected to the element of Tyrinth within it. He gauged the girl's distance, pulled the knife back over his shoulder, and launched the weapon toward her.

The girl ducked into a nearby row of vines, as if sensing the oncoming blade.

"Oh, but sweetheart, that simply won't do you any good." He walked as he sent out direction for his blade, guiding it with his connection. His old friend. He heard a thump in the vicinity of the girl and knew his blade had once again been true. It was all too easy.

He turned around the edge of the row of vines and found his target lying in the dirt, heaving around the blade lodged in her back. He took his time getting to her. When he at last stood over the girl, she looked up at him and coughed blood onto her pale skin.

"Now, darlin', you probably could be saved. Maybe. If perchance you knew the whereabouts of your grandmother's special secret wine. You know the one? The one that isn't supposed to exist?" The girl struggled to breathe, wheezing. She coughed, spitting up more blood. "See. You hear the way you're breathin'? You feel that pain in your shoulder and chest? That's because that gentle organ is collapsing in on itself. I'll just bet a little golden elixir and you'll be fit as a fiddle."

"It's not real," she said.

"Oh? And I suppose you're not a Tyrmini either, are you?"

"What are you talking about?"

"Don't cast me as the fool. You think I just showed up here with no more than a rumor?" He was shouting now. He paused to gain control of himself. "Remember a boy named Treyor?"

The girl's eyes shifted again. This time he was sure he'd seen it. Violet to blue to black.

"Yes, I see you do," he said, ignoring the odd twitching of her eye color. "What a delightful monster. He had tales to tell. Tales of a girl who consorted with elementals and who'd broken him with an awesome display of unknown power. And then the tale went on that the grandmother of the girl had given him a bottle of golden elixir."

Luther pulled the empty bottle from the innermost pocket of his black and gold coat and held it down in front of the girl's eyes. She coughed again, as if she'd been fighting back her lung's protests. He wiggled the bottle to and fro to emphasize the very real existence of the empty bottle.

"That's an empty bottle," she pointed out. "That proves nothing."

"Aha!" he said. "Except I got to see the best proof of all. I smashed that young boy until he died. And then I forced this swill down his throat. Wouldn't you know, the angry little shit came back to life? Dead for a solid five seconds. Then gulp! And there he blinked and talked and spat vinegar at me for stealing what was rightfully his."

The girl wiped at her blood-soaked chin and sneered with red teeth. "Then I have you to thank for his attack on me."

"I think you have other things to concern yourself with, dear heart. Like that knife in your back." He gave the blade a gentle nudge with his connection to it. The blade pulled free and launched into his waiting hand. The girl screamed. Somewhere in the distance, a gentle, buzzing hum grew and shrank. He looked down the tunnel of vines. He thought he'd seen something. Something white and large...but he dismissed it as a trick of the moonlight.

He got down on his knees and got close to the girl. Close enough he could whisper and she would hear him. "But that's not all. I took that elixir back to the High King, and he had a sample. And just like that," Luther snapped his fingers together in front of the girl's nose, "the High King was ten years younger. Strapping, exuberant, healthy, whole. But nobody mentioned as soon as one partakes of the golden elixir, one is suddenly and inextricably addicted to consuming it."

Luther had been grateful he hadn't tested it on himself.

The girl gritted her teeth, eyes squeezed shut. Her body trembled. She opened her eyes and spoke with what looked like a lot of effort. "What's wrong with the High King that he needs an elixir to fix that the best physicians cannot?" the girl asked.

"Our blessed High King suffers with a lack of heirs to inherit the throne. A problem he hopes to remedy with the elixir."

"Oooohhh," Riana said, coughed, then continued. "How embarrassing."

"Never mind," Luther said, knowing there was more to the story than he was willing to speak aloud. "Take me to the elixir and you'll be healed. Or don't and die." He reached deep into himself and drew on the fire that always stayed just below the surface. He blew onto the blade and watched it ignite in blue flames. He was a true student of Mylah, the greatest Tyrinth and fire Tyrmini that ever was. Mylah—Tyrmini and traitor.

"You're Tyrmini," the girl said, and her breath rattled in torn lungs.

"Indeed I am. I am Tyrmini, Captain of the High King's personal Tyrmini retinue." The flames caressed the black blade. The fire licked against his fingers and danced away like a shy lover stealing a kiss. He held the blade out to a nearby vine. The flame leapt toward the vegetation, eager for a meal.

"No," the girl cried.

Luther pulled the blade away from the vines. "You'll show me?"

CHAPTER THIRTY-TWO

Riana ground her teeth. Sweat glistened on her forehead. Fire bloomed on the right side of her body, in her chest, shoulder, and back. She had to think, and think fast. Think through the pain. Think through the blood leaking out of her back and into her lungs. If she did this right, maybe she could keep her grandmother from this man's torment.

But what could she do? She had no elixir, and the man was clearly powerful enough that he had secured his position as the High King's personal bodyguard. No, he was the leader of the High King's retinue of Tyrmini bodyguards. Riana was sure that had not come without practiced skill with his elements. She'd manifested her power thrice and still had no clue what she was doing.

I am Magloryn. Magloryn. I am Magloryn.

The piece inside her that had snicked into place swelled within, giving her solidity, providing peace even in the face of awful pain.

She watched the blue flame sizzle against her blood still coating the black blade. The man regarded her with what Riana read as detached determination. To him, it seemed, Riana was not a person; Riana was a steppingstone to a goal. And the goal was not Riana. The goal was the golden elixir. Riana didn't think there was any left, but this man didn't know that. And he didn't know where it was kept.

"Yes," she said at last and coughed against the seizing of her lung as she exhaled to produce the one word. It was the third time in her life she wondered if she would die.

A grin widened across Captain Luther's face. The blue flame danced in the reflection of his eyes. He snuffed the fire, put the blade in its holster on his belt, and bent over her. Riana cringed at his closeness. He scooped her up by the left side, draping her arm around his neck and muscled shoulders. He smelled of some sort of burnt plant. Like trees had been lit ablaze and he'd walked among them as they burned. Riana recoiled from the odor, thinking of death, wondering how many people the man had tortured with his tie to the elements.

Riana yelped as the pull against her injured body sent a new wave of pain through her. She hacked, tasting more blood, her head swimming. She labored to pull enough air into the injured lung and drive away the circling darkness. Once her body adjusted to standing, she motioned them toward the TyrMinHai.

Haltingly, they trudged up the aisle of vines. The world was all blues and greys and blacks. Dots of stars in the sky overhead cast small illumination next to the moon's half reflection on the Tyrinth below. Riana allowed the man to drag her along. He didn't seem burdened by her weight nor the awkward stance in which he held to support her. Riana noted how solid his body was, like a mountain.

"If you're leading me into the forest in hopes of fooling me, Sugar, you'll wish I'd just have killed you. Speak now if it ain't or I'll take 'til dawn to finish you."

Riana shuddered against the man, but stuck with her plan, knowing if she didn't pull this off right, she'd suffer torture and death at the hands of the man who currently kept her standing. "Oh, no," Riana said, wheezing and fighting back another rattling cough, struggling to keep the pain from overwhelming her. "The elixir is out here."

Darkness swallowed them entirely as the trees eclipsed the light of the stars and moon. Riana had seen signs of the antoli. The man had missed it, too busy torturing her. But could she really put the creature's life in danger? She shuffled on, deeper into the forest, her chances of escape and survival slimming the further she went.

"I can't see a Light-Forsaken thing," Captain Luther growled. At that, he propped Riana against a tree and rooted around in the underbrush.

While he searched, Riana steeled herself for what she must do next. Bark bit into her soft palms, but the presence of the tree was reassuring, as if it were lending her strength. She coughed, tasting more blood, struggling to maintain an even flow of air against the pulling, stabbing pains in her chest. She trembled with fatigue and blood loss. Somewhere deeper within her dwelled the power she needed. So far, she'd only used it with an involuntary call for protection. Now she must learn how to call the power with her conscious mind. And she had to learn fast.

In the darkness of the TyrMinHai, she dove deep within herself. She imagined diving into a lake or the ocean. As she swam through the murky waters of herself, she passed several underwater caves. The one she was looking for appeared ahead of her mind's eye, illuminated in white light, shimmering with every color imaginable and some she couldn't fathom. Once she was in the cave, she swam forward toward an altar. Propped on the altar was a single white feather with a silver quill.

In her mind's eye, her hand closed around the talisman. The individual barbs of the feather brushed her hand, sending tingles racing up her arm, down her spine, and lighting her crown with light that she could somehow feel. The light poured into her, filling her up. She let it coalesce into her cupped right hand and shivered as the power crackled through her.

In the physical reality, branches snapped, Luther grunted, and at last the forest was bathed in a red glow of fire. The flames contrasted utterly with the white light Riana held firmly in her hand. Luther rose from his crouched position on the ground and turned toward Riana. Riana took as deep of a breath as she could manage and hurled the ball of light at her captor.

Every muscle in her protested at the movement. Her ball of light sailed through the dingy, red glow of fire toward Captain Luther. His eyes widened, mouth gaped, as he tracked Riana's weapon.

Luther cringed, eyes squeezing shut against the impact of the ball of light. It splattered against the Captain's brass buttons and black jacket in a shower of sparkling colors. Luther waited, eyes still closed, then blinked rapidly to clear his vision. He looked at Riana, stunned.

The world swam around her, her eyes closing of their own accord as her body gave out. As she hit the forest floor, the Captain barked out a laugh. Footsteps crinkled in the pine needles and dead leaves. The last thing Riana was aware of was his voice in her ear.

"And here I was worried you'd be somethin' fearsome."

CHAPTER THIRTY-THREE

Sela Starliss hadn't seen her granddaughter since Riana had gone to bed the night before. She rushed out of the house and headed to the winery in the dark before dawn while fear gripped her in a stranglehold. She prayed to all the powers that controlled the elements that the girl had wandered there in the night.

"Ha!" she yelled at the gentle mare, who twitched her ears back, but sensing Sela's fear, spurred forward in a jolting trot. The carriage rattled her bones, which were sore and hot after her restless sleep. She chided herself for not waking and checking on her charge, sure that's why she'd slept so soundlessly. With that vile High King's emissary visiting her later today, Sela could only guess at what trouble may have found Riana.

The old woman's heart squeezed in her chest, pumping a sudden burst of blood into her veins. Her pulse wah-wah-wahed in her ears, competing with the clop of the horse hooves and grumbling roll of the cartwheels on rock. She pulled onto the road leading to the winery through the rows of grapes. Tears slipped from her eyes and slid into the temples of silver hair.

Chilled, sea-kissed wind rushed at her face as she made haste toward the vineyard. The sun lightened the sky in the barest hint, turning the eastern horizon to deep green. No one would be at the winery yet. Except, she prayed, for Riana. When she pulled the horse and cart to the hitching post, her heart fell into her stomach.

It was not Riana who waited for her.

She ambled out of the cart as quickly as her stiff joints would allow. He grinned at her as she approached.

"It's nothin' personal toward you, darlin'," said Luther. "Or the girl. I should hope you'd understand when royalty pushes us to do things we don't want to do. They have a specific means to twist our scruples, goad our shadowy selves, and force our hands to the application of abhorrent actions."

Sela Starliss couldn't speak. Her tongue was locked to the top of her mouth and her jaws were resolutely cemented in place.

Captain Luther continued. "Yes, indeed, there is less sleep and more haunting of my soul, as of late, my dear, sweet Mrs. Starliss. But it's too far gone to worry about that dirty old soul of mine. Yours, however..." He trailed off as he pulled something from under the golden cravat in his black jacket.

Sela's heart sank to see it was the empty, tear-shaped bottle of elixir. The cold morning bit at her exposed cheeks and neck. Fog slowly gathered and rolled in

"I should have known the boy would squeak. I should have let him die."

"Indeed, you foolish woman," said the man. "Now, hand over every drop of this elixir. When you do, I'll point the way to your granddaughter. She just might still be alive."

Sela's knees buckled and before she could stop her body, it folded to the ground. "Might?" she asked, her voice barely above a whisper. Her stomach squeezed in on itself; her heart stuttering dangerously fast. She inhaled slowly, trying to supply air to her brain so she could wisely handle the situation. And maybe save her granddaughter.

"Aw, now, hun. I hate to see a woman cry," said Captain Luther.

Sela wasn't aware she'd been crying. She swiped at her face and pulled back her hand to observe the glistening tears gathered on her fingers.

"Truth be told though, she wasn't in great shape when I left her. I think we better move along if you want a chance at getting to her in time."

"It's all gone," Sela stuttered through the tears. She watched Luther's eyes darken, his mouth forming a sneer. Before he could speak, or something else, Sela quickly added, "But, there may be something else."

"The elixir is all that I want. What do you mean it's gone?"

"The Baron. He's consumed too much too quickly. But, there's the tree. And there might be some fruit left."

"Show me."

CHAPTER THIRTY-FOUR

Warm, moist air blew across Riana's face. She tried to ignore it, because waking to the new sensation woke her to immense pain. The breeze blew again, followed by a wetness smearing against her cheek. She lifted her hand to swat it away, but her hand fell limply to her side.

She squeezed her eyes tightly shut and inhaled. Her lungs protested and she coughed, tasting the metallic tang of blood. Her body absorbed the feel of the ground beneath her, the twigs digging into her back, as if in mockery of the knife wound there. She tentatively explored her surroundings with her fingertips and found the soft caress of moss. Her head rested at an awkward angle against a log.

An undulating purr vibrated first through the ground and then into Riana. It roused her enough to open her eyes. Staring up from the ground, Riana's view of the sky was blocked by the massive, eyeless head of the white, shaggy creature known as antoli. Above the antoli's head, the sky was lightening from dark to light blue.

Her heart beat with heavy thuds inside her chest, as if it really had to work hard to maintain any rhythm. Riana's head pounded along with it. She wanted to slip back into the sweet bliss of sleep. She closed her eyes again, meaning to let the darkness embrace her. The antoli nudged her with its enormous wet nose, growling deeply.

Riana dragged her eyelids up with a dragon's effort. The antoli looked down at her and grunted twice. It tossed its head back, the long strands of its hair shaking away from its snout and the place eyes should be.

"I—" Riana tried to say 'I'm dying and won't you please leave me alone,' but burbling hacks of bloody coughing cut her short. She hoped it would make the point.

The antoli growled again and stomped its front feet against the ground, sending a shock wave of vibration through Riana. Riana's heart responded with a jolt. She gasped against the sudden energy flooding her system. And with the energy came the realization.

Captain Luther was nowhere to be seen. He probably thought she was dead. Riana was surprised she wasn't. But if the captain wasn't near Riana and he was looking for the golden elixir, there was only one other place he would be.

As fear took over where only a desire to let go had been, Riana let the wave of panic fuel her enough to attempt to rise. It was no use. She was sure the swimmy feeling in her head and utter exhaustion was due to blood loss. And the fact that she couldn't pull in a proper breath. She was worthless like this. And even if she made it to her grandmother in time, what would she do? Throw another glitter ball at him?

The thought of that wicked, black knife and the way the flames eagerly danced toward the vineyard's grapevines made her push all those thoughts aside. She had to try.

I need help, she thought. No sooner had the thought crossed her mind then the antoli lowered its body next to hers, laying its head gently over her outstretched arm. Its rumbling purr tickled her side. Riana wondered if the antoli was comforting her in the last moments before she died.

When Riana didn't move, the antoli growled. The sound rumbled through her, deeper and more intense than the gentle tickle of its purr. Riana looked at the creature next to her. It raised its eyeless gaze toward her, snuffed and lowered its head again. Then it scooted its body into Riana and finally she understood.

It meant for her to ride it.

CHAPTER THIRTY-FIVE

When Sela reached the far north quadrant of the vineyard after thirty minutes of walking, she cut west. She led the captain down a dirt trail that ran east to west between the tree line and the vineyard. It was only she who knew the location of the tree that grew Kaely's fruit. Sela had hoped to share the information with Riana before she died, but she imagined that wouldn't happen now. Once the captain found out there was no fruit left, Sela was sure he would kill her. But if she did this right, perhaps the elementals would take care of the captain.

Maybe they wouldn't show up to rescue her. Why would they? She wasn't like Kaely or Riana. She was just a cranky old woman who had the pleasure of knowing truly extraordinary people with amazing and beautiful power. She counted herself lucky to have known Kaely and to witness her magic in action, healing people, nurturing elementals, growing the most beautiful plants and flowers and trees. She reminisced about their childhood as she cleared the last grapevines.

This had been their playground. They ran the alleys of the vineyard and ruled in the heart of the TyrMinHai. That was where Kaely had experimented most with her power. That was where she had produced food for dying elementals. It was her garden that had grown cures for people in Landsend, and it was there where she'd plucked the fire nymph's fruit to heal Sela's father. Sela's memories washed over her, coating her in shame, in sorrow, in mourning. She missed her friend and always wondered what life would have been like if Tyrmini were not outlawed.

Her heart throbbed. Riana was the only hope of changing that. She was the only chance the Tyrinth had to right the imbalance of power caused by the High King.

Captain Luther followed as the sun rose behind them on the eastern horizon, a knife-edge ray of light cutting above the line of budding vines.

"How long has my granddaughter been hurt? How long ago did you leave her to die?" Sela asked.

"Oh, well," Luther started, "I'd say it's been two hours. Maybe more."

Sela slowed her forward movement long enough to sneer at the man. Luther's expression was flat. "What are her injuries?" she asked.

"Her injuries are severe. Like yours will be if you're leading me on a merry chase instead of taking me to the fruit."

"You've doled out enough threats for one morning," Sela said. "I'm taking you to the tree. I wouldn't risk my granddaughter's life." Sela kept walking. After another several minutes, she took a turn into the TyrMinHai past a hulking evergreen.

There was no path here. No marker, except the tree which Sela knew so well she thought of it as an old friend. Once under the cover of trees, the path disappeared and Sela ambled more carefully over the bramble and undergrowth. The trees muffled the sound of the Dreavynan and dampened the light of morning. The air here was rich with the odor of pine, close and still.

Sela picked over fallen branches, crunching across forsaken needles and stepping around pine cones which had more than once twisted a much younger ankle. She had the fleeting thought that if she twisted an ankle now, she'd probably break a hip. Getting old was strange. Frailty didn't suit her. She straightened her shoulders and moved on, using a boulder for support to step over a rotting log. Its splinter-filled interior was revealed through a hole that was encrusted in vivid green moss.

Behind her, Luther barely made a sound. She checked over her shoulder to make sure he was still there. He wasn't even looking at his feet and caught her gaze with a hungry stare that set Sela's nerves dancing. What did those wide-open eyes anticipate? She twitched her gaze back in front of her, but it was no use. She could still feel his stare on her, burning a hole into her heart.

"We're almost there," she said, her voice scraping through the quiet air.

"Very good," he said. Hunger laced his voice, but also fatigue. Sela thought it had the same air of weariness she felt. She glanced over her shoulder once more. Luther was looking out through the trees, his face suddenly alert.

She glanced in the direction he stared but saw nothing. She moved on, taking a turn west at the sound of the slough. The trees opened up in this area, giving Sela more confidence in her steps. She passed through the grove of madrone at a quick pace and came to a halt only when she reached the wild hedge.

It was twice her height and stretched half a mile in either direction. The trees, who seemed to part to make way for the wandering wall, bowed in the direction of what lay beyond the hedge. Sela walked another hundred paces before she stopped and faced the monstrous shrubbery. Here in this portion of the hedge the leaves grew in a circular pattern. It was evident to her, but she was sure no outsider would pay it a second glance. Not that there were outsiders here. Most folks were wise enough to believe the myths and steer clear of the TyrMinHai. And so, the tree had stayed safe all these long years.

Sela situated herself directly in the center of the hedge and reached an arthritis-smitten hand toward its dark leaves. She passed her palm over the heart of the hedge and waited.

"What're 'ya doin'," the captain asked, running his words together while he peered over Sela's shoulder.

Sela knew he couldn't know about the real key to the hedge. She made sure of it.

"I'm opening it," she said mildly.

The leaves vibrated, first slowly, then shook wildly. Folding limbs creaked out from behind their cloaking leaves. Sela stepped back and watched as the foliage twisted, pulling in on itself and revealing the secret wonder that lie beyond.

Sela walked through the arched doorway, and despite everything in her screaming to keep him out, she allowed the henchman to the High King into Kaely's garden.

Directly in front of them, a lush carpet of thick, green grass cut a path through beds of plants that overflowed their boundaries and snuck onto the cool green blades. Flowers the color of fresh blood bloomed in a vast array of ferns. Their long necks sloped into green stalks. Sela led Luther past the plants, noting a fat bumble bee descend to the lip of the flower. She glanced back at the High King's right-hand man while tingles of foreboding paced up and down her spine.

The captain's face was a rapt mask of utter astonishment as he too watched the unexpecting bumble bee tremble on the lip of the flower. The scarlet petals vibrated, then squeezed closed on themselves, twisting over the bumblebee and turning a shockingly vibrant violet. When the frantic buzzing of the bee stopped, the flower slowly bloomed again, shifting back to its gruesome crimson once more.

A second hedge within the first wall curved away. This hedge was lined by beds of rich soil from which a variety of plant life sprouted. The air was thick with moisture and elemental power. Sela's head felt full of air, light and yet heavy with an insistent energy at the same time. Kaely had told her the sensation would be more pronounced for a Tyrmini. This was the moment she'd been waiting for. She swiveled her head over her shoulder. Captain Luther grunted, then yowled, stumbling into a copse of vine-ridden bushes boasting fresh blooms. He pressed fingertips into his brow bone as he fell to the soft grass.

"You've tricked me, woman!"

Sela stared at him as he rocked himself through the pain.

"Don't be a baby. Just wait a bit and the pain will ease."

"Ya coulda warned me," he complained.

"You could have not left my granddaughter for dead," she shouted at him, hoping her raised voice would inflict more pain.

She let him sit there rocking and pressing his hands into his face until slowly he became accustomed to the intensity of the elemental power concentrated in Kaely's garden. At last he looked up at her, his eyes a red-rimmed mess of over-spilling tears.

Breathing heavily, he pushed himself to standing. "Any other little surprises I can expect?"

"No," she lied. "Now, if you're finished, we'll continue."

She turned and continued walking, not waiting for his response. After a few moments, his footsteps dragged behind her, followed by grunts of exertion. Sela smiled to herself. Kaely had been so clever. Right up until the end. And the best was yet to come.

They meandered through the hedges and overrun flower beds of exotic trees, plants, flowers, vines, fruits, and vegetables. The vivid array of colors, shapes, and textures smeared together as the time spun away. Flashes of Riana popped and faded in rapid succession in Sela's mind. She moved with purpose, forcing the captain's breathing to heave like a blacksmith's bellows. Once he even tripped over a sneaky tree root.

Sela did not assist him back to standing.

When they'd wound their way into tighter and tighter corridors, Sela picked through the vegetation with greater care. At last, she led the way through a space no larger than her body that hooked back then sharply forward. She squeezed through the foliage, careful to pick her feet up and place them over the roots and vines on the garden floor.

Captain Luther cursed with such a dreadful accent Sela couldn't make out his precise words.

The branches and leaves squeezed down on them, forcing them to prostration. They crouched low, pushing aside the exploring fingers of vegetation. Sela forced herself to slow down; breaking an ankle on an upturned root would not help her get to Riana faster. Just before her knees tired of the awkward posture, she pushed through the last arching festoon of waxy leaves and emerged into the heart of the TyrMinHai.

The grass was lush and emerald, as it always was. Berry bushes, apple and peach trees spotted the open space. Sela remembered when Kaely had grown them, as snacks for when they'd come here. The fruit trees were healthy and beautiful, but they paled in comparison to the giant occupying the center of the circular space.

The tree's smooth bark was dark, almost black, as though it had been charred. The tree's trunk twisted slightly before branching out to a wide canopy of golden leaves. They shimmered in a breeze, catching and reflecting light in a cascading pattern that danced across the lawn.

Sela turned to her captor and presented Kaely's Tree. She clasped her hands in front of her waist and watched the captain as he cast his gaze far into the branches and leaves.

Luther's breath hitched as his head tilted up to take in the height of the giant. It was as big as ten of them. Luther's voice rolled through the glade like red wine and dirty gravel. "What lovely colors she wears. Yes, indeed."

Sela took a second to look at the tree and realized the man and the tree both boasted black and gold.

"Why indeed, indeed," the man's inflection on his repetition drew the word out like spreading butter over a warm biscuit, as long as the butter was slightly spoiled. "Where's the fruit?"

Sela didn't speak for two spent breaths. "The tree is dying, Captain. As I'm sure you can see. There may be some fruit left on its branches, here in the autumn of its life."

The captain moved in front of Sela so quickly and silently that she lurched away from him in the sudden shock of his proximity. There was an electric stillness hanging in the air as Sela stared into his dark eyes in defiant silence.

"Show me," he said, pronouncing the two words slowly, as if he spoke to an imbecile.

Sela gestured to the tree. "There in the far branches. You'll excuse an old woman; I'm not the tree-climber I used to be."

The High King's right-hand man stared at her hard and long. Sela took several breaths but refused to bat an eye or swallow the building saliva in the back of her throat. His gaze finally broke. He stepped back and surveyed the woman in front of him.

"It's quite a deed to live so long as to have such fine silver hair as yours. White as your granddaughter's. What's her story?"

Sela finally swallowed and hated herself for it. Against her will, her nose wrinkled, her disgust for the man whom she knew slaughtered children on a frequent basis rose within her. "She's an orphan. Dropped on the docks in a crate that used to hold wine bottles. My daughter found her. When my daughter died, I took Riana in and raised her."

Captain Luther, right-hand man to the High King, the person in power to execute all Tyrmini on Aelos, raised his eyebrows. "Is that all?" he asked.

"That is all I know," Sela asserted. And she was proud of herself. Proud of her ability to lie so quickly, so smoothly, and with so much relish. If lying was truly a sin of the Maker, she hoped she'd rot in the throne of Widdawah for all her lying, if it meant that Riana's life was protected.

The captain smiled slowly. First one corner of his mouth rose and then another, until his lips disappeared and his teeth shone. "Well, I'm sure it is," he said at last. "I'm sure, I'm sure that's all you know, you lovely mistress of grapes and wine." He pressed in closer to her. His breath hot in Sela's face.

At last he backed away and sidled past her to the section of tree whose branches Sela had referenced. His footsteps were nearly inaudible as he moved over the soft green grass to the tree branches.

Sela knew what he would find there and hoped the High King enjoyed rotten fruit. There was next to zero shelf life for the fruit.

Captain Luther stood under the branches, boasting several golden globes of fruit. He glanced over his shoulder where Sela stood staring at him. He grinned at her and then launched himself into the air. The ground where he'd been was raised, rich soil breaking through the vivid covering of grass. Luther grabbed a branch and, using momentum, swung himself onto it. The tree creaked in protest but didn't break. Standing, he pulled his jacket straight and reached for the fruit.

The tree vibrated as Luther pulled the first fruit free. Luther steadied himself, glancing quickly around him. "What's it doing?"

"The tree is a living thing, sir. It does not like its fruit pulled. We only ever collect what has fallen. You're hurting it." Sela felt tears prick her eyes.

Luther grunted, then continued pulling the fruit. The tree groaned as its body was torn. Sela looked away.

When the tree's crying ceased, Sela looked up and found the captain on the ground again, tucking the fruits into a handkerchief and gently sliding them into an interior pocket.

"Now, tell me where my granddaughter is," Sela said.

"When will the tree bear again?" Luther asked.

"I do not know. It's never been bare."

"How long will this last?" he asked, touching a hand reverently over his breast where the fruit was nestled safely there.

Sela chewed her thoughts. The fruit would last months if fire was applied to it. Even longer when she applied her wine-making skills. It had always been a tricky process. She refused to remove the fruit until it fell from the tree, and then she had to harvest, juice, and barrel it within days.

Kaely's fruit wasn't like grapes. It had to be handled with delicacy and precise measurement. The oak had to be just so old. The batches had to be just the right size. There could be no additions of other fruits. The juicing process could not be too bruising to the flesh, or the yeast that grew on it would be destroyed and the wine wouldn't ferment. It was a science; one Sela had mastered only after years of trial and error. But now all of that was useless with the tree dying.

Sela weighed out whether a lie was needed. "As fruit, it will spoil within days," she said.

The captain looked at her incredulously. "You knew and you drug me all the way, down deep into this King-forsaken magical rabbit hole?" he roared.

"Please calm down. The application of fire should preserve the fruit for months; enough time for you to make it back to the High King." And out of my life, Sela thought. Enough time for her to spirit Riana away. Enough time, perhaps, to unite her with Myla—if she could find the Tyrmini woman who'd delivered Riana to her that fateful evening sixteen summers ago.

"Fire?" Luther asked, a new grin sliding onto his face. "Well, it just so happens I have some of that." He pulled a fruit from his pocket and held it in front of Sela. While he held eye contact with her, he pulled the knife he'd brandished earlier from its scabbard. He waved it in front of Sela's face, causing her to flinch away.

Sela watched as flames appeared and bathed the dark blade in blue fire. Holding the fruit in one hand, he carved it with the flaming dagger. It did the trick. The juices sizzled and ran. The flame seemed eager and quickly enveloped the whole fruit and the man's hands. Sela backed away, the heat rolling toward her in an insistent wave.

"The fire is hungry," Luther said. "Did you know fire Tyrmini are the most feared? Doesn't matter the combination, though we are mostly fire and Tyrinth or fire and air. If there's fire, there's fear." Luther carved the first fruit and let the slices drop into the cool grass where the fruit smoked before the flames were smothered.

"I can only imagine," Sela said.

"Yet, you don't seem so shocked. Not too shocked at all. This little garden here makes me think you've known a Tyrmini or two in your long years."

"I watched my best friend's murder when I was sixteen. I'm not shocked to see men like you in power doling out punishment to innocent young people. Like Riana."

His eyes widened. Sela couldn't believe it. She'd spoken the unspeakable, almost admitting Riana's difference.

"I knew it. I knew there was more to her and you had that knowledge locked away behind those sea blue eyes." He advanced on her, knife gripped in his hands.

Sela backed away but ran out of room as she bumped against the trunk of Kaely's Tree.

"I hold you in contempt of the High King for fostering a Tyrmini," he said. He raised the blade.

CHAPTER THIRTY-SIX

"Don't you dare touch my grandmother," Riana screamed and immediately suffered a wracking coughing spell.

The captain whirled, eyes gone so wide the knife glinted in their reflection. Fear flashed over his face, and then, as his eyes swept over her, his fear turned to a sneer. Riana knew just how bad she must look. But there was that thrumming call echoing up from some deep part of her she had yet to access correctly.

Magloryn. I am Magloryn. Magloryn. I am Magloryn.

Like a chant, the rhythm of the repeating name moved her as surely as a tide moves a fallen tree down the river. Her ears rang against the crescendo of the name as she slipped off her mount, the antoli. The creature lent its body as a crutch while Riana maintained an arm over its sturdy back. Her head swam as stars blossomed in front of her eyes. She fought back nausea and when her near-syncope passed, she allowed her eyes to focus on the man who threatened her grandmother.

"I'll be slayed by the Maker," Captain Luther cursed. "Stabbed by a blessed elemental blade, but here she comes, here she comes just the same. And on an elemental creature while she's at it."

"Here I am," Riana confirmed. "Why don't you settle this business—it's with me and not my grandmother."

"I don't relish it, darlin'," he said, and moved toward Riana, one slight step.

The antoli growled and dipped its head, giant pink nose waggling back and forth in the direction of Luther.

"I'd rather you live, just as I do. And I'd let ya. I'd bring ya back to the Keep and let you test your mettle, earn the privilege of life. The thing is: I don't know if you've got any real power at all or if you're just a magnet to elementals."

As if in answer, a soft buzz warmed the garden. Riana smiled as a horde of fire nymphs flooded between her and the captain. They hissed at the High King's right-hand man. The queen was center to the swarm. Her voice rang out in the morning light.

Hurt our mother tree, Riana interpreted. *Hurt our sister.* And here the queen pointed at Riana. Riana was immediately covered in gooseflesh and a tear pricked her eye. She had been claimed by the nymphs. *Hurt our grandmother, you die. Leave—we let you live.*

The queen brandished a curved black sword. Compared to her body, the weapon was long but thin, like a thorn. The throng of nymphs growled, hissed, and cried, and all their vocalizations built a cacophony in the den of their great tree.

"They say you've hurt their tree and me. If you hurt my grandmother, they'll kill you. If you leave now, they'll let you live," Riana translated the queen's words to Luther.

"They—speak?" he asked.

"Yes," Riana said, although that wasn't entirely true. Their song held intention. They really had no words. Riana's translation was rough and didn't carry the same intensity of emotion. Riana wasn't sure how you could mistake the nymph queen's threat.

"Does that thing speak?" Luther asked, his eyes trained on the antoli.

Riana turned toward the creature. The creature's head swiveled toward Riana. It waggled its nose then sneezed, its head shaking with the effort.

"Perhaps you better worry less about which elementals can speak and which elementals are going to end your life."

Luther chuckled, then said, "I'm not scared."

There was a silent moment, then the queen banged the hilt of her sword against her charcoal black breastplate. She sang a series of notes, and when her song ended, she burst into flames. Her army of nymphs banged their own chests, sang one simultaneous note in reply, and then they too ignited. Riana blinked and stumbled back from the wall of heat and flame that danced in the air before her.

Beyond the roar of flame, Luther laughed.

When he was done, he spoke: "Oh, my dear, my dears. There is nothing so safe to me as the flame. Dare you threaten a most powerful fire-Tyrinth Tyrmini with fire?" He laughed some more.

Riana hung her head. Of course. Fire nymphs could do nothing against a Tyrmini such as him. Her guts squeezed in on themselves. She tried to breathe, but the attempt was so frail she pitched sideways and slipped from the grip of the antoli to the hard ground. The antoli growled and bent to the Tyrinth to lay at Riana's side.

What can I do? she thought. She peered through the curtain of fire nymphs, all awash in yellow, orange, and blue flame. The queen's fire was so electric blue it was almost white. The queen yipped, a quick note of utter conviction, and then the army of nymphs surged toward Luther.

"No!" Riana screamed, hoping they would hear her, listen to her, see her. But they charged forward anyway. Luther's first arcing swing of his knife caught three nymphs through the belly. Black blood spattered against their comrades. Luther was swarmed by nymphs. Their fiery swings found purchase, then were extinguished in a small stream of smoke.

He backed slowly away from them, every step bringing him closer to Kaely's Tree.

Grandmother Sela lurched toward Riana, arcing her way around the cloud of fiery nymphs that surrounded the High King's Captain of the Tyrmini Guard. "Riana." She fell to the ground next to Riana. She cast a hasty glance over her shoulder at the battle happening between the fire nymphs and the Captain. "I'm so sorry," she said. "I'm so sorry I haven't told you everything before now. And now there's no time."

"Grandmother, please," Riana started.

Her grandmother shook her head, tears streaming from her sea blue eyes. She reached into the front of her dress and pulled on a necklace. It broke free. She shoved it into Riana's hands. "You must go back to the winery. You must keep reading. I've written everything I know, and it's stored there. Please. Please don't ignore who you are any longer, Riana."

"Grandmother, stop. What are you saying? Stop. Just stop. We'll get through this."

Sela opened her mouth to say something else when an enormous creaking wail erupted through the grove. Sela turned. Riana looked past her grandmother. The fire nymphs screamed as Kaely's Tree caught fire. The antoli howled.

Luther stood bathed in flames. The fire nymphs were gathered around the tree, trying desperately to extinguish the fire that ate at their mother tree. Riana made eye contact with the captain. He made one small movement, and then he was standing over her grandmother. He grabbed her silver hair and yanked her head savagely back. Without pause, he wrapped his other arm around her shoulder. Riana inhaled, a scream building. Luther pulled the blade through Sela's neck.

Riana watched as her grandmother gurgled. Blood erupted from the wound. Riana screamed as she was sprayed with her grandmother's lifeblood. Her grandmother's eyes found hers. They were knowing and full of regret. Blood poured down her soft blue dress, which soaked it up eagerly. She choked, gagged, and then slumped forward, falling next to Riana in the grass.

Riana's stomach turned to steel and fire as horror shot through her, escaping in a violent scream.

"I am sorry, my dear, but your grandmother's been keeping secrets from the High King. And he just won't tolerate such a thing."

Riana could feel a deep dam beginning to break. The rising luminescence of her magic washed away the detail of her surroundings. Captain Luther shifted toward Riana.

"You killed her," Riana said through a wrenching sob. She wasn't aware of the movements she took, but found herself standing.

Captain Luther backed up a step. Riana barely registered it. There was a chorus in her head that accompanied the steady rhythm of her heartbeat in her ears.

I am Magloryn. Magloryn. I am Magloryn.

And now a second verse had joined the first and chased it around.

You killed her. You killed my grandmother. You killed her.

Captain Luther's eyes grew wide as Riana stepped toward him. He backed away once more. There was a gust of air near her legs that sent her hair swirling. The captain stepped back, but his legs bumped against the antoli. The creature growled, barked, and bit at the captain's arm. To put space between himself and the creature, he stumbled toward Riana.

Riana's intention rose within her, aching to be loosed.

I am Magloryn. Magloryn. I am Magloryn.

You killed her. You killed my grandmother. You killed her.

On went the song, circling around inside her as the war drum beat the interior of her chest.

"You don't wanna be a killer, dear heart," Luther said. "Trust me. You can't ever return once you've gone there."

Riana barely heard him speaking.

"Now, listen. I'll let you come with me. Bottle up that power ya got boiling, and I'll let you live. You can trial your powers with the other Tyrmini. You could make your way to the top of the ranks in service to the High King."

This, Riana heard. "In service to the High King? Do you mean to murder my grandmother in the name of the High King yet grant me mine in the next breath?"

"Darlin', I don't make his rules, I just abide by them." He made a swift hand movement and then was grasping the blade. It still glimmered with her grandmother's blood.

"I'll make my own rules," she said. Her arms rose. Light burst out of her palms. The light was fashioned as spears. They flew toward the captain, and in less time than it took to blink, he was skewered. He looked down, took in the pulsing blue and white length of pure energy jutting from his body, and gasped. He touched the spot where the energy had stabbed him in the chest and pulled away bloody fingers.

Riana exhaled and let the link with the energy dissipate. The spears of light evaporated, but the damage remained. Captain Luther tottered, then fell to the ground. He coughed up blood onto the lush grass of the glade. Behind him the fire nymphs' mother tree was ablaze, sending a solid black column of smoke into the bright morning sky.

Riana watched the captain as he struggled to breathe, reaching into his coat. Riana knelt, knocked his hand away, and confiscated the object in his pocket. She unfolded the handkerchief and found it full of Kaely's fruit. "I don't think so, Captain."

"Please," he wheezed. "I have a daughter."

"And I had a grandmother," Riana said, her resolve solidifying her center to lead. She held no compassion for the man in front of her, but somewhere in the back of her mind, she knew she'd regret this moment. She re-wrapped the fruit and tossed it into the flames of the mother tree, as if in offering to what had been done to it. The man broke into a convulsion of wracking sobs, spewing blood. After a moment, he stilled. His gaze was on the sky, but Riana was sure he didn't see it. She reached over and closed his eyelids.

"May the Maker forgive you," Riana intoned, although she felt no forgiveness herself. Not with the body of her grandmother lying in the grass so close to his.

The fire was blazing. The fire nymphs had circled the tree. Any encroaching flames were snuffed out while they watched their mother tree die a horrific death, with nothing they could do to stop it.

Riana turned to her grandmother's body. She put a hand on hers, surprised at the warmth still there. Tears streamed down her face and she sobbed loudly, the muscles in her stomach turning so hard she thought she'd vomit. She kept looking at her grandmother, expecting her eyes to flutter open. For her to tell Riana she was okay after all. When that didn't happen, Riana threw herself onto her grandmother, pressing her cheek against hers and covering her face in hot tears. Riana thought the world could end and she would be all the happier. To live without her grandmother was no way to live at all.

The antoli walked to her side. Its warm body brushed against her leg as it sank down next to her. Riana wasn't sure how long she stayed like that, weeping loudly, the fire crackling nearby, two corpses, an air elemental and a throng of fire elementals as company. When she felt her grandmother's skin grow cold, she pushed herself up.

She looked around her. The tree still crackled and smoked; Luther's body no longer distinguishable in the heightened flames. The antoli still lay at her side. The fire nymphs still held the tree's vigil.

Riana turned back to her grandmother, horror-struck all over again that she was really gone. Something glittered in the flash of fire still raging. Riana bent over and picked the long, silver necklace her grandmother had given her. She'd dropped it in the chaos.

It was a miniature bottle and tucked inside was the tiniest replica of the fire nymph's tree. Riana stared at it in wonder. She looked at her grandmother.

"Grandmother, you had so many secrets. What's this new one?"

She turned the talisman over and over in her hand, and then decided. She pulled the necklace over her head and clasped it closed. Then she tucked the miniature bottled tree into her dress. Her tears streamed fresh, but she knew she couldn't stay in the spot forever.

Riana touched the antoli's side. "I have one more favor to ask of you, my friend."

The antoli nodded. Riana situated her grandmother's body onto the elemental, clasped the antoli's hair, and waited for the squeezing sensation to wrap around her.

CHAPTER THIRTY-SEVEN

For days afterward, time passed in a blur. The first three days she spent at Healer's Hall under Elynda and Mrs. Heilbee's care. After that, she was allowed to go home with Elynda and Mrs. Heilbee, who agreed to care for her wounds there.

Some days and nights Riana spent at Elynda's, but she couldn't count them under the blankets where she hid from light, dark, and friends alike. Her only company was her grief and the pain from her many wounds—physical and mental. And the ceaseless images of death she'd seen that fateful morning. One of the days she allowed Elynda to support her as they watched as her grandmother's pyre was lit in the fading evening light at Valiant Pointe. The lighthouse stood starkly white against the night, as if mocking her in her mourning black.

Elynda and Mrs. Heilbee kept her safe, applying many medical treatments for the knife injury. They helped her pack her room in her grandmother's house the day after the burning and move into her adopted father's house at the General Store. Sorrow wasn't bad enough. Healing from being nearly killed wasn't enough punishment. Grappling with having killed someone pushed her limits. Learning she would be forced to live with her Roy Fraely ladled misery onto anguish.

Riana shuffled down the short hall to the last room on the left, carrying nothing but a stuffed animal her grandmother had given her. Elynda followed behind her with the last box while Mrs. Heilbee waited outside. "Do you want me to stay and help you unpack?"

"No," Riana replied, even though the sting in her back warned her she needed the help. Holding the stuffed bear made her think about her grandmother. How she had given it to her for her eleventh birthday. She could feel the tears building inside her and wanted to be alone when she started crying. "Thank you. I—I don't know where I want to put everything yet."

"All right," Elynda mumbled. Riana could hear the worry in her voice, but she didn't know what to say to make Elynda feel better. She didn't know if she had the energy to try to make her feel better. Riana pushed the door open to her bedroom. Behind it was a small, plain bed that still lacked coverings, empty white walls, one small window, and piles upon piles of boxes and bags.

She sat on the bed and held the stuffed bear to the ache in her chest, embracing the memory of her grandmother.

Elynda's arm went around her shoulders, and Riana looked into her emerald eyes. There was so much shared sadness in them. Riana set the bear aside and wrapped her arms around her friend, resting her cheek on the blue cotton dress Elynda wore. Her arm and back ached with the movement. Her breath still stung the interior of her healing lung.

"Thank you for all of your help today," she said.

"Of course," Elynda's response was muffled into Riana's black-clad arm. "I'll be by first thing tomorrow to walk to school with you and help you carry your books."

"All right," Riana said.

"I love you, my friend," she said.

"Love you too," Riana said and managed to work her mouth into what felt like might be a smile. She meant it; even through all the muffling grief, she could hear the love in her heart—or maybe it was the sadness that made the love that much sweeter a song. "Come on. I'll see you to the door."

Riana still moved carefully, not wanting to tear the internal or external stitches. They passed through the curtain and swinging doors that led through the storeroom and into the store. The waist-high, glass front counter to the right spanned the entire wall. A variety of rare items Mr. Fraely acquired from the sea merchants who docked at Landsend's port occupied cases built into the counter: knives and daggers glittered on black velvet, as well as a variety of pocket and pendant watches. A small collection of jewelry and flasks lined cases further down.

To her left were three rows of dried foodstuffs, and lined along the wall were barrels of flour, sugar, brown sugar, and other grains. Riana and Elynda passed a few racks of clothing from different regions of Aelos. A white fur-lined leather coat dyed purple looked to be from the icy, mountainous region of Idalfyn on the northeastern coast.

Riana was surprised to see Captain Steph standing at the counter in front of Mr. Fraely who was behind it. Steph wore his dark blue uniform with the silver tassels on the shoulders that marked his rank in the Baron's Guard.

Mr. Fraely wore a white, pin-striped collared shirt with the sleeves rolled up to reveal his hair-covered forearms. His suspenders kept his pants in place, and a plain beige apron covered it all. He looked over his square spectacles at a pile of papers held in his stubby fingers. His eyes glanced up as Riana and Elynda passed by yet again.

"Have you gotten it all?" he asked. Riana thought he sounded irritated.

"Yes, sir," she said. "Hello, Captain." She nodded politely to the captain.

"Hello, Little Miss," he said and smiled sadly at her.

"What are you—?" Riana started to ask what he was doing here after eyeing the paper in Mr. Fraely's hands again. She wondered if it had anything to do with her grandmother.

"Run along, Riana," he said, interrupting her question. He eyed the captain with a stern set to his straight mouth. Elynda's eyebrows shot up to her hairline as she led the way out of the store and onto its front porch.

After the door swung closed behind them, Elynda turned to her. "That was odd."

Riana thought about the home she was forced to leave and all the wonderful memories she had in it. It was a safe haven for her. She hadn't wanted to leave it, and she certainly hadn't wanted to move back into the small, cramped room behind the General Store under her adopted father's supervision. She was here because it was the only place she had to live, and because he hadn't refused. He had made his feelings known when her mother had died.

"Why do you suppose he let me live with him, Elynda?" she wondered out loud.

"Because he loves you as his daughter?" Elynda asked.

"That's a question," Riana stated. Elynda picked up her hand and squeezed it.

Riana stared at her friend seriously. "Don't ever go away on me, okay? Whatever you do, don't leave me."

Elynda's eyes widened, then she stuck her chin up and said, "Never! I promise."

They hugged one more time, and then Elynda joined her mother in the carriage. Mrs. Heilbee waved at her as they headed down the road. Riana watched until they were out of sight. When Steph came out of the store, he stood beside her for a while in silence.

Steph looked down at her with his handsome hazel eyes and smile wrinkles.

"When is your birthday, Riana?" he asked.

Riana had to think about it. Time passed in a blur lately. "It's only two weeks away," she said, surprised.

"Two weeks," he said. "I'll be back in two weeks. Do me a favor and don't go anywhere." He skipped down the steps and mounted his horse, which was tied to the post. Riana stood on the porch and watched him ride away, wondering what on Tyrinth he meant.

Riana scuffed down the steps of the front porch and around to the back of the house. She shuffled through the field that spanned the space between the general store and the TyrMinHai, and sat down among the concealing grasses.

The sun melted into the Dreavynan. The sky turned dark blue, and the grass surrounding her grew gray in the fading light. She sighed and looked out at the dark shape of the tree line. On the edges of the forest, Riana could see the lights of the fire nymphs coming to life. Soon the buzzing sound of their wings filled the air around her.

All were of the naked variety. They'd buried their dead and stowed their armor. Their wings varied in an array of semi-transparent colors: green, blue, pink, purple, and golden. There was a glittering light that shone from their wings, and when they flew, it blurred to a soft halo of their individual color. They whizzed around her, greeting her with their smiling, round faces and large, black eyes.

Riana counted them as they approached: about twelve. Five days ago, it would have been twice as many. Captain Luther had cut much of their population. Riana could feel the air move against her hair as they flew past. She thought about pulling out her sketch pad, but just didn't have the heart.

"Hello," she told them. They hummed and purred. Several perched on her drawn up knees. Some gently grabbed hold of her wild, silver hair and swung back and forth as if it were a swing. She endured them, happy to be around them after weeks of missing their presence, missing the TyrMinHai, missing the vineyard, and most of all missing her grandmother.

Riana clapped her hand over the miniature tree captured in a bottle hanging around her neck under her black dress. Her grandmother's last unknowing gift: a tiny replica of the fire nymph's tree was a reminder of her grandmother's sacrifice for her.

It was as though a little piece of her grandmother were reaching through time and death to give her strength.

CHAPTER THIRTY-EIGHT

She escaped Mr. Fraely with the excuse that she needed to get something from school. She'd tried saying she wanted to visit the vineyard the day before, and he'd refused her. Of course, she was lying. Her grandmother would chide her for it, but her grandmother wasn't here to do the chiding. A thought that bubbled up inside her and spilled out of her eyes.

She was raw on the inside. She'd managed to live through the ordeal; she'd vanquished her foe—and her grandmother's foe—yet she had failed her grandmother and the fire nymphs. It was for them she had ventured out of the General Store. She wanted to check on them. She wanted to confirm the tree was really gone. She wanted to read the books stowed in her grandmother's secret library to conclude if there was another food source for the fire nymphs.

She also wanted to be away from Mr. Fraely.

Riana walked along the North Road, thinking while she fiddled with the pendant her grandmother had given her. It hung from its long, silver necklace, the whole of it easily concealed under her tunic. She didn't mind the light, misting rain that fell on her, nor the chill breeze that snaked down the road.

She pulled her cloak tighter. The ever-present hush of the sea tried sincerely to comfort her, and she lost herself for a time in the simple task of putting one foot in front of the other and listening to the Dreavynan. When she arrived at the vineyard, the winery building bustled with activity. Carts and horses lined the driveway, and men, women, and children walked sedately toward the building. Riana recalled there was a memorial for her grandmother today for the vineyard and winery workers. She had been invited.

She looked down at herself. She'd pulled on her leathers and tunic and cloak, choosing comfort over a dress. She was in no state to present herself, and she was in no mood. She wanted nothing more than the comfort of solitude the forest would give her.

Decided, Riana dove into the vineyard and chased her loneliness all the way down the long aisle of fragrant growing vines. She was un-seen, and she hoped un-missed. When she arrived at the edge of the field, she slowed her pace and walked over the barren stretch of ground that marked the beginning of the Starliss's acres of forest.

Riana had a sudden thought as she peered up into the towering heights of evergreens. Had the forest always been there, or had it been grown by her grandmother's friend, Kaely? Riana touched the pendant again, wondering if Kaely was the maker of the trinket as well.

At the edge of the forest, Riana heard the oncoming rain patter through the vineyard first before it found her in the open. She ducked and jogged through two towering trees that formed what Riana always thought looked like a gate. She inhaled deeply as the scent of the air shifted from crisp sea mist to the sharp punch of evergreen needles and the soft and spicy warmth of bark. It was like coming home. Coming home after walking in the rain, only the rain she'd walked through had been the mass of tears she'd cried in the past weeks. She moved quietly over the mushy litter on the forest floor. It was freeing to wander the forest in pants and riding boots without worrying about tripping over dress skirts and petticoats, not to mention the horrible lack of functionality of dress shoes her grandmother had forced her to wear.

Riana let the pang of sorrow twist in her, triggering guilt for feeling grateful she could wear boyish clothes because her grandmother was dead. She pulled the hood of her cloak lower and watched the rain water pour from its tip. She shivered and picked up her pace, hoping to dispel the chill.

It wasn't until she was nearly to the hedge that she realized where her feet were taking her. She had wandered to the center of the forest, to Kaely's garden. But the antoli had transported her before, and she had no idea where the entrance was amidst the mass of hedge growing like a wall to keep the garden safe. Riana was sure that's what Kaely had intended.

Riana ran a hand along the vibrant, waxy green leaves, marveling at the height of the overgrown shrubs. Her fingers prickled as if with a sudden surge of electricity. She stopped, marveling at the sensation running up her hand, to her shoulder, down her neck. The necklace she'd worn every day since her grandmother's death began to vibrate. Riana pulled it from under her tunic. She held it out, dangling from its silver chain. It moved in a circle at first, then shifted to her left, as if being pulled.

Riana turned and walked, following the direction of the necklace. Her body trembled as she drew close—to what she wasn't sure. When the necklace shifted to a specific point in the hedge, Riana stopped and faced it.

The leaves of the hedge shivered then shook wildly. Folding limbs creaked out from behind their cloaking leaves. Riana watched as the foliage twisted, pulling in on itself and opening into an arched doorway.

"The only thing it's missing is a welcome mat," Riana whispered to herself.

She ducked through the archway and wandered into the first layer of the labyrinth that was Kaely's garden. She followed the tugging direction of the necklace as it led her past wild foliage, snapping flowers, sneaking vines, and grasses the color of amethyst. There was so much she wanted to stop and draw, to create a catalogue of her discoveries in this aged magical treasure. But the necklace relentlessly pulled her on.

Riana squeezed through nothing more than a gap in a collection of foliage. The tunnel hooked back then turned sharply forward. She squeezed through branches and leaves, hunching low as the vegetation formed a rabbit hole path. She pushed aside the exploring fingers of vines. Just before she gave up, thinking the passage would dead end, she passed through the last arching festoon of waxy leaves and emerged into the heart of the TyrMinHai.

The necklace vibrated but lie against her chest, no longer pulling her in any direction.

Riana thought she might suffer a heartache, or maybe vomit, or pass out, or just dissolve into tears at seeing the place of her grandmother's death. Maybe she'd suffer all of those things at once. She looked around the center of the garden, at the mound of ash in its middle, and fought back the tears. After so many weeks, she was exhausted of crying. She couldn't bear one more salty drop of sorrow to track her face.

It was so sad to see the remains of the Mother Tree. She worried about her fire nymph friends and how they would survive without the sustenance the tree provided. Would they all go back to extinction? Would they die? Just like their tree? Riana paced toward the pile of ash, not with purpose, but to move as she thought about the sadness of the whole situation.

She felt like such a failure. She'd failed to protect her grandmother and she'd failed to protect the fire nymphs' tree. She'd exposed herself as a Tyrmini—or something—and then had killed someone in her search for vengeance. A horrible darkness blotted her insides, and try as she might, she couldn't wish it or will it away. It would always reside there, tucked away in her heart, making her cold, calculated, and unfeeling.

Riana nudged the pile of wet ashes with her muddy boot. Her necklace vibrated. She nudged the pile again and was rewarded with a soft buzz of electricity zipping through her breast bone, tingling the skin on her chest. She pulled the little thing to eye level.

Trapped in the bottle, the little tree was illuminated in growing light. When she peered even closer at the tree, she could make out the details. What was illuminating the tree were miniscule fashionings of the golden fruit. Fashionings so real, Riana could swear they looked like organic material. As if the tree was real.

Riana was struck with an overwhelming idea. A stupid, impossible, but undeniable urge. Her heart skipped with excitement and a dare-not-hope reigning in of her emotion. It was just too crazy. It was just too magical.

"But what have I got to lose?" she said aloud.

She held the bottle in one hand and unscrewed the tiny lid with the other, peering into the glass with rapt fascination. It couldn't work. Could it?

Riana held the bottle and lid in one hand and carefully shook the tiny, glowing tree into the other. She could smell a fragrant aroma. She looked at the tree, then at the pile of ashes. It couldn't be so easy, could it?

She reached her hand out. Her body was numb. She saw as if through a telescope as she placed the tiny tree, roots down atop the mound of black ash.

At first it just sat there. Then it fell to the left. Riana sighed.

What did I think would happen? she thought, chiding herself. She pulled the tiny bottle from the palm of her hand and reached for the miniature tree. When she moved closer, she halted. The little tree quivered in the soil and ash, its fruit shining against the black earth. Its leaves shivered as the roots dived into the mound.

At this proximity, Riana also noted small specks of shining material in the dirt. They glittered golden bright against the black remains of the Mother Tree. She recalled throwing the fruit into the flames and wondered...

The tiny tree was no longer tiny. Its trunk had expanded, its branches twisting out and up. Roots snaked deeper into the soil. Riana fell backward as the tree swelled in a sudden burst of growth. It creaked and groaned as its size doubled, tripled, quadrupled, and on and on. The roots churned through soil, shaking the ground beneath Riana, who sat stunned at the miracle before her.

As if this replacement tree, a baby tree maybe, had set off some sort of alarm, fire nymphs flew over the walls of the inner garden, the heart of the TyrMinHai, coalescing in a gathering throng. Their skin was a cold cobalt blue when they entered. Their bodies were emaciated. Riana scrambled out of the way as the tree matured—or maybe it was just filling the space it occupied, she thought. Or maybe Kaely had worked some magic on the tree to shrink it into the bottle, suspending it in its glass prison.

Riana clapped her hands to her ears as the groans of the tree grew deafening. The nymphs were ecstatic, flying to form a circle around the tree, bursting into flame and song, as if to usher in the birth of this new tree.

At last the groans resided and the rumbles faded. The nymphs' song continued as they flew slow circles around their source of food and comfort. Riana spied the queen. She approached the tree, tears streaming. The rest of the nymphs quieted. Riana saw mother nymphs with children nymphs, holding them close. Pairs of nymphs embraced or held hands. The queen, her bluish white fire opalescent in contrast to the deep black bark of the tree. The leaves were vivid green, unlike when Riana had seen the tree before it had been set alight, when the leaves were golden. This tree was in its early spring.

Globes of golden fruit hung ripe and heavy from the branches. There was enough fruit to feed them all. To feed them all and make the wine, if she wanted.

She stared in awe as one of the fruits dropped to the forest floor.

Fire nymphs erupted into cheers. Then another fruit dropped, followed by a third and a fourth. The nymphs flew to the fruit, settled in, and sliced into the golden flesh with their black blades.

Riana sat down in the cool emerald grass, marveling at the magic she'd just witnessed. Even through a generation, Kaely's Tyrmini magic had lasted. The vineyard had been forever altered, producing fruit that created wines of legend. The elementals had sprung back to life, and then grown—which the fire nymph had told her was due to Riana's presence. Even if that were true, Riana couldn't magic food into existence for elementals. She wasn't sure what she could do.

The memory of spearing Captain Luther through with weapons fashioned from what seemed to be light rampaged through her memory. She recoiled. Kaely had brought things to life. Riana took it away.

She sat in the clearing, soaking in the exultant feast of elementals. Captain Luther had destroyed the tree that fed the fire nymphs, and Riana had restored it.

With that realization came another. Riana wanted elementals to have a place on Aelos. She wanted people to be safe, and she wanted Tyrmini to be safe. It really wasn't that she was of two separate worlds, but one. She didn't want to choose between one world and another. She just wanted balance. Harmony on the one world in which they all lived.

Aelos was out of balance. Maybe she could help right it.

She raised a hand and called on the Light of Magloryn inside her. The energy flowed through her and wrapped her hand in flame-like essence.

Kaely brought things to life. Riana opposed those who would push Aelos to further imbalance. That didn't mean she destroyed things. She simply fought against those who would destroy the beauty of the Tyrinth, its magic and its inhabitants—whether they were mundane, magical, or elemental.

Riana let the Light soak back into her body and sat a little straighter. She was not proud of what she'd done, but perhaps it had been necessary to who she was and what she believed in.

Perhaps balance came with a price.

NOTE FROM THE AUTHOR

Did you like this book?

Readers rely on reviews to decide if a book is worth their time and money. Therefore, I greatly appreciate any rating or review you're willing to give, whether it's just clicking the number of stars you believe it deserves or writing out what you most enjoyed about the book. I can be found on amazon.com and goodreads.com.

Thank You!